RISING FORCE

KEN LOZITO

ACOUSTICAL BOOKS LLC

RISING FORCE

ISBN: 978-1-945223-09-9

The author greatly appreciates you taking the time to read his work.

Published by Acoustical Books, LLC

KenLozito.com

Cover art by Jeff Brown

http://www.jeffbrowngraphics.com/

CHAPTER 1

Zack sat in the cockpit of a Boxan strike-fighter configured for atmospheric flight mode. The wing cannons could shoot ion bolts as well as kinetic weaponry, but they were presently disabled. A fully armed strike-fighter also carried missiles whose payloads could be changed to suit their purpose in battle. The ship Zack was flying was for training purposes only. He'd spent a lot of time in training simulators and had recently been qualified to fly an actual strike-fighter.

"Let's take it up a notch. I want you to take us beyond the atmosphere," Etanu said.

Etanu was a Nershal, a humanoid species with dragonfly wings. They were skilled pilots and highly capable at calculating navigational coordinates. At one time Etanu would have sooner seen Zack dead than flying in the same vehicle, but things had changed. The Nershals lived their lives by a strict code of honor, and owing to the fact that Zack *wasn't* dead and that he and

Etanu had survived being held prisoner by the Xiiginns, they'd developed a strong friendship.

Zack brought up the flight configuration on the internal heads-up display. "Sounds good."

He increased the velocity and angled the trajectory ninety degrees. Zack couldn't feel any change in pressure thanks to the inertia dampeners. Without them, he would have been unconscious from the gravitational forces of such a turn.

Zack found it hard to believe that he hadn't seen Earth in over a year. The closest he'd gotten was eight months ago when he'd uploaded Drar command protocols to the Star Shroud, causing it to converge around the Earth's star system and form a protective barrier that not even the Boxans could penetrate. What he hadn't anticipated was that they wouldn't be able to disable the barrier in order to get home themselves. As a result, he and the rest of the Athena crew were temporary residents of the Boxan colony world.

Basic flying of the strike-fighter had been easy to learn. Its computer systems used adaptive protocols to tweak the controls to the nuances of the pilot. Unlike Kaylan and some of the others, Zack wasn't a pilot back on Earth, but the flight controls for the strike-fighter were much easier for him to comprehend than the Athena's shuttle, although perhaps not anymore because it had been a few months since he'd been on the shuttle. The Athena was orbiting the planet, but he'd been in constant contact with the ship's artificial intelligence, which had become their unofficial tenth crewmember.

Zack used his neural implants to access the strike-fighter's flight systems and gave the command to change the engine configuration for space flight mode. The main heads-up display showed the updated configuration and they passed through the edge of the atmosphere. He waited a few moments while their distance from the atmospheric edge increased, then used the maneuvering thrusters to swing the nose around to give them a view of the planet. Zack grinned. He'd been practicing that maneuver in the simulator and had botched his first few attempts when Kaylan had been flying with him.

"Excellent," Etanu said. "Perhaps I'll tell Kaylan that she distracts you too much on these flights."

"It's the only way we get to be alone these days, between combat training and whatever the Mardoxian Sect does when they snatch her away for their own training regimen," Zack said.

"And here I thought you just wanted to get away from the physical rigors of combat training," Etanu said.

Zack snorted. "This is more fun than that stuff. I'm not a soldier and I don't ever plan on being a soldier. Honestly, I just want to get back to Earth and be with Kaylan."

Zack took in the view of the Boxan colony world. Olloron was decent enough, but it was a bit dry for his taste. Water covered only sixty percent of the planet's surface and there was nowhere near the lushness when compared with Selebus moon, a secondary habitable world in the Nerva star system and home to the Nershals. Olloron was the only home the Boxan's had left and they defended that home fiercely. Zack couldn't imagine losing Earth, and given the state of Human technology, Humans wouldn't survive losing Earth either.

Zack swung the nose of the ship forty-five degrees to the right and sped toward the Athena.

"Where are you taking us?" Etanu asked.

"Home . . . Well, *my* home, that is," Zack said.

He needed to see the Athena. So much had happened to them aboard that ship that he sometimes felt lost without it.

"You'll get back to Earth someday," Etanu said.

"I know, but combat training isn't going to get me there any quicker. I need to spend more time trying to decipher what the Drar did to our ship. There are still vast parts of the Athena's computing systems that I can't access, nor can the AI," Zack said.

Etanu blew out a harsh breath at the mention of the AI.

"Come on," Zack said, "you need to learn to work with AIs. When done properly, they can be a tremendous help."

"Our experience has been less fortuitous when dealing with an AI than yours has been," Etanu said.

"That's because the AI you were working with was based on Xiiginn design and I think we can agree that anything they touch only benefits them," Zack said.

"So you think the Xiiginns wanted our artificial intelligence experiments to fail?"

"Maybe . . . Another way to keep you dependent on them, I suppose. Look, I don't expect you to change your mind, but I would encourage you to consider developing your own when you eventually return to Nerva," Zack said.

Etanu was silent, but Zack could tell the Nershal was considering what he'd said.

Finally, Etanu answered. "I'd do it with your help."

"Really! That's great. We could probably adapt a version of the Athena's AI for you to use. I mean, it was based on the Boxan AI that was used to manage the monitoring station in our star system," Zack said.

"Yeah, but you modified it and it's something different than what the Boxans created. Even Gaarokk agrees with that," Etanu said.

"You are correct," the AI said, its voice coming from their helmet speakers. "My origin is somewhat unique, but I would be happy to create a base AI that stems from my programming to suit your needs."

Zack glanced at Etanu in surprise. "Wait a minute, Athena. Did you just say you can create more of you as in—like a child?"

"The context would fit in this instance. Does this surprise you?" the AI asked.

"Damn right it does," Zack said.

"I'm not sure I understand," the AI replied. "Besides you, no other crewmember knows my programming as well as I do. Why shouldn't I be able to create alternate versions of myself for the Nershals to use?"

"I think it might be a bit more complicated than you think it would be," Zack said.

"I shall devote some processing time to the problem and provide you with a report," the AI said.

Zack looked up at the HUD and saw that Etanu was watching him from the rear seat.

"What?" Zack asked.

"You mentioned before how you'd like to return to Earth and be with Kaylan. I'm trying to understand what this means. You're with her here, but I don't think that's what you mean," Etanu said.

"Oh, I was thinking just the two of us taking it easy on a beach somewhere," Zack said.

"And you'd find such an existence fulfilling?"

"Well, yeah," Zack said, and his mouth hung open while he

tried to formulate his thoughts. "Just her and me on a beautiful beach. Bathing suits, drinks, the warm Caribbean waters, and no one trying to kill us. Yeah, I would like that very much."

"I don't think I understand you Humans at all. Here, in this moment, you are a designated mating pair, but you feel you can't be alone because the Xiiginns are hunting you. The Xiiginn aren't here. What's stopping you from doing as you wish right now?" Etanu asked.

Zack frowned. "Ma'jasalax and the other Mardoxian Sect members have her so busy that we barely have any time for each other at all."

"Have you communicated your desires to Kaylan?" Etanu asked.

Zack rolled his eyes. "What are you? The relationship police or something?"

"You didn't answer my question."

Zack shook his head and sighed. "No, I haven't talked to her about it."

He just wanted to get aboard the Athena and forget about Olloron, the Boxans, and the fact that they'd been kept so busy that they could hardly focus on any one thing for very long.

"You pride yourself on being able to solve problems and yet this one causes you to stumble," Etanu said, and a series of high-pitched grunts sounded from the rear of the cockpit.

"Are you laughing at me?"

The sounds from the Nershal came in longer bursts and Zack ground his teeth in frustration.

"Fine, laugh it up. Next time I see Kaylan, I'll just steal her away for a while," Zack said.

The Nershal's laughter ceased. "Now you're making sense."

As they got closer to the Athena, the white outer hull gleamed with a bit of silver and Zack drew in a deep breath, feeling his shoulders relax. He felt more at ease on the Athena than he did on the planet below them.

Zack harrumphed. Seeing the Athena was both a relief and a reminder of how far they had yet to go. The ship was tiny by Boxan standards, but thanks to the Drar it now contained more advanced technology than even the Boxans had. The Boxans had been able to help decipher some of what the million-year-old Drar AI had done to their ship, but though it had been eight months since that had happened, they were still in the dark as to the extent of the changes. One thing that had soon become apparent to all the crewmembers was the usefulness of the upgrades to their neural implants. The implants had been linked to their PDAs, and they still were to a certain extent, but they had the ability to function equally as well without them. As a result, the Athena crewmembers were able to multitask much better than they had before. Executing a task had required a fair amount of concentration before the upgrade, but now they could be performed almost as fast as it took to formulate the thought.

The security protocols had also been updated so only the Athena crew could access the computer systems of the ship. They'd been able to give the Boxans provisional access, but no matter what Zack did, the Boxans were severely limited in what they could do without one of the original Athena crewmembers present. Zack was aware of how the Boxans had tried to bypass the security protocols and access the ship's systems directly, so those security protocols had kept the Boxans honest.

"So this is what Hicks refers to as 'hearing you think.' You know, when you're so focused you start to forget things like slowing the ship down so we don't crash," Etanu said.

Zack's thoughts snapped back to the strike-fighter's controls and he slowed their approach.

"I was thinking of some things," Zack said.

"Like what?"

"When we first got here I thought we'd focus more on what the Drar did to the Athena, and for the first month or so things were like that, but not now," Zack said.

"The Boxans are sharing their knowledge and training all of you on their systems. It is a great gift," Etanu said.

"I realize that, but part of me keeps thinking that we're being kept busy on purpose."

"Why?"

"I don't know. To keep us here longer? We should have gone back to our star system by now to try and open the barrier," Zack said.

"It's not safe. Not with the Xiiginn fleet in the area," Etanu said.

"They can't be everywhere at once."

"The barrier is a blessing. It's the only thing that saved your home world from being invaded by the Xiiginns. What if you were to bring down the barrier and then not be able to re-engage it?" Etanu asked.

"Earth would be vulnerable to attack, I know. But still, I wanted to test some Shroud devices and there aren't any here," Zack said.

"They destroyed what they could when they lost Sethion and the rest are in comms blackout until the Xiiginn threat passes," Etanu said.

"A sixty-year blackout? That seems extreme to me."

"What did Gaarokk say about this?"

"He told me he would look into finding some Shroud devices we could experiment with, but to be fair, I only asked him about it last week. I got the impression that he thought it was a good idea," Zack said.

"Well then, you just need to be patient," Etanu said.

This time Zack laughed. "Perhaps I should send Udonzari a message that you've finally learned about being patient."

"I wouldn't," Etanu said.

Zack stopped laughing. "Why not?"

"Because he'll request that I come back to Nerva and join the fleet," Etanu said.

"I thought that would be a good thing. Since the Xiiginns have been ousted from Nerva, it should be safe to return now," Zack said.

"We didn't oust them. We appealed to the Confederation, and the member species voted for the Xiiginns to leave on our behalf," Etanu said.

"I thought the Xiiginns controlled the Confederation."

"They do, which is why the Nershal military has been on high alert. Our last clash with the Xiiginns revealed to them that we had allied ourselves with the Boxans," Etanu said.

"Plus, the Xiiginns needed their fleet to invade Earth, so you guys got a break. It's a good thing," Zack said.

"No, it's not."

Zack matched the strike-fighter's speed with the Athena's orbital velocity so it appeared they had stopped.

"What do you mean it's not?" Zack asked.

"Peace in our star system at the expense of yours in not a

good thing. No species should have to live with the threat of a Xiiginn invasion," Etanu said.

Zack nodded. He hated the Xiiginns as much as Etanu did, and the fact that he'd brought up the barrier and killed thousands of Xiiginns hadn't bothered him. Kandra Rene's face still haunted his dreams sometimes. The female Xiiginn had tortured him to get information about Earth and how he and his fellow Humans had arrived in the Nerva star system. At least Zack had been able to resist the Xiiginn compulsion capability. Brenda and Emma strongly believed it was because he loved Kaylan and that shielded him from the Xiiginn's pheromones. Jonah Redford hadn't been as lucky, but Zack was pretty sure Jonah loved himself and science above all else, and that hadn't shielded him. Jonah had fought it as best he could, but it wasn't until they were on the ancient Drar space station that he experienced any relief from his symptoms. Zack glanced at the top observatory on the Athena. Jonah's lab was there, and though the astrophysicist was no longer with them, there were still reminders of him in his lab.

Zack had searched for some clue as to how the Drar had been able to alleviate Jonah's symptoms. It'd been a far cry from a cure, but it might bring those who were afflicted with Xiiginn compulsion some peace. So far, he'd been unsuccessful. It wasn't as if the Drar had any specific data about the Xiiginns specifically, but their AI had been able to diagnose and treat the symptoms until Jonah died. The Drar had given them a tremendous gift that would take them years to even go through and catalog properly, and it would take much more than the crew of the Athena. The more Zack thought about it, the more he kept coming back to their need to get the Athena back home to Earth.

"Do you think the Boxans are lying about having no access to a Star Shroud device?" Etanu asked.

"Not Gaarokk. I trust him, but the others I'm not so sure of. I mean I don't think they'd lie to harm us, but some Boxans have a superiority complex that the others would say made a conflict with a species like the Xiiginns inevitable," Zack said.

"They're learning how to deal with that, I think," Etanu said.

"Yeah, but that perception is still there," Zack said.

He sent a command over to the Athena to open the airlock doors and had the strike-fighter's autopilot maintain the ship's position relative to the Athena.

"Are you ready?" Zack asked.

"I'm always ready. You're the one who forgets crucial pieces of equipment," Etanu said.

"Are you ever going to let me forget about that?" Zack said, remembering the terrifying experience of being exposed to outer space without a helmet.

He was about to open the canopy when a comms channel opened from the planet.

"Congratulations on making it all the way to the Athena, but now I'm afraid you'll need to come back to Olloron," Hicks's voice said over comms.

"Why? What's going on?" Zack asked.

"Kladomaor has returned and he'll be reporting on what they found back home," Hicks said.

Zack's eyes widened. "Alright, we're on our way."

Kladomaor had left them a few weeks earlier to do some reconnaissance near the barrier protecting Earth's star system. It had been a comms-silent mission—no communications allowed back to the colony—so they hadn't gotten a status update. Zack regained control of the strike-fighter and sped back toward the planet.

"Remember to angle your approach unless you prefer to kill us during re-entry," Etanu said.

"I know," Zack said, noticing that he was coming in a bit too steep and adjusting accordingly.

CHAPTER 2

Kaylan was in a simulated environment meant for training Mardoxian Sect members, whom their translator referred to as priests and priestesses. She was floating in a virtual world, surrounded by different types of metallic blocks. The blocks converged in front of her, forming an artificial landscape. She touched down on the smooth surface and felt gravity return to the simulation.

Kaylan ran forward, maintaining her awareness of the surrounding area. She had done enough of these exercises to know that the Boxans loved to change the playing field, forcing her to adapt or fail to reach her objective. As she ran, she extended her senses out from her. The artificial landscape changed, becoming uneven, and several tall shafts extended from the floor. Kaylan leaped, grabbing onto one of the nearest ones, and it propelled her to the top. She gazed down at the floor and watched as it disintegrated, revealing a dark nothingness beyond.

Kaylan pulled herself up and stood with her head held high. The Mardoxian Sect's training methodology forced their initiates to trust their instincts, allowing their reliance on the sixth sense to become instinctual.

Officially, Kaylan wasn't an initiate into the sect because she was Human but was allowed to train with them. Ma'jasalax had told Kaylan that their training would allow her to further develop her gifts, and the Boxan priestess had been right. Kaylan's concentration hardly ever wavered, and she'd participated in practice sessions where she'd had to navigate through the obstacles in front of her as well as monitoring a half a dozen other environments. At first she'd failed miserably, but after these many months on Olloron, she was mastering what she would have thought were impossible feats before.

Kaylan sat down and closed her eyes to begin meditating, breathing in smooth, even breaths and quieting her mind. Ma'jasalax had told her the brain was a machine that was always working and was her single most powerful asset. When she meditated, she sometimes imagined she was standing in the midst of a thick fog. She wasn't afraid, and she didn't try to control the fog but accepted her place in it.

In this case, the swirling fog thickened and Kaylan cocked her head to the side, listening to a faint sound in the distance. She focused on the source of the sound and felt as if she were drifting forward through the fog toward the origin of the noise. A harsh clang echoed around her, along with heavy footfalls crunching on gravelly ground. A Boxan blaster fired and she cringed. There was a deep rumbling of Boxans speaking in muted tones as if she were listening to them from the other side of a thick wall. Kaylan relaxed and didn't try to force what she was experiencing. Ma'jasalax had taught her that sometimes it was best to allow the things she saw to unfold.

The skin on her forehead chilled painfully as a sharp breeze blew against her face. Plasma bolts blazed through the air, and she felt as if she were standing on a frigid battlefield. Boxans in full power armor stomped loudly nearby. Kaylan peered through the fog but only caught brief glimpses of what she knew must have been there.

There was a loud clearing of the throat and Kaylan spun around. A Boxan stood there in strange red power armor that was unlike anything she'd seen before. The Boxan crouched down and placed its hand on the ground as if trying to sense something Kaylan couldn't see. Then the Boxan turned around and the helmeted head looked directly at her. Kaylan gasped. The towering form of the Boxan lurched backward as if surprised by Kaylan's presence. She heard a tone that was soft at first but steadily gained in intensity. Then the fog disappeared as if there were a giant vacuum that had sucked it all away, and the battle sounds faded.

The latch to the door moved and the simulator door opened. Noises from the chamber beyond barreled their way in, and Kaylan squinted. Light poured through the rounded edges of the doorway. The simulation chamber was soundproof, and it took Kaylan a few moments to get her bearings.

Ma'jasalax peered inside. "I didn't want to pull you out when you were so deep in meditation, but Kladomaor has returned. Our presence is requested in the High Council chambers to hear his report."

Kaylan grabbed the handle and climbed to her feet. The simulator was designed for Boxans, who averaged eight-to-ten feet in height. Her own five-foot-ten inches were a pittance in comparison. Her mouth was dry, and she took a sip of water from the canister she'd set outside before going into the simulator. She rolled her shoulders, stretching stiff muscles, and glanced at her PDA, then looked at Ma'jasalax in surprise.

"Six hours?" Kaylan asked.

"We decided to let you go on longer than before to see how it affected your performance," Ma'jasalax said.

Kaylan frowned. It certainly hadn't felt like she'd been in there that long, but it did explain why she was a bit stiff from sitting for so long.

"I saw it again—Boxans on a battlefield somewhere. They were fighting," Kaylan said.

Ma'jasalax led her away from the simulation chamber. "Do you remember any details?" she asked.

"Someone was wearing red power armor, but it looked different than what I've seen here in the colony. I think the Boxan saw me or sensed me somehow. They reacted to my presence," Kaylan said.

Ma'jasalax gave her a sidelong glance. The Mardoxian priestess came to a stop and approached a wall terminal where a holoscreen flickered on. Kaylan watched as a cycle of Boxan power-armor images flicked past the screen.

Kaylan pointed to one. "That's pretty close to what I saw."

She leaned in to get a better look and then nodded up to Ma'jasalax.

"It's traditional combat armor from before the war with the

Xiiginns. More decorative than practical," Ma'jasalax said. She closed down the terminal and waved for Kaylan to follow.

"I don't know why I keep seeing a battle. I don't even know where it is," Kaylan said.

"It may not be taking place anywhere. You're quite gifted and it could be that you're seeing another Boxan's experiences. Most of the Boxans here have seen combat and every Boxan is required to learn basic combat skills," Ma'jasalax said.

Kaylan's brows squished together. "I don't understand. How could I see another Boxan's experiences?"

"You're participating with the other Athena crewmembers in combat training as well as what we're doing here, plus working on understanding what the Drar AI has done to your ship. Your vital signs were showing a sleep pattern," Ma'jasalax said.

"Sleep . . . You mean I'm dreaming instead of seeing an actual event taking place?" Kaylan asked.

"Yes," Ma'jasalax said.

Kaylan chewed on the inside of her cheek in thought. They were all working hard, but it had seemed so real. She'd heard the battle as if she were standing there on the battlefield. She'd felt the moisture on her skin and knew the Boxan in the red armor had seen her. She glanced at Ma'jasalax but didn't say anything. It was a strange thing to suggest and Kaylan wondered if Ma'jasalax was testing her in some way. They were all working hard. Other than the two of them sleeping in the same bed, she had hardly any time to spend with Zack.

They went through the doors into the warm, arid outdoor air and blazing sunlight. This was a marked difference from the high humidity the Boxans preferred, like their home planet of

Sethion. Olloron was a world with hotter temperatures due to its orbit being closer to the star in this system. The planet had large landmasses and oceans that covered about sixty percent of the planet's surface, but when compared with the Earth that had over seventy percent of its surface covered in water, it made for a much dryer atmosphere.

Kaylan followed Ma'jasalax over to the transit pad they'd use to quickly travel to the High Council chambers. The Boxans had been residents of this planet for fifty years. It had begun as a small outpost, secreted away, and it was that secret that had saved them from the Xiiginns. Kaylan had asked Ma'jasalax whether they would have considered going to a star system like Earth if they hadn't had Olloron. The Mardoxian priestess had given her a vague answer, but it still left Kaylan wondering what the Boxan's future plans were. They couldn't fight a war with the Xiiginns forever.

Kaylan used her PDA to check the location of the rest of the Athena's crew and all of them were heading for the general assembly, but Kaylan frowned when she saw Zack's location. He'd gone back to the ship again. He'd been withdrawing from the others and making regular trips back to the Athena. She sometimes found that the others would do something similar, herself included. The Athena was their link to home and sometimes being on their ship made them feel closer to home than being on the surface of the Boxan colony world did.

The transit pad hovered above the ground and then slowly rose into the air over the Mardoxian building complex. The wind blew Kaylan's dark hair back, giving her a momentary reprieve from the heat. They headed toward a large dome-shaped building that other transit pads were approaching. The pads had no railings, but they didn't need any; the sensors wouldn't let anyone fall off during their short flight.

Kaylan glanced up and saw a strike-fighter flying over them, and her lips lifted a bit, knowing Zack was inside. He'd flown with Etanu today since she'd been training with Ma'jasalax.

She turned back toward the dome, eager to learn what Kladomaor had found during his reconnaissance mission back to Earth's star system. The decision for them not to go with Kladomaor had been difficult to make, but ultimately they needed to focus on their work here and learn all they could about what the Drar had done to the Athena. And Kaylan marveled at what they'd been able to figure out. The Drar space station had remade the Athena by merging their technology with what had been built on Earth. There were some systems that not even the Boxans understood. Prior to entering the Drar space station, the Athena's hull hadn't been in the best of shape, which Hicks kept bringing up as a risk to all on board. All of those issues were gone. The hull material was in pristine shape, made of a radically advanced ceramic composite. They'd found references to the new composite formulas, but it would take them time to reproduce it.

While the artificial intelligence on the Drar station had enhanced their ship, it hadn't included any weapon that would give them an edge in combat—at least not directly. There was no big gun they could use to take out hordes of Xiiginns, and to Kaylan that was quite a telling statement on the part of the Drar AI.

The transit pad slowed its approach and landed just outside the domed building where the Boxan High Council met. As

Kaylan stepped off, alarms blared near them, along with the sound of strike-fighter engines as Zack brought it down for an impromptu landing in a clearing a short distance away. Boxan soldiers raced over to the craft while Zack and Etanu exited the ship. Kaylan watched as Zack gestured over to where Kaylan and Ma'jasalax waited, and the soldiers let them pass.

"Nice landing, although I don't think they appreciated it," Kaylan said to Zack.

Zack grinned. "Etanu mentioned something about surprise landings and that there wouldn't always be a designated area for them."

"Don't you blame this on me. I was referring to what you'd do if your ship was damaged and you *needed* an emergency landing," Etanu said.

Zack rolled his eyes. "I set it down right over there and everything turned out fine."

Kaylan had been around Zack long enough to learn some of his behavior patterns. He was getting restless and these little moments of rebellion were indications that he needed a change.

"Zack," Kaylan said, "landing a strike-fighter in the middle of a populated area isn't the best way to treat our hosts."

Zack blew out a breath. "Fine, I'll move it after we're done here."

They headed inside and Kaylan fell into step next to him. She leaned over so only he could hear. "It was a good landing."

"Thanks," Zack said with a half smile. "Maybe when this is over we can take a ride?"

Kaylan nodded but wondered whether the Boxans would allow Zack to keep flying after his little stunt. If anything, the

Boxans were rigid in their rules of expected behavior from their guests.

They met up with the rest of the Athena's crew and Hicks worked his way over to Zack.

"Why didn't you join us this morning?" Hicks asked.

"I'm not doing combat training anymore," Zack said.

"How come?"

"I know the basics and that's enough for now. I'm going to spend more time working with the Athena's systems," Zack said.

Hicks nodded. "That's fine. We just didn't know where you were."

Zack glanced at Hicks for a moment. "Etanu was giving me a flying lesson."

"Excellent, but I did want to tell you that you might have liked what we were doing today," Hicks said.

Zack's brows pushed forward. "What were you guys doing?"

"We got to use their exoskeletal suits," Hicks said.

Zack's eyes widened. "The ones that make you super strong and jump really high?"

Hicks nodded.

Kaylan grinned as she watched the warring emotions on Zack's face. It must have been every little boy's dream to put on a suit of armor that could make them super strong and impervious to danger.

Since this briefing pertained to them directly, Kaylan and the others were ushered to a designated area set aside for them near the front. The Boxans were a large race of beings and made every effort to be sure their guests were comfortable, which included appropriately sized chairs for them to sit on.

Ma'jasalax went over to where the Mardoxian Sect representatives gathered in the High Assembly. There was a deep, quiet murmuring throughout the vast hall, but there were only about fifty Boxans in attendance. The Boxan High Council was made up of seven members that included their leader, who was a Boxan named Awan.

Awan glanced over at Kaylan and the others. "Thank you for coming on such short notice. When we received Kladomaor's communications, we anticipated that you'd be as eager to hear the news as we are."

"Thank you, High Councilor," Kaylan replied. The crew of the Athena had decided that she was to speak for them.

A door on the far side of the chamber opened and Kladomaor entered, followed by Gaarokk and some other members of his crew. Kaylan had noted that Kladomaor preferred to work with the same crew when he embarked on missions, but she'd later learned that the Battle Commander was a bit of an outsider even among his own species. He was the only living Boxan to be brought back from the brink of madness at the hands of the Xiiginns and their compulsion ability. It was fair to say that Kladomaor was once a war hero who was no longer entirely trusted by his own race. Ma'jasalax had vouched for him, and it was through the High Council's respect for the Mardoxian Sect that Kladomaor was still able to serve.

Kladomaor walked over to the designated speaker's area and glanced at the Athena's crew. His facial features could have been chiseled from stone for all they gave away.

High Councilor Awan brought the assembly to a start. "Battle Commander, please report your findings to us."

"We returned to the Sol System to study the Shroud barrier and have learned that it possesses the same energy signature as the barrier we encountered at the Drar space station. There were no offensive capabilities, but that was expected. The sequence of code used to realign the Shroud device and change its composition wouldn't give it offensive capabilities," Kladomaor said.

"So the Earth is protected for the time being," High Councilor Awan said.

"That's true, but I have more to report," Kladomaor said.

"Please continue."

"We ran a multitude of tests on the barrier and it's capable of withstanding an assault from our most powerful weapons; however, the barrier is shrinking," Kladomaor said.

Kaylan stood up. "How fast is it shrinking?"

Kladomaor turned toward her. "We're not sure. We've left sensor equipment to monitor and measure, but it will require another mission to retrieve the data."

"Are the Xiiginns still there?" Kaylan asked.

"There was no Xiiginn presence detected, just a vast field of wreckage from the ships they weren't able to salvage," Kladomaor said.

"Were there any survivors from the Dreadnaughts?" Kaylan asked.

"No, unfortunately not. The Dreadnaughts were completely destroyed, but we did find a data recorder jettisoned prior to the battle," Kladomaor said and turned back to the High Council. "Prax'pedax sent non-essential personnel, tech platforms, and orbital defensive platforms back to Earth before engaging the Xiiginns. There's an excellent chance that there are surviving Boxans and Humans alive in the Sol System."

High Councilor Awan shifted his gaze to Kaylan. "What do you think your race will do?"

Kaylan glanced at the others, unsure what to say. Anything she said would be pure speculation. "I'd like to think they would be working together."

Hicks stood up and the high councilor nodded for him to speak. "The data we collected prior to leaving showed that the Xiiginns were sending asteroids to the interior of the star system. They were likely targeting Earth. A clear and present danger like that would have caused the cooperation of Earth's militaries. They would have joined together to mitigate the attack. Assuming they all survived, and with the help of the Boxans, my guess would be that they're building a fleet to protect themselves."

Kaylan looked at the Boxans on the High Council and got the impression that none of them were pleased.

Kladomaor cleared his throat. "The data recorder also contained Prax'pedax's personal logs. He was aware that he'd broken protocol for dealing with a less advanced species. He recognized, as I have, that in order to survive we must work with species like the Humans."

"Prax'pedax operated outside of his mandate to protect the Earth. Those protocols are in place to ensure a safe path for all those involved. We intend to work with the Humans, but Prax'pedax's actions may have put them in even more danger," High Councilor Awan said.

Zack let out a bitter laugh while coming to his feet.

"What are you doing?" Kaylan asked.

"No, I finally get it. I see what's going on here," Zack said to Kaylan. "They're angry that Prax'pedax deviated from protocol and took an action that was outside the confines of the council." Zack turned toward the council. "He was there and he decided that the best course of action was to share your precious technology with us so we could all have a fighting chance against the Xiiginns. Does that about sum it up?"

"Zack," Hicks warned.

"No," Zack said. "I want them to answer. We're here right now today because they tried to control the galaxy with an iron fist. Tell me, what were Prax'pedax's orders if the Xiiginns defeated your ships?"

Kaylan's face flushed until she realized the implications of what Zack was saying. She stood by his side and faced the High Council. "It's a fair question and one that needs to be answered," she said in a steely tone.

High Councilor Awan shifted his feet and faced them fully. "Yours is a species that we cannot allow to fall to the Xiiginns. Your species is the only other race we've encountered with the Mardoxian potential. Battle Leader Prax'pedax was tasked with protecting your planet at all costs, but if he was unable to complete this task then he was to prevent the Earth from becoming an asset to the Xiiginns."

Zack growled in disgust. "Unbelievable . . ."

Kaylan's mouth hung open in disbelief. She looked at Ma'jasalax, who was watching her intently. Kaylan was prepared to work with the Boxans and make this alliance work, but this was too much.

"I realize that our stance appears to be harsh and I understand your initial response," High Councilor Awan said.

"I don't think you do. Not really," Kaylan said. "How can you expect us to be in alliance with you with these kinds of contingency plans?"

"We expect you to respect our judgment," High Councilor Awan said.

"This is bullshit," Zack said.

"Hold on a minute," Hicks said. "If our survival was at stake, do you think our own governments would react differently?"

"Yes, we would because we're not all military. Not everything is a damn objective. We don't quantify life as a numbers game," Kaylan snapped.

"You are exactly right," Ma'jasalax said, drawing their attention. "And not only that, Prax'pedax agreed as well," she said and then faced the High Council. "Prax'pedax's record shows a strong alignment with our original ideals. He represented the best among us and yet, upon meeting with the Humans directly, he changed his mind. He saw something in them, much as Kladomaor and I have, that has influenced us to question some of our stricter protocols."

"These are the protocols that have allowed us to survive," High Councilor Awan said.

"No doubt Prax'pedax thought the same thing, but do you see their reactions?" Ma'jasalax said, and the Boxans in the chamber swung their gazes toward the crew of the Athena. "They are but a few, but I would place a strong probability that their reactions are aligned with the rest of their species. If we persist along this path, no species will enter an alliance with us."

There were a few moments of heavy silence. High Councilor Awan glanced at the other members of the High Council and then turned back toward Kaylan and the others.

"We respect the counsel of the Mardoxian Sect and each of us will spend time in quiet meditation considering the implications of our actions."

The Boxan high councilor waited.

"Thank you," Kaylan said in a neutral tone.

She glanced at Zack, who was seething, and the rest of the crew had guarded expressions.

"When will another team return to the Sol System? We need to understand how long the barrier can last before the system itself is in jeopardy," Kaylan said.

"We will send a regular team to investigate shortly and then compile and analyze the data here. Is that acceptable?" High Councilor Awan asked.

Kaylan nodded.

"Good. I have a request here from our scientific division. They're asking that the Athena be docked and its components studied directly," Awan said.

"Unacceptable," Kaylan said. "In fact, some members of my crew have expressed interest in spending more time on the Athena to study the Drar improvements. Those efforts were previously put on hold to allow you to perform your remote analysis while you educated us on some of your technology. Now that we have that foundation, we're in a position to better understand what was done to our ship."

The high councilor paused before answering. Clearly, he hadn't expected Kaylan's response. "Of course. We understand and shall assist however we can."

Kaylan nodded and found that she wanted to put some distance between herself and the Boxans. She caught Kladomaor watching her and she had the impression that there was more he wanted to say to them. She turned toward the rest of the crew.

"I think we need to talk about a few things."

The rest of them agreed. Kaylan looked back at the Boxans,

thinking that for all their advanced technology and their dry, logical approach to anything in their path, they seemed to be forgetting a very important thing. All life wanted to live and would struggle to do so regardless of everything else. The Boxans had spent too much time surviving and not enough time living, and their race was suffering because of it.

CHAPTER 3

Eight months had passed since the Earth was almost destroyed, eight months since the skies above Earth were forever changed. Ed Johnson still caught himself looking up at the new moon as if he still couldn't quite believe it was there. At the same time, he thought it was a daily reminder of the danger Earth was in. Ed drained the last of his bourbon and set the cup down. The brisk air of the Blue Ridge Mountains had more than a chill to it, but he'd always found that the rooftop patio of his secret hideaway held some semblance of peace—a place to recharge his batteries with its scenic views of the surrounding forests and a clear view of the stars. He gazed at the new moon, which was visibly smaller than the old one but no less beautiful. Some astronomers wanted to call the new moon Hephaestus, blacksmith of the gods who made weapons of divine strength, and Ed supposed their efforts on the mineral-rich new moon fit the name. Mining efforts had been underway for several months while tech bases were constructed so they could finally build spaceships of their own. He should be pleased with what they'd accomplished in such a short span of time, but he wasn't.

The Earth had been given a reprieve from an alien fleet that wanted to invade, but the fact that they were completely cut off from the rest of the galaxy even confused the Boxans. Boxan scientists had surmised that the barrier surrounding their solar system had to do with the Star Shroud, but even they were at a loss as to what had happened. The Star Shrouds were designed to filter out artificial wavelengths from penetrating a star system's interior while allowing outbound observations to occur without interference. They were a miracle of engineering that most scientists had trouble coming to grips with. Physicists from the mid-twentieth century had theorized the existence of a Dyson sphere, which was a hypothetical mega-structure built around a star to capture the energy coming from it, but even Ed understood that the Star Shroud was way beyond those theoretical concepts.

Zack Quick had been the first to crack the signal the Shroud devices used to communicate with one another. The young hacker had sent all his findings back to Earth before the Athena disappeared, but nothing he'd sent back had allowed them to communicate with the Shroud devices since the barrier. Not even the Boxans were able to control them. They were still deploying tiny monitoring drones that would report back to Earth about the barrier.

The barrier was the source of many debates around the globe. Since the barrier was in place, wasn't the Earth safe now? The barrier had blocked the Xiiginn ships from reaching Earth, so why did they need to devote all their resources to building ships of their own? Thankfully there were opposing arguments that were much more sensible.

"Ed, the meeting is about to begin," Iris called to him.

Ed turned around and crossed the rooftop patio to where Iris Barrett, his personal assistant and bodyguard, had set up mobile communications. Iris clicked her wrists together to activate the controls and several holoscreens came on. After a few moments, a view of General Sheridan sitting at the head of a long conference table came into view. The General wore his army fatigues, and his short, gunmetal-gray hair showed white around his ears.

Officially the Earth Coalition Force, or ECF, was under the dominion of the United Nations Security Council, which Ed found interesting because China and Russia still hadn't ratified it. In reality, the ECF existed in a gray area of international politics. Most of the ECF funding was coming from the other permanent member states of the UN, like the United States, France, and the United Kingdom, along with non-permanent member states like Japan, among many others. It wasn't enough, and this UN Security Council meeting was a long time coming. Here, they could finally nail down more support for the ECF.

"Hello, William," Ed said.

Another holoscreen came up and showed the UN Security Council chambers. A large circular desk was in the center of the room where nations could come and work together to maintain peace and security.

"Let's hope Rebecca Sharp is on top of her game today," Sheridan said.

"She's good and always on top of her game. She wouldn't be an ambassador if she weren't," Ed said.

Sheridan arched a brow and leaned toward the screen. Their comms channel was encrypted so there was no chance that someone else could be listening in on them. "Did her appointment to the UN involve you in any way?"

Ed chuckled. "You give me too much credit. It's in our best interest to know who all the power players are."

"So what's this going to cost us?" Sheridan asked.

"A lot. The Chinese are tough negotiators," Ed said.

"And the Russians?"

"They'll likely follow China's lead, but we need their help," Ed said.

Sheridan snorted.

"Believe what you want, but China has one of the largest workforces in the world, which is something we need to build a fleet."

"You know, I've spent a majority of my career neutralizing threats from them and getting into bed like this will change things. We're not going to become allies overnight," Sheridan said.

"We have to change; otherwise, there won't be many of us left."

General Sheridan eyed him for a moment. "I know what they're going to ask for and I'm sure you have a good idea as well."

"Of course. They'll want access to Boxan technology, as well as a few slots on your senior staff."

"And you'd be okay with that?"

Ed knew it didn't matter what he'd be willing to accept. Sheridan just wanted to know his perspective. It was the mark of an excellent leader to consider other viewpoints when making decisions.

"What I'd be okay with has little bearing on any of this. Can you function with those terms? Do you think the ECF would thrive with those terms?" Ed asked.

"What good will it do if we build our own ships to start shooting each other with? That's not going to stop the Xiiginns."

"First, we have to build a fleet. Then we have to be able to hold our own against the Xiiginns. Whatever comes after that will be someone else's problem. I do think that both the Russians and the Chinese can bring a valuable perspective to the table," Ed said.

"What's that?"

"Both of them have had to contend with how to counter a superior military force for a long time. They've spent years developing ways to outthink a more powerful enemy. It's this perspective that will be valuable to the ECF," Ed said.

"While gaining a technological advantage that is leaps and bounds over what they had before," Sheridan said.

"So will we. One thing history has taught us is that having an advantage and strategically executing an advantage are two different things. It's what we're able to do with the technology and our ability to keep it in working order that will prove which of us is going to last."

They watched the UN Security Council session. Rebecca Sharp deftly steered the meeting to the primary agenda and events unfolded much as Ed expected they would until it came time for China's UN Ambassador to present the People's Liberation Army's top pick to join the ECF: General Heng Shang.

Sheridan leaned back in his chair, shaking his head. "They can't be serious. Shang was indicted for fraud and corruption."

Ed brought up Shang's dossier on his holoscreen. Shang was one brutal SOB with a record for placing a high priority on seizing the initiative in conflict regardless of the cost. He also knew how to get the most out the men working under him and he'd never missed a deadline or a target that he was ordered to attain.

"Screw this. They can give us another candidate. I won't work with that man. He'll have no place on *my* staff," Sheridan said.

Ed took a deep breath. There were worse candidates but not much. "Just listen to me for a second," he said.

Sheridan looked squarely at the camera, his face red with anger. "Make it short."

"You can deny their candidate, but if you do, the negotiations will get bogged down for months. We're already on borrowed time and we're not sure when our time is going to run out. We don't need a perfect army to go to war with and we only have this one chance to get in front of this thing without massive casualties," Ed said.

Ed felt as if there were a train thundering in his ears while he watched Sheridan think about what he'd said. Suddenly, the holoscreen went dark. Sheridan had cut the connection, and Ed swore.

There were contingency plans should the ECF fail at this juncture, but it would put their manufacturing model out five years without help from the Chinese and the Russians. If they had global support, they could have ships completed within another year. They didn't have time to crawl or stumble. They had to learn to run—and run as fast as they could.

Iris closed down the mobile communications center and turned toward him. "What do you think he'll do?" she asked.

Ed shrugged. "I'm not sure. I know what I want him to do, but Sheridan is in a tough position. The repercussions of his decisions will affect generations to come."

"You know I have five older brothers," Iris said.

Ed shook his head. "I didn't know that."

"Yup and they were all strong-willed and fought with each other constantly. It wasn't until our mother put them to work that they started to get along."

"What did she have them do?"

"She bought an old car that needed a lot of work and told them that if they could fix it up, they could drive the car. So, grumbling and cursing and a few bruises later, they eventually fixed that car up. Then they fixed up another car and word got spread around. Eventually they opened a repair shop that they all still operate to this day," Iris said.

"So you think if we just force them to work together they'll work their differences out? I'm not sure that's going to work in this case," Ed said.

"It would be nice if it did. If you want my honest opinion, I don't think the UN Security Council is scared enough. We had a close call with that asteroid, but the fight has hardly come to our backyard," Iris said.

"Sheridan gets it. He understands what's at stake."

"You're right. He does to an extent. Heng Shang can deliver results. We may not like the method, but at least we'll be alive to have the preference. Sheridan should make use of Shang but also try to keep him honest," Iris said.

"I had no idea you were so pragmatic."

“That’s crap and you know it. One more thing that was made clear from that meeting, the UN Security Council doesn’t get what’s at stake. They still think there’s a way for them to survive what’s coming without banding together,” Iris said.

Ed headed for the door to the house. “Well, we’ll just have to change their minds, won’t we?”

CHAPTER 4

Michael Hunsicker had more or less taken up permanent residence on Armstrong Lunar Base. He'd been back to Colorado to visit his grandkids but only for a short period, and his children understood why he needed to leave them again. Since getting back to Earth, he felt he had a new lease on life. He visited Kathryn's grave and told her about all he'd been through. He would always miss her but now felt more at peace with her passing than he ever had. And it wasn't long before he was recruited to join the Earth Coalition Force on loan from NASA, as it were. He was the foremost expert and liaison to the Boxans.

During his short stint back home, he'd noticed how people still watched the new moon with a sense of trepidation. Michael approved the way General Sheridan hadn't sugarcoated the news that the Xiiginns had sent the behemoth-sized asteroid to destroy the Earth. The Boxans believed the Xiiginns used the asteroid as a ploy to divide the people of Earth. Misinformation was a strategy the Xiiginns often employed to achieve their goals. The ploy had nearly worked and had been almost catastrophic for Earth.

After weeks of analysis, it had been generally accepted that after the Boxan Dreadnaughts were destroyed, it was the Shroud barrier that had prevented the Xiiginn fleet from reaching Earth. The Boxans confirmed that the engine farm that had propelled the new moon toward the Earth was of Xiiginn design, and the barrier prevented any 'abort' signal the Xiiginns would have sent to prevent Earth's destruction. It had been a carefully orchestrated gambit, with the Earth caught in the crosshairs. Those engines had been disabled and the materials repurposed for the mining stations that had been built all over the new moon.

Over the months, the lunar base had become more of a colony, with additions to the existing base being added to accommodate the additional ECF personnel working up there. The Boxans had also built their own habitats on the lunar surface, even though there had been many offers for the Boxans to come to Earth. They did go to the planet surface but only for short periods of time. Michael had asked Chazen about this behavior and the Boxan had simply said it was for the best at this point. The Boxans did, however, make themselves available to advise the new technological centers springing up all over Earth. It would be a joint effort to build the ECF's first fleet to protect the planet.

It didn't make sense to bring all the materials mined from the new moon down to Earth's surface in any significant capacity. Near the mining outposts, the Boxan tech platforms left by Prax'pedax were being put to good use. The platforms had enabled them to get to a point where producing the materials needed for ships was taking months instead of years. The ECF engineering division had even been able to build their own tech platforms based on what they'd been taught by the Boxans.

A reminder message appeared on Michael's internal heads-up display and underneath came a text message from Alyssa.

::Breakfast?::

::You bet. I'll be right there.:: Michael sent back.

He finished dressing and left his room. Alyssa Archer was the commander in charge of running Lunar Base. Since he'd first arrived here from Pluto, he and Alyssa had become fast friends. They were both in their fifties. He was a widower and she was divorced. They enjoyed each other's company and both of them had decided not to make it any more complicated than that. She had a strong, no-nonsense attitude that he liked. At this stage in his life, he didn't want to try to guess what she was thinking, and she had never been one to hold her opinion back.

Michael's stomach growled. Bacon and eggs, followed by a cup of coffee, were calling his name. Perhaps he'd even indulge in some toast. With his mouth watering, he closed in on the officer's mess hall, but before he could reach it Allyssa walked out and waved over to him.

"Change of plans. We've got to meet with the Mirae Corporation's representative now instead of later," Alyssa said.

Michael glanced longingly at the mess hall, smelling the rich aroma of breakfast food.

Alyssa tossed a protein bar toward him and he caught it.

He looked at the prepackaged block that was supposed to tie him over. "Thanks," Michael said.

"Don't be such a baby," Alyssa said and quickened her pace.

Michael tore open the package and bit into the protein bar that was ostensibly some mix of coconut, chocolate, and peanut butter, but most of all it lacked any kind of flavor. Hopefully, there'd be some coffee in the conference room on the ECF wing of the base.

"Why'd they move the meeting up?" Michael asked.

"All red-line projects get priority, and right now we've got a bunch of Mirae mechs here that we can't use," Alyssa said.

They came to the security checkpoint and used their neural implants to authenticate, after which the doors opened and they entered the new ECF wing of the base. The hallways were larger and the ceiling much higher in order to accommodate the Boxans who also worked there. The gray, lunar-rock walls had been smoothed down but still had a bit of roughness to them.

They entered the command center, and if the ECF wing had been a ship, then the command center would have been the bridge. It was a large, semi-circular room with different work areas for the various teams assigned there.

Michael spotted Colonel Kyle Mathews speaking with Chazen and one Boxan soldier whose name he couldn't recall.

"We need to get the mechs up and running ASAP," they heard Colonel Mathews saying.

Michael and Alyssa walked over and Kyle greeted them.

"Great, you're here," Kyle said. "Maybe now you'll tell the Mirae Corp representative to find a way to get these things working before I order them scrapped and used for strike-fighters."

"What's the problem?" Michael said and glanced down through the window at a cavernous work area. Off to the side were two lines of hulking robotic mechs that were made by the Mirae Corporation based out of South Korea. The manned mechs could be adapted to a variety of tasks from combat to working with heavy materials.

"In layman terms, we're having power issues, and the onboard computers seem a bit flaky," Kyle said.

A man named Lewis was about to speak, but Kyle cut him off.

"I know it's more technical than that, but ultimately that's what the problem is," Kyle said.

They headed over to the conference room located away from the command center and the automatic door shut behind them. Holoscreens powered on and a comms channel was opened planet-side.

Three men appeared onscreen. All had short dark hair and wore dark suits.

"Hello, Pak Jun-Seo. Are you able to see us?" Alyssa asked.

"Loud and clear, Mrs. Archer," Pak Jun-Seo said.

"It's Miss. I haven't been a misses in a long time," Alyssa said.

"Apologies," Pak Jun-Seo said and then introduced his two companions. Mae Hyo was the head robotics engineer and Kam Min-Su was the department head for the mech's operating system.

After the introductions, Pak Jun-Seo focused his gaze on Michael.

"It's our honor to be speaking to you, Mr. Hunsicker," Pak Jun-Seo said.

Michael bowed his head slightly and the Koreans returned the bow in kind.

"I've had our teams here review the reported problems and we do have some options to present," Pak Jun-Seo said.

Lewis cleared his throat and Alyssa nodded for him to speak.

"If you have a software patch for the mech operating system, you can transmit that here and we'll review and test it before it gets deployed to the other mechs."

"This will not be possible," Kam Min-Su said.

"Why the hell not?" Lewis asked.

"The code is proprietary and only Mirae employees are authorized to update the kernel of the mech's operating system code," Kam Min-Su said.

"You've got to be kidding me," Lewis said and glanced over at Kyle.

The Colonel looked as if he were about to spit fire. "You guys realize that we're working from the moon. This isn't some operation where we can just come and get you to fix your damn broken mechs."

Michael suspected the Colonel had been about to call the mechs something else entirely.

Pak Jun-Seo regarded them calmly. "We do realize this complicates things, but this is the only way we can vouch for the proper operation of our mechs."

Colonel Mathews turned away, shaking his head. "Mute the call," he said.

The comms tech running the meeting told the Mirae representatives that they needed a minute.

"Call muted, Sir," the comms tech said.

"This is bullshit," Kyle said.

"It is," Alyssa said. "And they won't be the first to try this tactic with us."

"Well, we can't give in to this crap. Even if I wanted their employees here, Sheridan's staff would never authorize it. The

ECF may be a new organization, but it's still run like a military branch," Kyle said.

"What choice do we have?" Michael asked.

He didn't have a head for this sort of politics. He knew how to solve problems directly in front of him, but this was an entirely new arena for him.

"I'm sure that with a little bit of time I could update the code myself," Lewis said.

Michael glanced at the engineer. He had brown curly hair and looked to be in his thirties. Lewis's statement about updating the code himself reminded him of Zack Quick. It wasn't the first time he'd thought about the hacker-turned-astronaut. If Zack had been here, Michael was sure he would have already updated the code and gotten the mechs working before the rest of them even knew there was a problem to begin with.

"How much time would that take? And then we'd run the risk of introducing other problems with our fix," Michael said.

"What about the Boxans? Could we ask for their help?" Lewis asked.

Both Kyle and Alyssa shook their heads. "We can't go running to the Boxans to sort out our issues for us. We should be able to handle this ourselves," Kyle said.

"I say we hand this up the chain. We give Sheridan the options, along with our recommendation, and let them decide," Alyssa said.

Michael nodded. "The ECF is supposed to be bringing in people from all the nations supporting the effort."

"Yeah, but in the meantime this sets us behind," Kyle said.

Alyssa was commander of the base, but this was EFC-related,

and currently Colonel Kyle Mathews was the ranking officer, so the decision was up to him.

Kyle glanced over at the comms tech. "Open the channel back up."

The Koreans turned back toward the holoscreen. "We await your decision," Pak Jun-Seo said.

"I'll authorize four of your techs to come here to fix our mechs. The one condition I must insist on is that Kam Min-Su and Mae Hyo be the two leads that come as well," Kyle said.

Kam Min-Su's skin paled and he glanced at the others nervously.

"Acceptable," Pak Jun-Seo said.

Kam Min-Su swallowed hard. "I'll need some time to gather my team and the equipment we'll need."

"You have one hour," Kyle said. "I'll have a shuttle brought right to Mirae headquarters to pick you and the other two members of your team up."

Kam Min-Su was about to reply when Kyle cut the comms channel.

"Do you think Sheridan will go along with this?" Alyssa asked.

"He cares that we get things done. I'll send him an update and he can countermand the order if he wants, but he won't. I have operational authority here and he needs those damn mechs working," Kyle said and looked at Lewis. "When the Koreans get here, I want you and Alan to be with them at all times. They may have bartered their way onto this base, but this is going to be a knowledge-sharing job for them. If they don't like it, then I'm sure I know a few people who can properly convince them for me."

Michael felt his lips curve upward. He was glad Kyle was in charge of this. He'd get results and knew how to apply the right amount of pressure to get the job done.

"Why bring Kam Min-Su and Mae Hyo here?" Michael asked.

"Because they're department heads who know the ins and outs of those mechs. If Mirae Corp wanted to get cute and barter their way onto this base, I'm sure as hell going to get the most out of this deal," Kyle answered.

Michael watched the colonel for a moment. He'd seemed angry before, and while he was still annoyed by the Koreans, it hadn't distracted him from what was important. Kyle Mathews was one of the reasons Earth was still here and the rest of them still had a place to call home.

"Come on, I need you to kindly ask the Boxans to pick up a few people for me," Kyle said, grinning.

Michael snorted and knew this wouldn't be the last time a country or corporation would try to use their position of supporting the ECF as a way to muscle their way inside.

CHAPTER 5

Kaylan stood on the Athena's bridge with Emma. The crew rotated coming back to the Athena, and it felt much like a homecoming. They'd been given living quarters on the planet that were quite comfortable, but the Athena was the only place they could really call their own.

Emma sighed. "It feels good to be back doesn't it?"

"Yes, it does," Kaylan agreed.

"I have to admit that when we first got to Olloron, I couldn't wait to get off the ship and feel solid ground beneath my feet. Now I just want to get back home," Emma said, and there was a catch in her voice.

"We'll get home," Kaylan said, giving Emma a hug, "and Tom will be waiting for you. You'll have your wedding."

Emma laughed. "I feel so stupid," she said and pulled away, wiping her eyes. "I know we'll get home. I have to believe it, but I just miss him so much. I keep replaying his last video message to me. He was holding our dog at our favorite park, trying to get him to wave at the camera."

Kaylan's eyes became misty as well.

"How are you and Zack doing?" Emma asked.

"Oh, . . . we're fine," Kaylan said a little too quickly and knew Emma wasn't fooled. "We try to be discrete, but lately there just hasn't been a lot of time and sometimes . . . he can be . . ."

"Zack," Emma supplied.

"Yes!" Kaylan laughed. "What would you do if Tom were here?"

Emma frowned. "You mean after I jumped his bones all night because I haven't gotten laid in over a year?"

Kaylan felt her cheeks redden. Emma was usually so well spoken with her British accent that to hear her like this was sometimes disarming.

"I don't know if he and I being in a confined space like a ship would be best for our relationship. Don't get me wrong. I love him, madly, but sometimes . . . men," Emma said.

Kaylan didn't mind being near Zack, but she also understood what Emma meant. Her sister Iris loved her husband but needed her own space to help balance it out.

"Have you thought what you and Zack will do after we get back home?" Emma asked.

"Take a vacation on a beach somewhere far away and not be bothered by anyone else for a while. That's what I'd want, but given all this, I doubt we'll be any less busy than we are right now," Kaylan said.

Emma nodded. "Indeed, all this," she said as she went over to the conference table and turned on the holodisplay. "I wanted to talk to you about the Boxans."

Kaylan walked over. "What about them?"

"I've been doing my own analysis of Olloron and the Boxan population," Emma said.

"Okay, what have you found out?" Kaylan asked.

"It's strange. The Boxans don't reproduce fast, but on their home planet, their population numbered in the billions, according to their records. Here, on Olloron, there are only a few hundred million of them. They've been here for fifty years, give or take, and their population hasn't changed that much," Emma said.

"Well, they *have* been fighting a war," Kaylan said.

"I've accounted for that, but even with that, their population isn't growing and cannot be sustained on this planet," Emma said.

Kaylan's forehead wrinkled. Emma was a biologist and this was her field. "Are you sure?"

"Yes. I've run my analysis half a dozen times and it all indicates that Olloron cannot sustain the Boxans for more than a hundred years at the most. That's assuming they can even maintain their population. One of the reasons I wanted to come up here was to have Athena look at my data models to see if they're correct," Emma said.

Kaylan watched as Emma transferred a file from her PDA and uploaded it to Athena's data storage.

"I'd be happy to look at your work, Dr. Roberson," the AI said. "Analyzing . . . complete. Your findings are accurate."

"How could they not know this?" Kaylan asked.

"Empirical evidence would suggest that the Boxans already *do* know these facts and have not acted on this knowledge," the AI said.

Kaylan pressed her lips together in thought. Could an entire species be in denial about their situation?

"I can't believe they would simply ignore this problem. Do you know if they've tried to find another colony world?" Kaylan asked.

"I tried looking on the systems we have access to, but if they're looking, they're not devoting a lot of resources to it," Emma said.

"Perhaps they have a way to extend their time here on Olloron?"

Emma shook her head. "Unlikely because this planet isn't mineral-rich like Earth. It's only capable of sustaining limited forests and tundra, but even the oceans aren't teaming with life. If it were as simple as bringing water to this planet, that would be one thing, but the low mineral content of the soil suggests this world has already been depleted. It also doesn't have a moon, so no tides. The moon and the tides back on Earth are essential for life to flourish."

Kaylan studied the data onscreen. The Boxans weren't just losing a war with the Xiiginns, they were in danger of going extinct forever if they didn't find a safe place to live.

"They're stuck in this rigid cycle," Kaylan said.

Emma nodded. "And that's why we need to be careful, I think."

"Why is that?"

"They've had to make really tough decisions—so many that I

can't even imagine how they've managed to keep it together as long as they have. But when a society gets into this cycle of surviving and only surviving, they see everything as a tough choice that requires sacrifice. It becomes almost instinctual. I don't think all the Boxans feel this way, but this perception is certainly shared by many of them," Emma said.

"Well, they've lost a lot."

"They have, but they might lose even more if they don't deal with this problem now. They need to find a permanent home," Emma said.

"I want to talk to Ma'jasalax about this and see what she thinks. It could be that the Mardoxian Sect is trying to steer the High Council in this direction," Kaylan said.

"They do seem to be at the heart of many things . . ."

The rest of what Emma said suddenly became muffled in Kaylan's ears as she closed her eyes to a flash of light and heard the distinct sounds of a blaster being fired.

"Kaylan, are you alright?" Emma asked while shaking Kaylan's shoulders.

Kaylan opened her eyes. "I'm all right."

Emma frowned. "Maybe I should call Brenda."

Kaylan shook her head. "No, it's nothing. I'm fine. Just a bit tired, I think. I've had some strange dreams lately."

Emma looked at her for a long moment. "What have you been dreaming about?"

Kaylan told her about the Boxan in the red power armor and being on a battlefield.

"I'm not surprised you've got Boxans on the brain. We all do, but are you sure this isn't your ability rather than a dream?"

"I'm not sure," Kaylan admitted.

"Maybe you should try and use a Mardoxian chamber to see if that gives you a stronger vision. If nothing happens, you'll know it was just a dream," Emma said.

Kaylan smiled. "That's a good idea. I think I'll give that a try."

CHAPTER 6

Kaylan and Zack had spent the night alone aboard the Athena and were eating breakfast in the mess hall.

"You know we have this ship that we could use to just fly right out of here," Zack said.

Kaylan shook her head.

"Or take the shuttle and find some remote part of Olloron that the Boxans haven't been to yet," Zack said.

"I need to get back down to the surface," Kaylan said.

"Let me guess. Ma'jasalax."

"Yes, I do need to see her. It's about what Emma told me yesterday."

Zack nodded. "I get it. Well, I don't really get it. Why would anyone stay somewhere that wasn't going to keep them alive? That doesn't make any sense to me, but . . . you know what? It does make sense to me," he said, his eyes lighting up.

"Really," Kaylan said unconvinced.

"Yes, really. When my mom left us, my dad and I couldn't

stay in our house. We couldn't afford it anymore. The one thing my dad insisted on keeping was a 1968 Dodge Charger. It was a beautiful car. God, I miss that thing. We'd work on it on weekends and stuff, but what I didn't know at the time was that it was worth a fortune. He could have sold it and made a lot of money, but he didn't. It was like this was the one thing he could hold onto. It was almost like he would lose his identity if he sold that car. He held onto it even when it didn't make sense to keep it any longer, but it was his. I'm wondering if there are some similarities with the way the Boxans feel about Olloron, as a way of holding onto their identity." Zack said.

Kaylan eyed him for a moment. "You're equating an entire species' determination to stay on a planet they can't survive on with your dad's car?"

Zack nodded with a smile. "Yes, I am. This was a colony world. They already lost their home planet. There's only so much loss a person can take before they throw in the towel and just hold on or let go."

As the seconds went by, Kaylan found that Zack was making a lot of sense. His dark, penetrating eyes regarded her and he saw her finally get his point. Sometimes she wondered what Zack would do if he had the Mardoxian trait like she did. He already had the uncanny ability to see right to the heart of any matter and put it in simplified terms that anyone could understand. It was something she admired in him.

"Whatever happened to the car?" Kaylan asked.

Zack's ears turned red. "I had to sell it when he died."

Kaylan stroked his forearm. "That's not your fault."

"I didn't even think about it, about how much that car meant to him. I was actually happy that it sold because it paid a lot of bills, but still, I should have . . ."

Kaylan pulled him into her arms. "You were so young. I remember what it did to you. How could you have known? We should try and find the car when we get back."

Zack frowned. "Are you serious? The car is gone. Who knows where it could be?"

Kaylan rolled her eyes. "You manage to decode an alien signal, but a car with a VIN number is beyond you? Don't be an idiot. We'll find that car when we get back home."

Zack sighed heavily. "Why's this so important to you?"

"Because it's important you, dummy," Kaylan said.

"Do you have any idea what it will cost? It's a collector's item —" he stopped himself and then shook his head. "No," he said and stepped away from her. "I don't need charity."

Kaylan shook her head. "We're going to argue about this here? Now?"

Zack stepped back from her and put his hands on his hips. "Your family has enough money to rival small countries. I get it."

Kaylan crossed her arms and narrowed her gaze at him. "I don't know how you can go from brilliant to idiotic in seconds. Yes, my family is wealthy and I have a huge trust fund. I'm not going to apologize for that. If you want to be with me, then you'll need to come to terms with it, you jerk. How dare you accuse me of making you a charity case," she said, stalking toward him.

Zack backed away, bringing his hands in front his chest in a placating gesture.

"I'm with you because I love you, even when you do this. I don't need to buy your dad's old car for you because you'll be able to do it yourself. You're a damn hero, Zack. Whether you want to admit it or not, you saved Earth from the Xiiginn fleet."

"It was all of us," Zack said.

"We were all there and we contributed, but it was you who uploaded the command to the Star Shroud. It was you who had the insight to apply what we found at the Drar space station and gave the people back home a fighting chance to live. And I'll make sure they all know it was you," Kaylan said.

She'd gotten so close to him that she brushed against his chest.

"God, you're scary when you're mad, and I'm strangely turned on right now," Zack said.

Kaylan punched him in the stomach.

Zack coughed and laughed at the same time. "Alright. I'm sorry. I'm an idiot. I can't be brilliant all the time. Do you have any idea how hard that is?"

Kaylan cracked a smile and the rest of her ire drained away. Kissing him goodbye, she headed toward the shuttle.

A short while later Kaylan landed the Athena's shuttle on the landing pad where Efren and Katie met her. After a quick greeting, Efren went straight aboard the shuttle, but Katie lingered for a moment.

"How's he doing?" Katie asked.

"Burying himself in his work," Kaylan said.

Katie had long since gotten over her fling with Zack, but they were still friends. Kaylan had noticed that Katie was spending quite a bit a time with Efren, so maybe there was something there. They all took whatever comfort they could find in each other.

"I'll check on him later," Katie promised, and Kaylan thanked her.

Kaylan took a transit pad to the Mardoxian complex. She had Emma's data analysis on Olloron in case she needed it, but she didn't think she would. There was no way anyone in the Mardoxian Sect would have missed this. The question that remained was why no one was doing anything about it.

The transit pad brought her down in the middle of the Mardoxian complex. Boxans preferred a dome-shaped architecture and Ma'jasalax had told her that the dome shapes were efficient, but on Sethion there were vast cities. Kaylan had spent a little bit of time learning Boxan history and they'd come from an incredibly lush and fertile world. Sethion was larger than Earth but not by much. Most of the planet was forested and the forests were brought into the vast cities. The pictures she'd seen were amazing and she wished she could have witnessed it in person.

Kaylan accessed the info terminal to find Ma'jasalax's location and then probed with her senses to see if she was actually there. She was, but she wasn't alone. Ma'jasalax was with Hodak, the head of the Mardoxian Sect. Kaylan swallowed hard. If she wanted answers, his were probably the best she was going to get.

Kaylan walked through the building. The hallways were sparse, with most buildings designed for necessity rather than comfort or history, and there weren't very many Boxans at the Mardoxian complex at any given time. Ma'jasalax had told her that they were purposefully spread apart to keep the actual numbers of Boxans with the Mardoxian trait a secret. All Boxans had some level of the Mardoxian trait, but not all of them were adept at it like Ma'jasalax. Kaylan suspected that the same would apply to Humans. She knew Dux Corp had a recruitment protocol for the program that followed Stargate, but she had no idea what it was. She also had no idea how she stacked up against the other members of that secret organization, but Ma'jasalax insisted that Kaylan was gifted even by Boxan standards.

Outside the door she needed to go through was a heavily armed Boxan soldier. He must have been Hodak's bodyguard. All Mardoxian priests had them. Ma'jasalax's guard had died protecting her when she was captured by the Xiiginns. She should have been assigned another bodyguard but hadn't, and it was also unclear why Ma'jasalax's old bodyguard hadn't carried out his duty to end her life rather than risk a Mardoxian priestess being captured by the Xiiginns.

"They're expecting you, Commander," the Boxan guarding the door said.

The door opened and Kaylan walked through. The room beyond was much like the resonance chambers the Boxans built on their starships. The resonance chamber was an artificial garden filled with plants that were native to Sethion. Those plants would never survive in Olloron's dry atmosphere.

"Welcome, Kaylan," Hodak said.

The two Boxans knelt on the ground, facing one another.

The door closed behind her and Kaylan continued toward them and knelt down, sitting on her feet. "Thank you," she said.

"Ma'jasalax tells me that your progress through our training regimen has been exponential. I'm very happy to hear this and you should be proud of your accomplishment," Hodak said.

"Thank you," Kaylan said. "I'd like to discuss something with both of you."

Ma'jasalax's large ears twitched and her long braids shifted. "What is it you wish to discuss?" she asked.

"Emma Roberson is a foremost expert in multiple fields of biology. She's been running some analyses on Olloron and has come to realize that its viability as a long-term home world for the Boxans may not be possible. I have her data, but neither of us can imagine that this is something you're unaware of," Kaylan said.

Ma'jasalax exchanged glances with Hodak, who gave a slight nod.

"You are, of course, correct. Olloron is merely a resting place while we regroup," Ma'jasalax said.

"Have you located any other worlds you can migrate to?" Kaylan asked.

"I can say we're aware of the situation but have prioritized stopping the Xiiginns rather than finding another world to migrate to," Hodak said.

"Why wouldn't you look for a new home? Could you return to Sethion?" Kaylan asked.

Hodak's body went rigid. "Sethion is beyond our reach. To return there would condemn our species to death. There's a reason the star system is under quarantine. Also, with the Xiiginns in control of the Confederation, we couldn't stand against the combined forces of the Confederation."

"I know your war is with the Xiiginns, but at some point you'll need to defend yourself, even from those species that are misguided," Kaylan said.

"Was Jonah Redford misguided?" Ma'jasalax asked.

"No, he was a pawn, a victim," Kaylan said.

"That's how we feel about the other species in the Confederation," Ma'jasalax said.

"If you're not looking for another colony world, what will you do if the Xiiginns discover this place? What if, despite all your precautions, they find out where you are? You owe it to yourselves to look for another home—a better home than this place," Kaylan said.

"We shall persevere as we always have. Our fleets would defend this place and throw back any attack made by the Xiiginns," Hodak said.

"Are the other Boxans aware they can't stay here in the long term?" Kaylan asked.

"Scientists are aware of the situation. Key members of the High Council and Battle Leaders are aware," Ma'jasalax said.

"Why don't you appeal to the Confederation for help? Not all the different species can be subservient to the Xiiginns. Aren't there other allies?" Kaylan asked.

"We've tried in the past. The price for their help is always to grant access to the Star Shroud network across a multitude of star systems. Primitive species would fall victim to the Xiiginns, and we won't condemn those species to their mercy," Ma'jasalax said.

Kaylan glanced at both of them. Zack was right. The Boxans had become a race of beings that was fixated on making tough decisions. They were so rigid that they wouldn't find a more suitable home world to live on. What was worse was that she didn't think she could convince them.

"I realize this appears harsh, but we have a different perception of time than you do. For the foreseeable future, we will remain here," Hodak said.

Kaylan looked at Ma'jasalax. She knew this was wrong. The

Boxans had backed themselves into a corner and wouldn't do anything to get themselves out of it. Is this how a species like the Boxans eventually went extinct? They were alive, but Kaylan felt that something needed to change. Her mind kept returning to Sethion. She felt that it was the key to the Boxan's survival. She had to learn all she could about it, but she wouldn't get answers from Hodak or Ma'jasalax so she let the matter drop.

CHAPTER 7

In an area between the planets of the star system that was home to the Humans, remnants of a Xiiginn warship floated in space. Passive scans hadn't detected the minuscule amount of power still operating within the wrecked starship and Mar Arden had a difficult choice to make. They'd survived inside the mysterious barrier that was protecting this star system from their fleet and they'd managed to remain undetected for many cycles. Their survival required all of their ingenuity, as well as the promise that what they would find on Earth would be worth something of great value to the Confederation. With the limited number of shuttles he had at his disposal, he'd made only a single foray to this star system's interior planets. The Boxans had left the Humans their Orbital Defense Platforms that were more than capable of detecting their attack shuttles if they'd suspected that the Xiiginns were in the area. Secrecy was their primary weapon, especially with only a few attack shuttles and a converted section of the warship hull that functioned as a lifeboat for the surviving crewmembers.

Mar Arden waited in his chambers for Hoan Berend and Kandra Rene to arrive. Hoan Berend had been much more amiable since Mar Arden had put him in his place. Now the ship commander did his bidding without question, and rightfully so. It had been Mar Arden's actions and quick thinking that had saved them from the rest of the Xiiginn fleet's destruction. He still couldn't fathom how the barrier had been created, but he knew it had something to do with the Star Shroud.

Standard Boxan protocol for observing a less advanced species would put their monitoring station on the furthest planet in the system, and it just so happened that this planet was more than half a system away from their current location. But it wouldn't have mattered to Mar Arden if it had been much closer. He wouldn't risk going there. It was the ultimate sort of irony that after all this time fighting with the Boxans over their Star Shroud monitoring stations, they had finally found an intact one and they weren't even going to investigate it. Mar Arden had little doubt that the Boxans and Humans were watching the monitoring station and should his presence be detected there, the Boxan monitoring station would self-destruct. He'd seen the Boxans use such tactics before in other star systems.

The door chimed and Mar Arden authorized it to open, revealing the squadron of loyal soldiers that stood outside his door at all times. They were in a survival situation and he wouldn't chance another Xiiginn trying to take his place if the opportunity arose. Only one other had tried, and Kandra Rene had made short work of him. Hoan Berend had also ensured that no one else made any such coup attempt. Mar Arden had always found that fortune would favor those who were better prepared.

Hoan Berend and Kandra Rene entered the room, the elder Xiiginn coming in first as befit his rank. Mar Arden invited them both to sit. Kandra Rene had just returned from an important assignment.

"My mission took longer that it otherwise would have if we'd had our sensor array intact," Kandra Rene said.

"I'm well aware of the limitations of the attack shuttle," Mar Arden replied.

Kandra Rene nodded. "I have an accurate model of the barrier. I didn't risk tampering with any of the Shroud devices."

"That's good, because if you had, no doubt the Boxans would be sweeping the area now, looking for us," Mar Arden said.

Learning that there were still Boxans in this star system made their work here even more delicate than if they'd had to contend with the Humans alone. It seemed that the Boxan Battle Leader in charge of the Dreadnaught group had emptied their ships of non-essential personnel and sent them back to Earth. Mar Arden approved of the tactic. The Boxans would only sacrifice Dreadnaughts for the highest priority of species. He still didn't understand what made the Humans so valuable to the Boxans, but that would come in time.

"According to my analysis, the barrier doesn't encompass the entire star system," Kandra Rene said.

Hoan Berend frowned. "There are gaps in the barrier? Perhaps we could signal the fleet through one of these gaps," he said.

"Apologies, Commander, what I mean is that the barrier will

cut off the ninth planet's orbit within the next fifty cycles," Kandra Rene said.

Mar Arden considered that for a moment. "Interesting. The power requirements for maintaining the barrier must be extremely high. Otherwise, whoever re-aligned the Star Shroud would have accounted for the ninth planet's orbit."

"I don't think they had time," Kandra Rene said.

"What do you mean?" Mar Arden asked.

"You already surmised that a new species is taking a hand in our war with the Boxans. There was the anomaly that was detected toward the end of the battle and then the barrier went up. This is not a coincidence, and if the Boxans had this kind of power, why would they waste two Dreadnaughts standing against our fleet?" Kandra Rene said.

"It could have taken them time to power the devices. It also could have taken them time to get the configuration uploaded through the Shroud network," Hoan Berend said.

"Those are possibilities," Kandra Rene acknowledged.

Mar Arden was impressed with his student. She could present her thoughts and still recognize that there were other possibilities. "I agree with you," Mar Arden said to Kandra Rene.

The Xiiginn perked up at the compliment and her tail flicked in the air behind her, but she immediately got her emotions under control and brought her tail to rest.

"I've managed to identify asteroids that have a significant amount of ice on them," Kandra Rene said.

"Excellent," Hoan Berend said. "I'll let our salvage crews know."

It was always a matter of resources. Their stock of provisions would sustain them, but a warship's design called for liquid water to be stored in the aft section of the ship, and that happened to be the part of the ship that had been sheered in half when they'd raced through the barrier as it was forming.

"We need to decide what our next move is," Hoan Berend said.

Both Xiiginns waited for Mar Arden to speak.

"Why do you think the Boxans are so invested in the Humans?" Mar Arden said.

"They tried to recruit the Nershals against us because they could resist our compulsion. Perhaps it's something similar," Hoan Berend said.

"The Boxans have ever been trying to nullify that particular vulnerability, but we have conflicting reports on whether the Humans are vulnerable to compulsion," Mar Arden said. His gaze drifted toward Kandra Rene.

The Xiiginn sucked in a harsh breath. "I failed to use compulsion on the Human, Zack Quick. He was able to resist me on multiple occasions. He could sense what I was doing and was able to deny me," Kandra Rene said.

"And yet Sion Shif was able to successfully control one of the other Athena crewmembers," Hoan Berend said.

Mar Arden pressed his thin lips together. "I don't believe that one Human resisting your compulsion calls your skills into question. It could simply be that some Humans are vulnerable while others aren't. It's something I look forward to learning more about," Mar Arden said.

Hoan Berend frowned. "So you mean to go further into the system then?" he asked.

"Of course. Getting to Earth was always the plan, but I'm reluctant to leave any Xiiginns behind," Mar Arden said.

"Mercy?" Hoan Berend said with a hint of disbelief in his voice.

Mar Arden shook his head. "Necessity. Carrying out my plans once we reach Earth requires a certain number of us and attack shuttles don't have the capacity to bring all of us there."

"Then how do you propose we get to Earth? Or even within the vicinity of the Human home planet?" Hoan Berend said.

Mar Arden drew in a deep breath. "What we really need is a way to move within this system without being detected. As slow as we are, we would only make it to the field where a failed planet never formed. And even that carries some risk as we've detected some Human activity in the asteroid field."

"Most likely mining activities," Hoan Berend said.

"Agreed. Surveyor probes and such," Mar Arden said.

There were a few moments of silence before Kandra Rene cleared her throat.

"We need to test their reactions, probe their defenses. Nothing that would give us away but enough to get their attention," Kandra Rene said.

Mar Arden let out a satisfied smile. "I concur."

Hoan Berend frowned. "There's a lot of risk for this effort."

"We'll need contingency plans should we be discovered," Mar Arden said and noted Hoan Berend's surprised expression. "Earlier, I said I was reluctant to lose resources if I don't need to. I didn't say I would risk losing my chance at Earth for the sake of all the Xiiginns we have with us."

"Understood. I'll make some preliminary lists for you to approve," Hoan Berend said.

Mar Arden looked at Kandra Rene. "I'll expect you to come up with a plan for getting the Boxan's attention."

Kandra Rene frowned. "Just the Boxans? Not the Humans?" she asked.

"We don't know how many Boxans made it back to Earth, but let's assume it was a few hundred. They'll be occupied with getting Earth ready to defend itself from attack," Mar Arden said.

Hoan Berend tapped his fingers on the table. "So a few hundred Boxans, some technical resources, and a species that can barely travel through their own star system. And you believe they're focused on defending themselves from attack?"

Mar Arden nodded. "Yes, and it's thanks to Garm Antis. Our illustrious supreme leader insisted that we send large asteroids through a wormhole towards Earth."

"His intention was to arrive at Earth in time to prevent the massive asteroid from destroying the planet and make the Humans believe the Boxans were somehow responsible," Hoan Berend said.

"Not the best plan Garm Antis could have enacted. The Humans were able to stop the asteroid and have no doubt surmised the vast resources in terms of materials it contains—more than enough for them to start building their own fleet. Couple that with a few hundred Boxans with the technical knowhow to give the Humans a head start and this could go very badly for us," Mar Arden said.

Hoan Berend shifted uncomfortably in his seat. "The Boxans wouldn't have a choice but to abandon their long-held principals about sharing advanced technology with a more primitive species."

"Yes, Garm Antis practically threw them together," Mar Arden said.

"There was no way Garm Antis could have anticipated something like the barrier around the star system," Hoan Berend said.

Mar Arden shrugged. He was seeing how far he could push the warship commander about their supreme leader before he'd push back. "I can't see the Boxans committing such resources to the Humans because some of them can resist our compulsion ability. They already have the Nershals, or at least the Nershals were still fighting a civil war regarding which side to take."

Kandra Rene's eyes flashed. "The Mardoxian potential! It has to be."

"It's the only reason I could think of as well, but I was curious to see which of you would bring it up first," Mar Arden said.

"We'll need to confirm it and that won't be easy," Hoan Berend said.

"After we get to Earth . . . but think about it. We could finally find the genetic link that gives the Boxans the advantage they've used for hundreds of years. Once we confirm the Mardoxian potential in Humans, we can then work toward implementing it into our own species, and that will take test subjects," Mar Arden said.

Hoan Berend let out a hungry growl of assent and even Kandra Rene was intrigued. Mar Arden found that the proper motivation was the best way to get the most out of his resources, and now that they were properly motivated, it was time to move forward with the next step in his plan.

CHAPTER 8

Ed Johnson glanced at his ECF visitor's badge, which showed a picture of him beside a prominent blue stripe. The clipped cadence of Iris Barrett in her Louboutin heels sounded next to him, comprising his entire protective detail at the ECF branch headquarters. At five foot, eleven inches she had more advanced implants and enhancements to strength, speed, and vision than most military drones used for reconnaissance. Iris was an army of one.

General William Sheridan no longer operated from NORAD but had taken over a state-of-the-art facility within a hundred miles from the Cheyenne Mountain complex.

Ed and Iris waited for the remaining two members of their party to go through the security checkpoint.

Alicia Murphy was a thick-set woman who was barely five feet tall. Her brown, curly hair hugged her round face, and her thick glasses were part of her disguise. Walking past her in public, no one would give her a second glance. Her gray business suit and pale pink shirt allowed her to blend in with either a crowd at a shopping mall or a corporate office.

Blake Allen was the last one through. He was only a few inches taller than Alicia and had a small belly pressing up against the belt of his pants. Add a thinning head of hair above a black necktie and most people wouldn't notice him any more than Alicia. No one would guess they were both exceptional viewers who were highly respected in the Dux Corp upper echelons. Blake and Alicia were here to join the ECF. They had no family ties and were dedicated to doing their part to help protect the Earth.

They were escorted farther inside the buildings where Ed saw Sheridan speaking with a Boxan soldier. When the Boxans had first arrived, they'd rarely come planet-side, but now that things were getting up and running on the New Moon and Lunar Base, groups of Boxans had been making regular trips down to various ECF complexes across the globe.

Their escort asked them to wait while he notified Sheridan they were here, and after a few moments, the lead general of the ECF waved them over. Ed led the way and shook hands with Sheridan.

General Sheridan gestured toward the Boxan soldier. "I'm not sure you've met in person, but this is Scraanyx, Strike Commander for the Boxan military."

Ed gave a slight bow to the Boxan.

"Michael Hunsicker speaks highly of you. A pleasure to make your acquaintance," Scraanyx said.

The Boxan's great size and deep voice took Ed a moment to register. It was one thing to know there was a being that was ten foot tall but it was quite another to have it standing in front of you. Ed introduced Iris, Alicia, and Blake.

Scraanyx bowed to Alicia and Blake. "It is an honor to meet those who have the Mardoxian potential," he said.

"Welcome to the Earth Coalition Force, and thank you for joining us," Sheridan said to Alicia and Blake, then shifted his gaze toward Ed. "We need to talk about testing centers for ECF recruitment. We know Russia had their own remote-viewer program that was part of the old KGB."

Ed nodded. "I'm aware of the program. Wasn't anywhere near as effective as ours."

"You and I both know that if we add anything regarding telepathic abilities to the ECF recruitment bulletin, we'll get nut-job applicants instead of quality applicants," Sheridan said.

"That's why we didn't use those terms as part of the recruitment process," Ed said.

"Yeah, but we need a way to attract people who may have this ability," Sheridan said and looked at Scraanyx. "How do you find members of your race who have the Mardoxian potential?"

"Having the Mardoxian potential is among the highest honors for Boxans. There are no pretenders, but without Thesulia we have no one here who could aid in validating the claim," Scraanyx said.

Ed drew in a deep breath. They'd learned that Thesulia was a Mardoxian priestess who had stayed with Prax'pedax to help fight against the Xiiginn fleet.

"Their sacrifice will not be in vain, I promise you," Ed said and turned toward Sheridan. "Alicia and Blake can help with testing potential recruits, but you don't need to start from scratch. We have lists of potential candidates you can choose from."

Sheridan frowned. "Do I even want to know where this list comes from?" he asked.

"It's not what you think. Most countries have a form of standardized testing for children throughout their school career from the elementary level all the way through college entrance exams," Ed said.

"Telepathic abilities can present themselves in a number of different ways," Alicia said.

"How?" Sheridan asked.

"Intuition, for one—being able to read into a situation and still achieve your objective. These are things that are emphasized in basic training found anywhere from militaries to law enforcement agencies around the globe," Alicia said.

"We target the people who stand out to determine whether they'd be ideal candidates," Ed said.

"What makes an ideal candidate?" Sheridan asked.

"There are some who are open to the possibility of certain telepathic capabilities, but then there are others who don't cope with it very well," Ed said.

"Where does Kaylan Farrow figure into all this then?" Sheridan asked.

Scraanyx cleared his throat. "The Athena commander is known to us. A highly revered Mardoxian priestess has validated the claim of her skills."

"Michael Hunsicker's reports from the first leg of the Athena mission to Pluto categorized Kaylan's abilities as repeatedly demonstrative. When they first arrived at the Boxan monitoring station, it was as if Kaylan had already been there. I'm willing to wager that Kaylan's abilities have only become more refined during her time with the Boxans," Ed said.

Blake raised his hand, indicating he had something to add. "We've seen those reports and they're nothing short of amazing. Kaylan Farrow was able to remote-view to a place millions of miles away, and their mission update also describes how she used her ability to help locate the Athena crewmember held captive by the Xiiginn."

Sheridan nodded. "What I'd like to know is whether Kaylan's the exception or if she's the standard we can expect others to be able to achieve."

"Right now, she's the exception," Ed said. "Even the Boxans have indicated that telepathic capabilities among the Mardoxian Sect vary."

"My understanding is that they put their Mardoxian priests on the bridge of their ships and the captains will defer to them as part of their strategy in battle," Sheridan said.

"That is correct," Scraanyx said. "There is no challenge to authority, but a battle commander would be remiss if they were to ignore a recommendation made by anyone from the Mardoxian Sect."

Sheridan frowned. "I acknowledge that you have a system in place that works for you. We'll build our own fleet, but I'm not sure how this will fit within our command structure."

"They'll need to prove their worth," Ed said.

"We wouldn't advocate that you adopt our model for commanding your fleets, but the Mardoxian potential is something that can help your species realize its full potential. And it will be something the Xiiginns will try to take from you," Scraanyx said.

Ed had seen that whenever a Boxan referred to the Xiiginns there came with it the deep loathing of one's enemies. Soldiers returning from war often demonstrated this form of hatred that had enabled them to do what they'd had to do to survive. For all intents and purposes, the Boxans'd had to become a militaristic society in order to survive. Ed understood the necessity of it and at the same time hoped that Earth's fate wouldn't require the same price for survival.

CHAPTER 9

As the head liaison between Humans and Boxans, Michael Hunsicker was also on point for General William Sheridan's visits to the lunar base. And Michael knew it was just a matter of time before the head of the Earth Coalition Force ventured onsite.

On the lunar base, they had no formal ECF uniform other than the jumpsuits they wore for their everyday duties. The official ECF uniform was dark blue with a phoenix-emblem patch on the side. Since Michael was no longer a member of NASA and was officially part of the ECF, his old military rank of Air Force Colonel had carried over, but he wasn't sure what ranking structure the ECF would settle on because once they had a fleet there was talk of them following the US naval command hierarchy. There were no colonels in the Navy. Ultimately, Michael didn't care. He had a job to do, and whatever rank the ECF brass saw fit to give him would be okay with him. He'd been an Air Force colonel and, later on, a mission commander for two of

NASAs most historic missions—one to Mars and the second to Pluto.

ECF staff lined up along the corridor for Sheridan's visit and base commander Alyssa Archer stood at Michael's side.

"Stand up straight, the boss is coming," Alyssa whispered.

Michael snorted.

Those in the military snapped a salute as the four-star general came through the airlock doors and entered the ECF wing of the lunar base. Two of his armed escorts walked ahead of him. Sheridan swung his mighty gaze at Michael Hunsicker and walked directly over to him.

"I feel like *I* should salute *you*," Sheridan said and stuck out his hand.

Michael shook the general's hand. "It's nice to finally meet you, General," he said.

"I should have come here much sooner. As it is, we hitched a ride with Scraanyx," Sheridan said.

Michael nodded. "If you'll follow Alyssa and me, we'll be the ones showing you around."

Sheridan shook Alyssa's hand as well. The rest of the ECF staff was dismissed and Michael proceeded to show the general around. He'd been in numerous meetings with him, but this was the first time they'd met face to face. By the time they got to the main conference room, Colonel Mathews had caught up with them.

"Apologies, General. I was at the new moon making sure the engineers from Mirae Corporation were situated and working on getting the mechs online," Kyle said.

"Understood, and I approved their transfer last week. They'll be here for as long as you need them," Sheridan said.

Chazen and Scraanyx joined them in the main conference room where they sat on reinforced benches designed to take the weight of a Boxan, who could weigh nearly a thousand pounds —and more than that when they wore their powered armor.

"Thank you all for coming," Sheridan said. "All of you here, along with the rest of the people in your departments, are our boots on the ground. We're getting to the point where we've amassed materials sufficient enough to ramp up our shipbuilding capabilities. We're all part of the ECF, and we'll only continue to grow with the best people our planet has to offer. Futurists would say that an organization such as ours has the potential to outlast the countries from which it began. It sounds nice, and hopefully, hundreds of years from now, the people will look back at what we've started and acknowledge what will be done here. There are some who think we'll fail, that the Earth Coalition Force will not succeed. Humans have never come together as a whole, but there are people from around the world here, and there'll be more now that China and Russia have officially joined the ECF and will be contributing resources to us. We all need to learn to work together, and our efforts here and now will have long-lasting effects far beyond what will happen once we leave here. We're the line that stands between the Xiiginns and the people of Earth. Perhaps, in the future, there will be another species that will threaten our lives," Sheridan said glancing at the Boxans. "I hope not, but the ECF will be the ones to defend our planet and our right to exist in the galaxy."

Michael glanced around at those gathered in the large assembly area. Most sat a little straighter, and even Chazen and Scraanyx were caught up in Sheridan's speech. The Boxans stood up and brought their fists to their chests.

"Battle Leader," Scraanyx said, addressing General Sheridan with title reserved for the most eminent leader in the Boxan military. For a Boxan it was the highest form of praise.

"Colonel Matthews, show us what you've got," Sheridan said.

Kyle Matthews stood up and engaged the holoprojector. Three-dimensional images of six starship designs came into view.

"The ships you see before you are of Boxan design but aren't the Dreadnaughts we saw when the Boxans first arrived. Those ships are beyond our current capabilities so we propose that our approach to starship-building will be to start small," Kyle said and took control of the holointerface. He swiped the ships to the side, and a smaller, two-person craft came into prominence. "This is a strike-fighter. We plan to merge the Boxan strike-fighter with our own advanced military space vehicles. Actual production of these ships has already begun. Strike-fighter training programs have begun at places like Sacramento Bay and RAF Cranwell in the United Kingdom. We even have a few simulators here. Cadets who go through the training on the ground will finish their training up here.

"Some of you may be wondering why we would start with such a small attack spacecraft, but one thing history has taught us is to start small and build from there. This will hold true even with the help from the Boxans, although with their help we'll be able to develop much faster than we normally would have. Strike-fighter squadrons are something we can do quickly, setting up fighter bases here and on the new moon. We'll eventually put them elsewhere as well, such as on carriers that we'll build. Again, we'll start small and take our cues from established practices throughout history, but this time it will come from our navies. Although some ship designs may need to be merged, the ships we build will serve our first and ultimate goal, which is to defend the Earth from the threat of invasion. Destroyer-class vessels will be first, then cruisers, and eventually battleship carriers. Those will be our ships of the line. Eventually, we'll get to the big behemoths the Boxans have built, but we can't just start building ships indiscriminately. Our ships must be built to stand against Xiiginn warships and tactics. There'll be some things we'll need to start over, acknowledging our weaknesses and making them our strengths. We're new to space warfare, and one of the things we need from you is your ideas. The Boxans and Xiiginns have been fighting for a long time. Perhaps there's something we can offer that the Boxans haven't considered."

Michael listened as various ECF members put forth their ideas. The Boxans had already been sharing all they knew about the Xiiginns and their arsenal. More than once Michael had found himself thinking about Prax'pedax and his foresight to send as many Boxans back to Earth as he could.

After the meeting, Michael was reviewing his messages and saw an alert about several drones tasked with monitoring the barrier having gone offline. They were running diagnostics on the system and the nearest drone would be sent to investigate.

CHAPTER 10

Over the past few days, Kaylan had dedicated her time to learning what she could about Sethion, the Boxan home world. Finding the coordinates to the planet had been relatively easy, but with them came a warning that the planet and star system itself was under quarantine. Any attempt to go to Sethion without proper authorization would result in that ship being treated as a hostile force. Not only would the automated defensive platforms throughout the system destroy anyone trying to enter the system, but also anyone trying to leave. Learning that bit of news had shaken her and left her restless ever since.

The Boxans had found themselves in the midst of a civil war that had spawned during what they called the Xiiginn uprising, which led to the Chaos Wars. Hordes of Boxans had fled Sethion, but when Boxans under the Xiiginn influence attempted to learn of Olloron's location, the High Counsel had to act. In order to preserve the lives of the remaining free members of their society, they'd had to cut all ties from

Sethion. The Boxans had successfully ousted the Xiiginns from Sethion's star system, but the damage had already been done. Once a Boxan was under Xiiginn influence, there was no way to reverse it. There'd been a number of scientists who had tried and all had failed. The High Council had forbidden anyone else from returning to Sethion and condemned any Boxan left behind to a life filled with terror, loss, and brutality. Kaylan had seen the vids, and until then it had been hard to imagine what the wide-scale impact of a Boxan war would have on a planet.

Large portions of the planet had been destroyed, and such madness and savagery had spread that Kaylan wasn't sure how anyone could survive. The images in the vids haunted her and wouldn't abate no matter what she did. She knew there were Boxans still fighting for their lives back on Sethion and her visions of them weren't just dreams. She knew she should focus on trying to get back to Earth, but she couldn't let her intuition about Sethion go. Intuition and foresight were what the Boxans revered most about Mardoxian Sect members, and her gut instinct was telling her that there was still hope for Sethion.

Kaylan decided to start asking different Boxans about Sethion and whether they thought there was any hope for those left behind, but hardly any Boxan was willing to speak to her about it. Even Gaarokk, who had helped them in the past, refused to consider it. Earlier that day she'd gone to speak to Kladomaor about it and even he told her that Sethion was dead.

What she needed was proof. More than growing her abilities, she needed to find evidence that there were still Boxans unaffected by the Xiiginn influence there. Sethion may be lost, but the Boxans who had been left behind required a miracle, and if the Boxans here refused to answer the call, she'd have to go it alone while trying to convince anyone she could to help her.

Kaylan had arranged for Zack to meet her at one of the garden paths outside the city. What forests there were on Olloron were short and sparse, as if they were near the ocean shore. The roots weren't able to grow very deep and the nutrients in the soil weren't abundant. The Boxans had done what they could during their time here to create gardens that they cared for, but the plants that were native to this planet didn't vary all that much and were mostly brown or tan to match the dry landscape. Where the Boxans had brought irrigation, the plants thrived, but only to a certain point, and the gardens were pale shades of greens.

Kaylan's PDA buzzed on her wrist, signaling that Zack was getting close, and she heard the sound of a small craft approach and land nearby. Zack was spending most of his time on the Athena but would occasionally return to the surface to be with the others. He climbed out of the cockpit of a Boxan transport vehicle, a small gray craft that was used for training young Boxans and was readily usable by the crew of the Athena. They couldn't leave the atmosphere but were perfect for traveling short distances. She was glad Zack shared her love of flying. She'd prefer to race around in a strike-fighter, but her time had been limited.

Zack waved over to her and glanced around to see if anyone else was around, raising his brows in exaggerated mock surprise. "Are we all alone out here?" he asked.

Kaylan smiled. "I thought it might be a refreshing change of pace."

Zack came over to give her a quick kiss and then took her

hand as they walked down the garden path. They chewed the time away, talking about different things.

"I still haven't been able to get any Shroud devices to test with," Zack said.

"What are you trying to do?"

"I want to recreate the barrier but on a much smaller scale. The issue we're having is that the barrier is preventing us from disabling it from the outside," Zack said.

"So you think if you send the proper sequence to turn it off from inside the barrier, it would work?" Kaylan asked.

"That's the theory," Zack said.

"What if it didn't work? Whoever was inside the barrier would be trapped," Kaylan said.

"Well, gee, I didn't think of that," he said with a grin. "I wasn't going to be the one inside—and no one else for that matter. I'd put a transmitter inside that would send out the shutdown signal after a period of time. If it didn't work, then we'd know. I'm sure we could limit the power available to the Shroud devices so they'd cease to function after awhile," Zack said.

"Sounds like a good experiment, so what's the problem?"

Zack blew out a breath. "The problem is they don't have any Shroud devices here. I don't need the actual thing. I could scale the model down, so I've been looking at building my own."

"Couldn't Gaarokk help with that?" Kaylan asked.

"He is. We're trying to gather materials, but it's proving to be more trouble than I thought. Materials are scarce, so while Gaarokk is looking into that, I've been searching through the Athena's new Drar reference library for any clue about how to build them. The problem is that the Drars didn't call it a Shroud device," Zack said.

Kaylan nodded, finally understanding. The Drars had their own way of naming things. The Boxans had been able to help with some translating and conceptual understanding of what was being described, but it was a slow process.

"I need your help," Kaylan said.

"With what?"

"I'm trying to get information about Sethion," Kaylan said.

Zack frowned. "What kind of information?"

"I need to know if there's been any recent activity on the planet that would indicate there're Boxans still alive there," Kaylan said.

Zack's brows shot up his forehead. "You told me the other day about the quarantine zone and that no ship could get through. Sounds like a suicidal request."

Kaylan looked away. "That was the other thing I wanted to talk to you about."

Zack shook his head. "No," he said, taking a few steps away from her where he stopped and shook his head again.

Kaylan followed. "Come on, Zack. I know you can do this," she said.

"Kaylan, I promised them I wouldn't go poking around their systems while we were here. We're their guests. I may think the Boxans are a bit harsh at times, but we wouldn't be here if it weren't for them," Zack said and held up his hand. "And I mean that in a good way."

"What if there are still Boxans there who need help?" Kaylan asked.

"I'm trying to figure out a way to get us home. Why do we have to solve the Boxans' problems for them?"

Kaylan drew in a deep, steadying breath and lowered her

voice. They'd both been speaking too loud. "Because no one else will. The Boxans have washed their hands of it," Kaylan said.

"Yeah, and that should tell you something. It's like they suddenly decided, 'Oh well, the rest of you stuck on the planet are screwed. Bye, bye, see ya later,'" Zack said and continued to walk down the path.

"I know there are Boxans there," Kaylan said, and Zack stopped in his tracks. "Ones unaffected by the Xiiginn influence."

"How could you possibly know this?" Zack asked.

Kaylan closed the distance between them. "I've seen it. Those visions Ma'jasalax believes are dreams are real."

Zack frowned. "Let me get this straight. You think this recurring dream or vision thing is you seeing actual events as they're unfolding?"

"Yes," Kaylan said.

"And what do the other Mardoxian priests think of this?" Zack asked.

"I've only told Ma'jasalax, but I did bring Sethion up to the others and they won't even consider anything that has to do with going back there," Kaylan said.

"Just bear with me a second," Zack said. "I can't begin to explain how you can do the things you do—like how you found me when I was a prisoner or even how you knew I was alive—but we were in the same star system and you had an idea of where to look. I thought you needed a precise location to remote-view your way there."

"That's part of it, but this is different. I've been training with the Boxans for a while now and my abilities are growing stronger. Ma'jasalax told me that the most gifted of the Mardoxian Sect are brilliant strategists who are able to see events beyond what they appear to be. It's how I knew to disconnect the gravity tether in the wormhole while we were trying to find the Drar space station. I think my time here learning all that I've learned has enabled me to pick up on certain things—things the Boxans are ignoring. It's these things that are allowing me to focus on Sethion. I don't know how else to explain it. The visions are so intense. I can smell the air and hear the Boxans fighting," Kaylan said.

"Who are they fighting?" Zack asked.

Kaylan swallowed hard. "Each other, but each vision I have centers around one particular Boxan wearing old, traditional armor. It reminds me of when I first used the Mardoxian chamber and met Ma'jasalax," she said.

Zack regarded her for a few moments, considering. "Why don't you use one of the Mardoxian chambers and go take a look?" he asked.

"It's not that easy. For one, they keep the chambers on lock-down, so there's that to contend with, and if I told them what I want to do I don't think they'd allow it," Kaylan said.

Zack pressed his lips together. "I don't know," he said.

Kaylan flinched. "I'm surprised. I thought you of all people would help me with this."

"It's not that. I'm trying to be compliant with their conditions for allowing us to stay here. I'm doing it for you," Zack said.

Kaylan looked away from him. She knew he wasn't just being stubborn, but why did he have to become respectful of Boxan wishes now? At one time he would have relished the challenge, but he was more mature now. She liked it, but if Zack wouldn't help her, how was she going to find out what was happening on Sethion?

"Look," Zack said. "Let me think about it for a while—weigh out the pros and cons."

Kaylan took his hand in hers. "Thank you," she said. It was something at least.

CHAPTER 11

The day after Kaylan asked Zack for his help with extracting key bits of information about Sethion, he decided he would look into it. For a while now the Boxans had been trying to probe the Athena's computer systems. The first time it occurred, the Athena's AI had alerted him immediately. The fascinating part was that they'd been unsuccessful. He instructed the AI to keep a close watch on their attempts and log the activity. He'd known the Athena's computing systems forwards and backwards before going to the Drar space station, and the Boxans should have been able to gain access with ease. However, the Drars had remade the Athena, including the computer systems, and that was the reason the Boxans were having so many problems trying to gain access. He'd thought of accusing the Boxans directly of what they were doing but had decided not to. One of the many things he'd learned from hacking his way into corporate networks or securing his own network was that it was far more revealing to watch the attacker attempt to gain access, seeing what tools they had in their arsenal and what methods they used. Sometimes he learned something.

The Boxan's first attempts to gain access to the Athena's systems had been almost delicate, but as they were continually thwarted, their attempts had become more aggressive. Their recent request to take the ship apart to see how it worked was the latest effort at trying to gain access to the Drar knowledge that was wrapped up in the Athena, and it was one of the reasons Zack had decided to stay aboard the ship. Well, that and the fact that he wanted to figure out a way to get home—a way that wouldn't leave Earth vulnerable to Xiiginn attack. The crew of the Athena was united on that front. No one would think of jeopardizing Earth in their attempts to get home. He hadn't told the others about the Boxans' attempts to gain access to the Athena. He was handling it and they were focused on learning what they could from the Boxans.

Zack knew Kaylan was upset that he hadn't immediately committed himself to helping her with this, but he had needed to give it some thought. If he did this and they got caught, it could mean the end of their alliance with the Boxans. His intentions might be honorable, but his actions could be considered treasonous. What would they do if the Boxans kicked them off Olloron? Kladomaor would help them get home no matter what the High Council decided, but Zack would rather not put anyone in an awkward position. On the other hand, Kaylan truly believed she was seeing events that were unfolding on the Boxan home world, and that, if nothing else, was enough for Zack to at least do some poking around.

Zack headed for the training camp where Etanu would be. While the Nershal soldier wasn't one for espionage or intrigue, he was someone Zack felt could be somewhat objective about the Boxans. He opened a comms channel and sent the Nershal his location, and after a few minutes Etanu was flying overhead. His four translucent wings could propel him at great speeds, but they could also enable the Nershal to do some pretty precise flying.

Etanu raced toward him as if he were initiating a game of chicken. Zack stood his ground and Etanu's deep orange eyes narrowed. Zack knew Etanu wouldn't fly into him, but he was coming in so fast that Zack took a step back and heard the Nershal howl in triumph.

"Well, it was either that or let you fly into me," Zack said.

Etanu landed next to him. "You're a rare sight on the ground these days," he said.

"I missed you," Zack said.

Etanu frowned. "You weren't even close to hitting me. What would you have hit me with? You're unarmed."

Zack shook his head. "I mean that we hadn't spoken for a while and I desired to be in your presence," he said.

Etanu laughed. "I knew what you meant. I was . . . What is the term Hicks used? Oh yes, I was just pulling your leg."

"Dale Hicks, the gift that just keeps on giving," Zack said.

Etanu frowned. "I'm not familiar with this expression. I thought you and Hicks were friends."

Zack smiled. "Oh, we are. We have a mutual understanding and history of playing jokes on one another. I once changed the passphrase for getting out of the Athena's airlock to 'Zack is my superior in every way.'"

"What did Hicks do when he found you?" Etanu asked.

"He told me he'd get me back for that and to take off the passphrase," Zack said.

Sometimes he just had to entertain himself.

"What is it you wanted to talk to me about?" Etanu asked.

"I need to know your thoughts on the Boxans," Zack said.

"They're a very wise race of beings worthy of our respect," Etanu said.

"Has your opinion about them changed since you've been here?" Zack asked.

Etanu shook his head. "No. Why are you asking me these questions?"

Zack scratched the back of his head. "There's no easy way to say this, so I'm just going to go ahead and do it. Kaylan believes there are Boxans still on Sethion who need help."

Etanu's gaze hardened. The code of honor for the Nershals was a solemn thing. To a fellow Nershal, loyalty was almost instinctual. "Has she spoken to anyone about this?"

"Yes, and it's like they won't even consider the possibility," Zack said.

"But Kaylan has the Mardoxian potential. Surely her word would carry a great deal of weight," Etanu said.

"You'd think that, but no one is listening to her," Zack said.

"So why exactly are you asking me about the Boxans?" Etanu said.

Zack looked away for a moment to check that no one else was near them. "She asked me to dig up some information about Sethion to see if the Boxans have had any recent contact with them."

Etanu glanced over at him in alarm. "Please tell me you haven't done this?"

Zack shook his head. "I haven't done anything yet. You're the first person I've talked to about it, but I will say this: Kaylan is convinced there are Boxans still alive there. She knew I was alive when everyone else thought I was dead, and well, we owe her," he said.

"We?" Etanu asked.

"Yes, we. Kaylan was the one who contacted Udonzari and gave him our location on Selebus," Zack said.

Etanu nodded, remembering their time being held prisoner to the Xiiginns. "So what do you intend to do?"

"I intend to do what she asked me to do and see what there is to learn about Sethion," Zack said.

"What do you need from me?"

"Someone to watch my back would be nice," Zack said.

Etanu made a show of craning his long neck so he could see behind Zack.

"What are you doing?" Zack asked.

"I was watching your back," Etanu said.

Zack shook his head. "I hope you're joking around again."

"I think we should talk to Gaarokk about this," Etanu said.

Zack nodded. Of anyone, Gaarokk would be the most likely to help them. "Do you know where he is?" Zack asked.

"Yes, he's right over there inside the building," Etanu said.

They walked over and Zack's internal heads-up display translated the symbols to words he could understand. Gaarokk had been in a supply building, but the Boxan scientist was leaving as they approached.

"I was just looking for materials to build the Shroud device prototypes you wanted," Gaarokk said.

"Oh, thanks. Find anything?" Zack asked.

"No, unfortunately not. Whenever I try to requisition anything, the reason for the denial is always the same. Earth isn't in any immediate danger so the materials required are reallocated to other things. Shipbuilding, most likely," Gaarokk said.

"Did they say when they'd be able to get us something to use?" Zack asked.

Gaarokk shook his head.

"Understood. We have some questions for you, if you don't mind," Zack said.

Etanu glanced at him. "*You* have questions for him. I'm just here to watch your back."

Zack rolled his eyes. "Thanks."

Gaarokk frowned. "What is it you'd like to know?"

"The Star Shrouds that are still surrounding the star systems. Have you had any contact with them?" Zack asked.

"No, but with Prax'pedax's last communications and learning that there are Boxans trapped in those systems, the High Council is putting resources into checking them," Gaarokk said.

"Good, that's really good to hear. Do you guys monitor for signals from known star systems?" Zack asked.

Gaarokk eyed him suspiciously. "You already know we do. What is it you want to know?"

Zack blew out a breath and rubbed the back of his neck. "I want to know about Sethion and whether there have been any new signals detected from there."

Gaarokk's large flaxen eyes widened. "Sethion! First Kaylan and now you . . . Did she put you up to this?" he asked.

"No . . . Yes. Can you just answer the question?" Zack said.

Gaarokk grumbled and stomped away from them.

"She's not going to give up on this," Zack said.

Gaarokk stopped and turned to face him.

"Neither am I," Zack said.

Gaarokk drew himself up and Zack was reminded once again of how tall the Boxans were. Gaarokk, at eight feet, was considered short by Boxan standards, but he still made an imposing figure.

"You shouldn't be asking about Sethion," Gaarokk growled.

"What if she's right and there are Boxans still there? Don't you want to go back and check it out?" Zack asked.

Etanu placed a hand on Zack's arm and squeezed.

"If you persist in this—poking your nose where it doesn't belong—you'll be dealt with severely. Sethion is gone and we don't need you dredging it up for us. We know who we left behind. They're all gone. The only Boxans that remain are those under the Xiiginn influence. If there were signals, we'd be checking into it," Gaarokk said.

With that, the Boxan turned on his heel and walked away.

"Let him go," Etanu said.

"See. They immediately shut down at the mere mention of Sethion," Zack said.

"With good reason. Sethion represents a great shame for the Boxans," Etanu said.

"No, the real shame is if there are Boxans there who need help and their own species is turning their back on them. I'm sorry, Etanu. I know there's a significant risk with the Xiiginn influence, but that's not a good enough reason to condemn anyone to death," Zack said.

"So what do you want to do?" Etanu asked.

"Boxans monitor everything. They've spent hundreds of years leaving their little monitoring stations all over the galaxy. You honestly think they're not monitoring Sethion? I want to know if there have been any recent signals from whatever they have monitoring that star system," Zack said.

"The system is under quarantine," Etanu said.

"Yeah, but they're likely still monitoring it. They'd want to know if anyone was trying to go there or was trying to leave. It's worth checking into," Zack said.

"Even if it means incurring the wrath of the Boxans?" Etanu asked.

Zack sighed. "Let's hope it doesn't come to that. We may not learn anything at all."

"You don't believe that. Not if Kaylan is having visions," Etanu said.

"You're right. I don't believe it. I think we're going to find something, and if that makes the Boxans uncomfortable, then so be it. This is their mess," Zack said.

Etanu looked away and seemed to scan the area. "Where to next?" the Nershal asked.

Zack smiled. He'd known he could count on Etanu for help.

CHAPTER 12

Zack stood by one of the open info-terminals that were placed in most of the common areas of the buildings he'd been in. He brought up the access interface and glanced over his shoulder in consternation. Etanu gave him the thumbs up, a gesture Zack had taught him to let him know he was clear to proceed. The amber-colored holoscreen came up and Zack began searching for the comms control systems based on the current connections to the info-terminal. The list came up on the screen and he noted that the one he'd been searching for was present. He and Etanu had been to a few other buildings so Zack could validate the protocol connection hierarchy. All his time spent working with Boxan systems was being put to use, but it wasn't a whole lot different than computer systems back on Earth. All networks and systems needed a way to talk to one another and the method they used came under the protocols established for that system. Once you learned the different protocols, you could then disseminate the signal to look for something hidden. Of course, knowing the protocol he was looking for was only one part of what he needed, but it was an important step that led to the next, which was finding a way to authenticate that wouldn't leave a digital trail right back to him. If Zack used his own credentials, he might as well run naked through the Boxan High Council chambers while waving his arms and yelling that he was looking for information on Sethion, the thought of which didn't appeal to him. He needed to get in and out without anyone the wiser.

A message appeared on his internal heads-up display.

::*I could run the analysis for you and attempt to gain access.*:: Athena's AI said.

Zack focused in order to send a text reply without speaking the words. ::*Thanks, I appreciate it, but I don't want you involved. I don't want to give the Boxans an excuse to trace what I'm doing back to you.*::

::*Understood, but the way you're attempting to exfiltrate the data you need is inefficient.*:: Athena's AI said.

::*Yes, but the probability of being detected and having it traced back to us will be much less this way. Besides, I'll need you to clone the credentials we'll need.*:: Zack said.

::*Cloning the credentials will require you to be in proximity of the target for no less than ten minutes.*:: Athena's AI said.

::*Understood. Will initiate the process once a target has been selected.*:: Zack said.

Zack closed the translucent chat window and ended his session on the info-terminal. He returned to Etanu and they walked outside.

"Talking to your computer again?" Etanu asked.

Zack frowned. "How'd you know?"

"The skin on your forehead creases whenever you concentrate on communicating with text messages," Etanu replied.

Zack's gut clenched. Had anyone seen? He would need to be more careful in the future.

"No one else noticed," Etanu said, guessing his concern.

"The AI is just trying to be helpful," Zack said.

"I wasn't faulting the AI for doing what it does. I was informing you that you might want to work on not giving yourself away when you're talking to your computer," Etanu said.

Zack knew that Etanu struggled with trusting the AI. Nershals'd had a few bad experiences with artificial intelligence, but Zack was working with Etanu to adapt a version of the Athena's AI for Nershal use. He suspected it would take the Nershals years to learn to trust any AI, but eventually they would recognize that an AI is a powerful tool to have at their disposal. Medical doctors on Earth had been using AI constructs to help with diagnosing and proposing treatment options for more than twenty years. The doctors had the last say, but the AIs could inform the doctor of cutting-edge research and treatment options that would normally take months or years to become available.

"So what's next?" Etanu asked.

"We need to target a Boxan who has the access we need to learn about Sethion," Zack said.

"Gaarokk is a scientist. Wouldn't he have the necessary access?" Etanu asked.

"Maybe, but I don't think so. We need someone else . . . someone with more access," Zack said and frowned in thought. "The problem is that the information we're trying to access wouldn't be available to just any Boxan. They'd have to be someone important."

"Anyone on the High Council should work," Etanu suggested.

"They'll be the ones hardest to get close to. I need to get my PDA within a fifteen-foot radius for ten minutes to get what I need. I don't know if they'll even meet with me on such short notice," Zack said.

Etanu's large orange eyes widened at a sudden thought. "I know who would work with you. Hodak," Etanu said.

"The head of the Mardoxian Sect?" Zack said, trying not to raise his voice.

"Can you think of someone better?" Etanu asked.

Zack tried to think of someone but couldn't. "He'd likely have the access we need. We need to find out where he is and get him alone."

Etanu shook his head. "Not we. Just me. You've made your stance quite known, and if you suddenly show up asking questions, it may arouse suspicion."

Zack pressed his lips together. "How would this be any different if just you were going to talk to Hodak?" he asked.

"Unlike you, I actually have something to discuss with him," Etanu said.

"Like what?" Zack asked.

"The fact that they were secretly testing our species for the Mardoxian potential, for one. Also, I can ask him about the state of Nerva. That alone should give us the time we need," Etanu said.

"I didn't think that was a secret," Zack said.

"There was a small Mardoxian chamber on Ezerah's family estate, which might suggest that they were doing more than was previously known at the time," Etanu said.

“Okay, but are you sure? You don’t have to do this,” Zack said.

“Just show me how to work your PDA so we can get this done,” Etanu said.

Zack spent the next few minutes showing Etanu how to use the PDA. It was a simple process and the Nershal learned quickly.

“I’ll come find you after I'm done,” Etanu said and started to walk away.

“Wait,” Zack said. “How are you going to find him?”

“Don’t worry about it. The less you know, the better, wouldn’t you agree?” Etanu asked.

Zack didn’t think they would get caught, but there was still the possibility. He’d already tested copying a Boxan’s credentials and it hadn’t tripped off any alarms, but they hadn’t tried with a Boxan who had access to confidential information.

“It’ll be fine. If you don’t hear from me in a few hours, you’ll know I was caught. But you need to be visible so the Boxans don’t have a reason to suspect you,” Etanu said.

“I guess I’ll see what Hicks and the others are doing today,” Zack said.

As he watched Etanu leave, he was unable to keep away the sinking feeling that something was going to go wrong.

“Zack, pay attention!” Hicks said.

Zack had spent the last few hours with Hicks and Vitomir at the weapons training facility for small arms practice. He held a pulse rifle in his hands and had been waiting for his turn to fire his weapon at the targets on the course in front of him. The pulse rifle was configured for practice burst only so it would take out a target but not hurt anyone if he had an accident. Not likely to happen. Hicks was quite an effective teacher when it came to this stuff. Zack had never fired any gun before being recruited to the Athena mission, but the practice he'd gotten over the past few months showed how much he'd improved. He doubted he'd ever be anywhere near as skilled as someone like Hicks or Katie, but at least he could hit what he was aiming at most of the time.

"Sorry. I'm ready now," Zack said.

He brought the pulse rifle up and aimed it at the first target.

"Go!" Hicks said.

Zack squeezed the trigger and took out the closest target, then shifted his aim to the next target that was farther away. There were ten targets in all, but he had to shoot them in order before trying the more challenging targets that were even farther away. The pulse rifle fired three-round bursts and Zack went through the first five targets quickly, but he missed the sixth one.

"Just calm down and line up your shot," Hicks said.

The sixth target was six hundred yards away, but the targets farther away were much smaller than the ones that were closer to him. Zack lined up the sights with the target, but he couldn't keep still enough to get a shot off, so he rested against the platform in front of him and fired. The sixth target flashed red, indicating a successful hit. Zack aimed for the much smaller seventh target and couldn't hit it.

"That's time," Hicks said.

Zack blew out a breath and put the pulse rifle into safety mode.

"Not bad. You got the sixth target this time," Hicks said.

"I don't know how anyone hits the seventh one, let alone the others," Zack said.

Hicks regarded him for a moment. "They're called implants. You should have been using the vision enhancements option," he said.

"Isn't that cheating?" Zack asked.

Hicks laughed. "Of course not. I thought you knew that."

Zack glanced behind him, looking for some sign of Etanu. "I guess I missed it."

Zack stowed his practice weapon and followed Hicks and Vitomir out of the firing range. The sounds of weapons fire muted once the doors shut. A short distance away he saw Ezerah looking around, and upon seeing them, headed over.

"I can never tell whether Nershals are angry or not," Vitomir said.

"Being that she's scowling at Zack, I'd say she's angry," Hicks said and clamped a hand on Zack's shoulder. "What did you do this time?" he asked.

Zack took a second and thought about making a run for it, but considering that Nershals could fly, he knew he wouldn't get very far.

"Your guess is as good as mine," Zack said.

Ezerah closed on the three of them. "I wish to speak to you alone," she said to Zack.

"Is there anything we can help you with?" Hicks offered.

Ezerah's gaze softened when she looked at him. "No, I'm apparently playing messenger now."

Zack swallowed hard. "I'll see you guys later."

Ezerah didn't say anything to him while he followed her. Once they were outside, she turned toward him. "What are you and Etanu up to? He wanted me to give you this," she said and held up Zack's PDA.

Zack reached for the PDA, but Ezerah snatched it away.

"Not so fast. First, you answer my question," Ezerah said.

"What did he say when he gave it to you?"

Ezerah frowned. "Just that I needed to give you this. He looked as if he was running from someone," she said.

Zack's mouth went dry. The Boxans must have suspected Etanu was up to something.

"He was helping me with something," Zack admitted.

Ezerah's eyes flared. "That much is obvious," she snapped.

Zack drew in a quick breath and glanced around to see if anyone was watching them. "Please just give me my PDA."

"No. If you won't tell me what's happening with Etanu, I'll just give your PDA to Ma'jasalax or Kladomaor," Ezerah said and started to walk away.

Zack ran in front of her. "Don't do that. If I tell you, will you give it to me?" he asked.

Ezerah regarded him coldly. "First, you tell me," she said.

"Fine, we're trying to find out information about Sethion."

"Why? The planet is under quarantine," Ezerah said.

"I know, but I was asked to look into it," Zack said.

"By whom?" Ezerah asked.

"I can't tell you that. Now that I've told you what we're doing, will you give me my PDA?"

Ezerah softened her gaze. "Etanu wouldn't recklessly risk a slight to the Boxans. Perhaps I can help you."

Zack frowned. He didn't think he could convince Ezerah to give him his PDA without telling her what he and Etanu were doing, but she might not give it to him anyway after he did tell her.

"Kaylan believes there are Boxans still alive on Sethion and she asked me to try and find out if the Boxans were hiding anything about their planet," Zack said.

Ezerah looked away from him for a moment while she considered what he'd said.

"I'm telling you the truth," Zack said.

Ezerah turned back toward him. "Etanu has always told me you Humans are quite clever and your intentions seem honorable. Kaylan would never ask this if she didn't have a good reason," she said and handed Zack his PDA.

Zack took it and strapped it to his wrist. He started to power it on but decided against it.

"Did Etanu say where he was going?" Zack asked.

"No," Ezerah said.

Zack sighed. "Okay, I'll find him. Thank you for giving me this."

Zack walked away and noticed that Ezerah was walking next to him.

"I'm curious," Ezerah said.

She obviously meant to go with him. Zack had never spent much time with her. He wasn't sure if it was a female Nershal thing or just Ezerah, but he always had the feeling that she didn't want to interact with him at all so he stayed away.

"Where are we going?" Ezerah asked.

"I was going to find an info-terminal but one with a little bit of privacy," Zack said.

"I know a place. Follow me," Ezerah said and walked in front of him with a determined stride.

Ezerah led them past a series of Boxan training facilities. The Boxans they walked by hardly paid them any notice aside from an acknowledgment as they went about their own business. She led him into a building that had a large, open atrium with multiple info-terminals available for use, but they were much too visible. Ezerah came to a stop and looked around. Zack was about to tell her this place wouldn't work for what he needed to do when she started walking toward a corridor on the right. The corridor curved around, following the shape of the building, and there were closed doors on the interior wall. Ezerah went to one of the doors and it opened automatically. Inside was a large, empty room with a sloping pathway that led to a tall podium. The lighting in the room became brighter as they walked farther into the Boxan lecture hall.

"Doesn't anyone use this room?" Zack asked.

"They're done for the day," Ezerah said.

Zack glanced behind them at the door. "And you just happen to know this?" he asked.

"I've been using this room for a while to explore different interests of mine. I was supposed to serve on a Xiiginn warship when Kladomaor came to Selebus. A lot of what the Xiiginns have in terms of technology and knowledge stems from the Boxans. I'd never realized how much until I came here," Ezerah said.

Zack remembered when they'd first met Ezerah. He'd been convinced she was going to turn them over to the Xiiginns, but they'd proven to her that the Xiiginns were exploiting her species.

Ezerah walked up to the podium and activated a large holoscreen.

Zack powered on his PDA, checked Hodak's stolen credentials, and used them to access the terminal, getting immediately to work. He used the secret Boxan protocol he'd found earlier and ran a search on anything about Sethion, but nothing was found. Zack frowned and then tried using the star coordinates for Sethion's star system.

"Here we go," Zack said

Ezerah stepped beside him. "Those are check-in intervals from the quarantine zone," she said.

"So they *are* monitoring it," Zack said and pulled up the details for one of the more recent entries. "Looks like someone is trying to access the quarantine zone. Would this be the Xiiginns?"

Ezerah peered at the data he pointed to.

"That's not the Xiiginns. The ship signature isn't right. These are Gresans," she said. "They're a species in the Confederation. They challenge Xiiginn authority from time to time."

"I like them already," Zack said.

"You might not if you actually met them. They've been less than friendly to other species since the Boxans were cast out of the Confederation," Ezerah said.

"Any idea why they'd be trying to get through the quarantine zone?" Zack asked.

"I have no idea, but they're not getting through based on this information. Why would they keep trying?"

"Were they loyal to the Boxans? Could they be trying to help?" Zack asked.

Ezerah shook her head.

Zack set up another search algorithm to run in the background while he used Hodak's credentials to access something else. He found some historical records that came under the categorization of Xiiginn Uprising. He and Ezerah read the information as it appeared on screen.

"We had no idea how destructive the Xiiginns were to the Boxans," Ezerah said.

"Looks like the Xiiginns were integrated into Boxan society before they staged their uprising. They used their compulsion ability to break down the government hierarchy from the top down. This military group called Protectors keeps getting referred to. The Boxan Protectors were the first military unit to initiate a global conflict by murdering the heads of governing bodies," Zack said.

"The Xiiginns only told us that they brought justice to the Boxans. The Confederation species believed the Xiiginns were liberators," Ezerah said and sucked in a harsh breath. "It was all so contrived."

"The Xiiginns must have planned this for a long time. Years probably. I don't see any record of the Boxans asking for help from the Confederation," Zack said.

"They were too proud to ask for help," Ezerah said in disgust.

"Look at the timeline for these entries. I think by the time they knew what was happening, any help that may have come would already have been too late. Don't forget that while this was happening, the Xiiginns had coordinated attacks from other Confederation species," Zack said.

"The quarantine zone is enforced by a drone blockade. Look at all the conflicts registered as being prevented by the blockade," Ezerah said.

Zack scanned the on-screen data. After the initial burst of activity logged by the blockade when the Boxans first activated the system, there were occasional incidents of ships trying to make a run past the blockade.

"Are the locations for these ships right?" Zack asked.

Ezerah frowned as she read the highlighted entries. "Those are ships that tried to leave Sethion after the quarantine zone was put in place."

Zack felt as if something heavy had just sunk to the bottom of his stomach. The information onscreen showed that the drone blockade had prevented hundreds of ships from leaving Sethion. How could all those Boxans have been under the Xiiginn influence? He didn't know what the capacity of those ships was, but the number of dead must have been staggering.

Zack turned away from the holoscreen and leaned on the podium for support. He was having trouble wrapping his mind around what the Boxans had done to survive. No wonder they didn't want to go back there.

There was an audible chime from his PDA, indicating the search algorithm had finished. Zack looked up, and as he read the results, his mouth hung open. "Oh my God," he said.

"What is that?" Ezerah asked.

"These are communications requests," Zack said.

"Could they be automated?"

Zack pressed his lips together and ran a quick regression analysis on the data. "Looks like a majority could be automated, but there are outliers."

"Those look random," Ezerah said.

Zack nodded. "Or they could be comms requests that were manually initiated by a Boxan."

He scanned the data and noted how the comms requests had significantly decreased over time, but they were still coming in.

Zack swallowed hard. Not only did the High Council know they'd left Boxans behind, but they'd been ignoring them for who knows how long. He glanced at Ezerah, who looked away.

"We have to tell someone about this," Zack said.

"Who are we going to tell? Once you say how you got the data, they'll take you into custody," Ezerah said.

"Maybe, but I can't just pretend I don't know about this. I think I know who to contact, but I need you to do it for me," Zack said.

"Why would you need me for this? Shouldn't we go straight to Kaylan?" Ezerah asked.

"Not yet. We need some backup, but the Boxan we need to speak to is mad at me right now, and I think he'll ignore me if I try to contact him," Zack said.

"Very well. Who is it?"

Zack copied the data to his PDA and closed the session. The holoscreen flickered off.

"Gaarokk," he said.

A short while later Zack and Ezerah decided it would be best to simply find Gaarokk and speak with him instead of summoning him somewhere else, so they set off on their ambush of the Boxan scientist. Gaarokk wasn't difficult to locate as the scientist spent much of his time in the research laboratory he'd claimed for himself. When they opened the door to Gaarokk's lab, they heard him talking with someone, so they went inside and saw Gaarokk standing in front of a holo-screen, speaking to another Boxan. His back was to them and he was so focused on his conversation that he didn't hear them come inside.

"I need the materials for a research project. We're building a Star Shroud model to test some theories about the barrier surrounding the Human home world," Gaarokk said.

"Understand your need, but these materials have already been designated for the fleet."

Gaarokk slammed his hand down on the console. "This is ridiculous. I should be getting more cooperation. The Humans have shared what the Drars have given them with us in good faith. The quantities needed will have no impact on your production schedule and you know it."

"My orders come straight from the High Council. I would like to help you, but I'm not able to at this time."

The holoscreen flicked off and Gaarokk stood shaking his head. Zack felt sorry for the Boxan. Gaarokk was trying to help them and was getting the runaround.

Zack cleared his throat and Gaarokk turned around. Upon seeing them, Gaarokk's shoulders slumped.

"I assume you saw that?"

Zack nodded. "Yeah, we saw that. Thanks for trying."

Gaarokk blew out a breath that almost sounded like a growl. "I've been contacting different groups that would have access to the materials we need and none of them will help."

"It's almost like the High Council doesn't want us to leave," Zack said.

Gaarokk gave him a sidelong look and glanced at Ezerah.

"We have something to show you," Ezerah said.

Gaarokk gave Zack a suspicious look.

"Yes, it has to do with Sethion, but damn it, just listen to me," Zack said.

Gaarokk started walking away, his footsteps pounding into the floor.

"We found evidence that there are still Boxans on Sethion. They need help. I don't care what you say, I know this matters to you," Zack said.

Gaarokk stopped in his tracks.

"Here, look at what we found," Zack said and used his PDA to put the data they stole upon the holoscreen.

Gaarokk slowly turned around and looked at the data on the holoscreen, and the silence dragged on while the Boxan took it all in. The noise of shifting feet came from one of the dark adjacent rooms Zack hadn't noticed before and Kladomaor emerged from the darkness. His powerful gaze was fixed on the holoscreen. Zack knew the Boxan's military-grade neural implants were more advanced than what they had and could disseminate the data quickly.

"Where'd you get this?" Kladomaor asked.

The Boxan's menacing tone sent shivers down Zack's spine. "I used Hodak's credentials to get this data," Zack said.

"The head priest of the Mardoxian Sect!" Gaarokk said.

Kladomaor turned on his heels and stalked away at a pace that Zack wouldn't have been able to match even if he'd been running at an all out sprint.

CHAPTER 13

Dome-shaped buildings were scattered throughout the complex and Kladomaor blazed a path directly to the Mardoxian training headquarters. Each breath he took ended in a low growl. He didn't slow down at the security checkpoint and the soldiers gave him a wide berth. After months of cooperation, he knew Zack wouldn't have done what he did on his own, which meant someone had asked him to do it. The only person Zack would have broken so many of their laws for was Kaylan, and she wouldn't have made such a request unless she felt she'd had no other choice. All Boxans on Olloron knew they'd left behind a significant portion of the population, but in service of the greater good of the galaxy, it had to be done. A necessary sacrifice was what he'd believed, but now all he felt was outrage.

Kladomaor found Hodak with Ma'jasalax and Kaylan in the large atrium just inside the main building. There were other Boxans in the atrium, but Kladomaor didn't care.

"You!" Kladomaor shouted, his gaze fixed on Hodak.

Ma'jasalax looked over at him in alarm.

"What's the meaning of this?" Hodak said.

Several bodyguards closed in, but Kladomaor didn't hesitate. He was in full battle armor and would take them out if it came to a fight.

"Sethion! You knew there were Boxans left on the planet still fighting for survival and you ignored their pleas for help," Kladomaor said.

Hodak frowned. "What are you talking about? Sethion is quarantined and has been quiet ever since."

Kladomaor used his neural implants and military officer's credentials to take control of all nearby holoscreens. He then pushed Zack's data and analysis to every one of them.

"You lie," Kladomaor hissed.

Hodak's eyes flashed angrily. "Where did you get this? Where did this come from?"

The bodyguards that had been closing in on Kladomaor had shifted their attention to the Mardoxian priest. Kladomaor pulled out his hand cannon, the tip of which started to glow a menacing green as it powered on. Then he pointed it directly at Hodak. Reacting quickly, the Boxan bodyguards drew their weapons and pointed them at Kladomaor.

"If you think you can take me down before I kill him, go ahead," Kladomaor said. "Now answer my question."

Hodak looked stunned for a moment, then quickly recovered. "Put your weapons down," he said to the bodyguards. "I'll answer your question. The High Council is aware that there's Boxan activity on Sethion, but the only thing all that data you've found proves is that someone on Sethion is trying to contact us. We don't know if they're under the Xiiginn influence or not."

Kladomaor lowered his weapon. "There are no more Xiiginns on Sethion."

"Yes, but you of all Boxans should know that their influence can have long-lasting effects, especially when given a specific goal," Hodak said.

"We have to go back," Kladomaor said. "We need to know for sure."

Hodak regarded him for a moment. "We fight the Xiiginns on many fronts. Sethion is lost. There's nothing to go back to but pain and suffering."

Kladomaor looked at Ma'jasalax. "You've gone awfully quiet," he said.

"I think you've said quite enough for the both of us," Ma'jasalax replied.

Kladomaor glanced around. "Where's Kaylan? She was just here."

Ma'jasalax looked around in alarm and then over at the Mardoxian chamber in the courtyard beyond the atrium. The panels were glowing red, which indicated the chamber was in use.

"What is it?" Kladomaor asked.

"She's in the chamber, looking for answers. She kept having what she thought were visions of Boxans fighting a battle with each other. I thought it was exhaustion, but I may have been wrong. Kaylan was likely feeling the connection of another Boxan with the Mardoxian potential," Ma'jasalax said.

"On Sethion," Kladomaor said.

"That's impossible," Hodak said. "How would she even be open to the connection without using the chamber?"

"I told you she's extraordinarily gifted," Ma'jasalax said.

"We have to get her out of there," Hodak said.

Kladomaor brought his weapon up again. "If anyone moves towards the chamber, they'll be the first one I shoot. There'll be no cover-up of this information, not by you or the High Council."

Hodak motioned for the bodyguards to move away from them. Kladomaor headed over to the chamber entrance and turned around. He kept his plasma pistol in his hand and stood guard. Ma'jasalax stood nearby with Hodak and some others of the Mardoxian Sect. Each time Kladomaor caught Ma'jasalax's eye he had the feeling that nothing of what had just transpired had been a surprise to her.

CHAPTER 14

Kaylan slipped away from the gathering crowd of Boxans. Once she'd heard what Kladomaor said about Sethion, she knew Zack was involved. He must have found a way to get some real information about Sethion, and the revelation of it had sent Kladomaor into a rage. While the Boxans were looking at the data Kladomaor had put on all the nearby holoscreens, Kaylan made her way to the Mardoxian chamber in the courtyard. As she neared the pyramid, she heard the gentle hum of energy. Kaylan placed her hand on the panel next to the closed door and it opened. She cast a quick glance behind her to be sure no one was watching and then stepped inside. Glowing cyan lights raced up the cathedral-high ceilings, coming to a central point. Crimson lines of light also came on from twin points on the floor and continued around the base of the pyramid's interior.

Kaylan crossed the threshold and the door closed behind her. A dark blue beam shot down from the ceiling to a crystal sphere that rose from the floor. Kaylan sat on the floor and focused on the star coordinates for the Boxan home world. Within seconds her mind was thrust down an azure pathway. When she'd used the chamber to search for Zack back on the planet Nerva, she'd used her personal connection to Zack to find him. She had no such connection to Sethion. It was a planet that she'd only seen in the Boxan archives. Her only impression of it was through the mournful shadows in each Boxan she'd ever met.

The azure pathway receded in her mind and Kaylan found herself amongst the planets, orbiting a bright main-sequence star. She had a bird's-eye view of the inner system of planets and it took her a few moments to register all the hulking wrecks in the star system. Some of them were the size of small moons. She marveled at the sheer numbers and would have loved to have seen Sethion as a thriving star system.

She zipped past the floating spaceships. They were all dark and she couldn't tell if they were intact ships or merely remnant hulls left over from a battle long ago. Kaylan focused on the mustardy yellow orb well within the Goldilocks Zone that was the planet Sethion. Three remnant moons still orbited the planet but huge chunks were missing from each of them. Kaylan couldn't fathom how those moons had come to be in such a state.

Dark orbital platforms surrounded the planet. There were minimal indications of power and she wasn't sure what the platforms were used for. Orbiting close to the planet was a behemoth-sized space dock. Darkened scorch marks dotted most of the space dock's hull. The sheer scale of the destruction here was unimaginable. So much death in this bitter cold star system. She felt a deep pang in her chest at the loss of life.

Kaylan shifted her gaze to the planet's surface. Much of the land along the equator had a worn brown look as if the whole planet were one big scar. Sethion was a graveyard. How could anything survive here? Large brown clouds swirled beneath Kaylan and she circled the planet, looking for any signs of life.

She felt her heart beat faster as despair set in and the view of Sethion blurred in front of her. Kaylan took hold of her focus with an iron will, building an image of the Boxan warrior in the red armor standing alone amidst a field of battle. Pushing onward, Kaylan plunged through the atmosphere. Within moments she was above the corpses of massive cities. She thought she recognized remnant forms of architecture that the Boxans had brought with them to Olloron. Dome-shaped buildings between dirt fields on large, strolling campuses had once been home to lush plant life that must have been beautiful to see, but now there remained only the vestiges of a nuclear holocaust.

She kept thinking there was no way anyone could survive here for a few days, let alone the forty-plus years since the quarantine zone had been put into place, so she moved back from the cities and focused on the mountainous regions of the continents. There were no animals or plant life of any kind. Still, she searched. Those visions had not been figments of her imagination. They were real. There were Boxans here; she just knew it.

Something flickered from the corner of her eye. She turned toward it and saw storm clouds gathering over a city covered with ash and soot. Lightning flashed and struck the ground. A shadow moved along the ground, drawing her attention, and Kaylan sped forward. She heard the sound of a loud blast and one of the buildings near her came crumbling down. Kaylan was about to turn away when she saw multiple figures running from the building. Her eyes widened. The long shadows moved with the assistance of power armor, and they raced away from her. She tried to follow but lost them in the rubble. Someone was here. There were Boxans still here. She felt herself smile as she let the connection go and returned to the Mardoxian chamber on Olloron.

Kaylan rolled her shoulders and blinked her eyes, trying to get rid of the dryness she felt. She took a deep breath and blew it out, then pushed herself to her feet while the crystal sphere sank back down into the metal container. She walked over to the door, placed her palm on the panel, and the chamber door sank into the ground. Kaylan came up short as she met the flaxen-eyed stares of the Boxans waiting outside to greet her.

Kladomaor stepped into view. "It's alright. Come on out," he said in a remarkably calm tone.

She was still a bit disoriented and Kladomaor extended his large hand toward her. She took it and allowed herself to be guided forward, seeing Zack and Ezerah to one side along with the rest of the crew of the Athena.

Kaylan frowned. "How long was I inside the chamber?"

Zack came over to her side. "You've been in there for nearly ten hours. How are you feeling?" he asked.

Brenda Goodwin came over and handed her a bottle of water. Kaylan drank the water greedily and tasted faint traces of cinnamon. As she drained the bottle, she felt a hollow emptiness in her stomach. She was starving, but food would have to wait.

"I'm fine. I just needed to get my bearings for a minute," Kaylan said.

Zack looked relieved and Kaylan glanced at all the Boxans

present. Kladomaor stood nearest her and kept a watchful eye on everyone else.

"We need to know what you saw," Zack said.

Kaylan told them everything. She started with her view of Sethion's star system and proceeded to the state of the planet. Through her entire recounting of it, all the Boxans hardly dared draw a breath.

"I was about to give up. There seemed to be nothing alive on the planet surface, but then I saw them—Boxans running amidst the ruined buildings. I only saw them for a few moments, but it was enough. They wore protection and armor," Kaylan said.

Hodak stepped toward her. "Did you see anything else? Anything at all?" he asked.

Kaylan shook her head.

Hodak looked at Kladomaor. "See, there you have it. A few scavengers are hardly a reason to risk the colony," he said.

"It is to the Boxans left behind. There are more there. I know it," Kaylan said.

Hodak didn't look convinced. "I believe you saw something, but you're still new to your gifts—"

"I didn't imagine this. I saw the look on your faces as I described the star system, the breadth of the destruction that could only be possible if I had been there to see it. There are Boxans left behind who need your help and you owe it to them to send help. You owe it to yourselves as well," Kaylan said.

Ma'jasalax cleared her throat. "Kaylan is the most gifted student of the Mardoxian Sect I've ever seen. If she says she saw it, then that's precisely what we'll find."

Hodak drew himself up. "Is this what it's come to?"

"I only ask that you put the request to the High Council.

They'll listen to you. Will you at least consider it?" Ma'jasalax asked.

Hodak regarded Ma'jasalax for a moment and then glanced at the rest of them. "I'll consider it on one condition," he said.

Ma'jasalax glanced at Kladomaor, who gave a firm nod.

"No one in this room speaks of what they've witnessed until I've made my decision," Hodak said.

"When will that be, exactly?" Kaylan asked.

Hodak seemed taken aback by the question, but now that it had been asked he would be forced to give them an answer. "Two days at the most. I need to confer with select High Council members."

Kaylan glanced at Ma'jasalax.

"That is acceptable," Ma'jasalax said.

The courtyard and atrium cleared out and the crew of the Athena gathered outside the Mardoxian main buildings. Kladomaor and some of his crew met them, along with Ma'jasalax.

Ma'jasalax looked at Kladomaor. "Is two days enough time?" she asked.

Kladomaor frowned in confusion. "For what?" he asked.

"To steal a ship and return to Sethion," Ma'jasalax said.

Kaylan's mouth hung open. "Wait a second. I thought you didn't believe me. You said I was suffering from exhaustion."

"That's right, I did. A calculated risk, one would say, but when the vision kept recurring with growing clarity, I knew it wasn't a dream. Somehow you were sensing another Boxan with the Mardoxian potential on Sethion," Ma'jasalax said.

"Hold on a minute," Zack said. "How is it that she was able to do this and you weren't?" he asked.

Kaylan was wondering the same thing.

"I've said it before. Kaylan is among the most gifted of the Mardoxian Sect, surpassing those who've come before her in some areas and still learning in other areas. I knew she'd reach out to you for help and I knew you'd find a way to get the information needed to confirm what's happening on Sethion," Ma'jasalax said.

"So glad we could be pawns in your little game," Zack said.

"It was necessary," Ma'jasalax said.

Kaylan's mind raced with the implications of what Ma'jasalax had done and the events that had brought them here.

"You understand, don't you?" Ma'jasalax said to Kaylan.

"I do," Kaylan said and looked at Kladomaor. "Whatever ship you get has to be able to accommodate the Athena. There's no way I'm leaving our ship behind."

Kladomaor glared at Kaylan and Ma'jasalax. "What makes you think I can simply take any ship I want?" he asked.

Ma'jasalax's large ears quivered and it caused her thick, dark locks of hair to move. "Aren't you the famed Battle Commander?" she said.

Kaylan smiled. "We can do this. Together we can do this. We can make it to Sethion," she said.

Kladomaor sighed. "Getting there is the easy part, but getting through the blockade is all but impossible."

Zack grinned. "No place is totally secure. There has to be a way through."

"There's never a lack of enthusiasm on your part," Kladomaor said dryly.

"We have two days," Ma'jasalax said.

Kladomaor shook his head. "No, we have less than one day,

and if we're not gone by then I suspect we'll all be taken into custody."

"Why do you say that? Hodak said he needed two days," Kaylan said.

"I don't trust Hodak. He may not be on the High Council, but he holds a lot of sway," Kladomaor said.

"Okay, then let's get to work," Kaylan said.

She felt her stomach growl and knew she needed to eat, but that would have to wait or her next meal might be in a cell.

CHAPTER 15

Valkra pulled up the survey map on her helmet's heads-up display. The drones they'd used to scout out the abandoned city had been here weeks ago, but she couldn't remember a time when the cities of Sethion hadn't been the ruined skeletons of a bygone age. What buildings were left standing from the Chaos Wars were a brittle reminder of the greatness of Boxan ingenuity and superiority in the galaxy. Now those empty shells provided adequate cover for her and her squad, and nothing else.

Valkra sent a signal calling for a halt while she examined the survey map and her squad mates quickly found cover. She glanced around and switched the lens setting to standard live view as the thin yellow veil of a toxic cloud swirled above them. They'd picked this area to forage for supplies because the cloud cover was so minimal this time of year, something the dreaded Protectors would no doubt surmise as well. She switched her heads-up display to combat mode and her suit computer immediately began scanning ahead wherever she looked.

One of her squad opened a comms channel to her.

"Toxicity is rising," Ranem said.

Valkra acknowledged her second in command. They had a limited timeframe they could safely be exposed to Sethion's atmosphere. Without protection, they'd be dead in minutes. The powered armor they were using had been ancient before the Chaos Wars and had been a patchwork of quick fixes ever since. Everything that followed was a reminder of the Xiiginn's betrayal and the bitter wars that killed their planet.

"Let's make a sweep of the area. Remember, we're looking for useable materials for the fabricators at Haven. Use your suit computers to see the list and identify any high-priority items," Valkra said.

This wasn't their first salvage mission, but it never hurt to put a reminder in her fellow squad mates' ears of why they were here. She set a countdown timer and uploaded it to the others. This was all the time they had for scavenging before the toxic atmosphere compromised their suits. There was also the looming threat that the Protectors would detect their presence and kill them all.

Valkra activated her particle rifle and the rest of the squad did the same. The rifle's beam had a finite range but was incredibly accurate, even at longer distances. The Protector's armor could resist a single particle beam for a time, which gave the Protector an opportunity to kill them and was why they trained by firing multiple beams at a single target. This tactic would overwhelm even the elite military armor the Protectors used. Ranem carried the only phaze hand cannon in the group, which was a weapon of last resort. It had limited ammunition and the amount of energy released from the hand cannon would light them up on any Protector's sensors in the area, painting a large target on their backs.

Ranem had been with her for the many cycles since she'd first joined the foraging squads. Under her leadership their squad had the most successful record of finding the rare elements needed for the fabricators still in operation at Haven. But they were running dangerously low on supplies, which created the need for these foraging missions.

She moved ahead and checked the area. Once satisfied that it was safe enough to proceed, she waved Ranem ahead. They worked in teams of two and checked each building they came across, making their way to the base of a large building. Valkra knew that at one time structures such as these had been so tall that the upper levels were in the clouds, but these vast, stumpy remnants were all that was left of those unimaginably tall buildings.

They moved inside and the jagged walls opened up to the sky like a gaping maw.

Ranem came to a stop. "Gladium deposits detected," he said in an elevated tone.

Gladium was at the top of their list for its durability and strength. It was the base element for making ships and reinforcing the infrastructure of Haven.

"Go check it out. We'll cover you," Valkra said.

Ranem waved Tholev over, who carried a plasma cutter, and the two Boxans moved to the exposed innards of the building's superstructure where Ranem began moving large pieces of rubble. The servo gears of the power armor gave off a high-pitched whine as they struggled with the last piece. Tholev ignited the plasma cutter and then went to work cutting pieces of the beams out so they could extract the gladium.

Valkra moved away from them and kept her particle rifle ready. The area beyond the building was quiet, but she felt a growing sense of dread. They were blind down here. She'd learned long ago to trust her intuition and of late she'd been growing more restless. She signaled to the others that she was going to climb higher to get a better vantage point. Recon drones would have been helpful, but she'd lost the lottery for them on this mission and she'd have to rely on the other squads in the region to notify her of suspicious activity.

Valkra moved away from the others towards a large pile of rubble where she performed a squat-and-leap maneuver that threw her into the air. Grabbing hold of some twisted metal that jutted outward, she pulled herself up and reached across to the next piece. Valkra swung out with her foot and leveraged herself up. Hearing the faint sounds of the plasma cutter working, she glanced down. She was fifty feet above them. She looked up again and climbed even higher, enabling her jump to the partially intact roof of the nearby building. She squatted close to the rooftop and moved toward the edge of the building to peer downward. The streets below her were clear so she gazed at the city line. Scanning the area, she noticed movement a few hundred yards away. Her suit computer tried to identify it but she lost sight of it too fast. Valkra clutched her rifle and took aim while opening a comms channel to her squad mates.

"We're not alone. I have an unknown contact northwest of our position. Ranem, time to pack it up," Valkra said.

She scurried further along to see if she could get a better look at what she'd glimpsed a moment before. The recon map on her

HUD didn't show any of their teams in the area. Her targeting computer noted another contact, but this one was in a different position. Valkra ducked down and caught the faint glow of the plasma cutter still at work.

"Kill the cutter. We have hostiles in the area," Valkra said over comms.

She sent out a high-band alert notifying the other squads of the danger. The other squad leaders might not like that she didn't have clear visual confirmation, which was required for a mission abort, but she knew the Protectors were here. Nothing else moved on Sethion's surface besides them or the Protectors.

"Clear out of the building," Valkra ordered.

Tholev was packing the gladium deposits into a large container as quickly as he could and Valkra's eyes widened at the size of the deposits. If they could get this back to Haven, they wouldn't need to another foraging mission for months.

"Commander, we have movement behind us," Ranem said.

"Clear out to the south and I'll meet you there," Valkra said.

The squad began to move out and Valkra turned around and ran. She pounded across the rooftop and leaped across a wide chasm to the next building. Quickly closing the distance to the south end of the building and vaulting over the side, she held on with one hand and dangled in the air for moment, then dropped. At the last second, as the ground raced up to meet her, Valkra engaged a burst from her suit thrusters to slow her down and her suit absorbed most of the impact. She glanced down the street, waiting for her team to arrive, but she heard a noise behind her and ducked down behind a rocky pile of rubble. She pressed her back against the pile and shifted toward the edge so she could peek around the corner, turning around to bring up her particle rifle. Craning her neck, she tried to find a target, but her view down the street faded after a hundred yards. She scanned, using all the known visual frequencies, but couldn't see anything. Valkra sucked in a deep breath. She heard the familiar sounds of her squad rounding the corner and raised her hand, gesturing for them to take cover.

"What have you got, Commander?" Ranem asked over comms as he and the rest of the squad took cover.

Valkra peeked around the corner again. A splatter of acid rain had begun pelting down and there was a harsh hissing sound whenever it made contact with anything. In the gloom, she saw the hissing vapor rise from objects ten feet off the ground.

"Contact!" she cried and fired her rifle.

A bright yellow particle beam sliced through the air and slammed into an armored Protector, momentarily disrupting the stealth field.

"Ranem, I need that hand cannon of yours. Down that street one hundred yards," Valkra said.

Ranem climbed to the top of the pile of rubble and took two shots. Plasma bolts belched from the heavy hand cannon and slammed into the approaching line of Protectors. Ranem slid down the rubble and hit the ground next to her. Around the corner where the rest of her squad was, she saw flashes of particle beams being fired. The noose was tightening around them. Across the street from her was an alleyway that seemed like a good escape route and Ranem was already poised to head that way.

"It's a trap. That's where they want us to go," Valkra said.

They raced to the corner where the rest of her squad was fighting for their lives. Valkra glanced behind her, knowing that at any second now more Protectors would be coming. Two shots from a heavy hand cannon would only have stopped two of them, at best. She peeked around the corner, seeing the glistening sheen of the dark Protector armor hissing in the acid rain, and fired her rifle at the nearest Protector, adding her beam to the others. The Protector tried to find cover, but the five particle beams were overwhelming his power armor. The other Protectors dove for cover.

"Fall back," Valkra ordered.

The squad followed her as they moved down the street and Ranem brought up the rear, providing covering fire as they went. Tholev carried the large container of precious gladium. Valkra bolted to the right, only to find that the street was completely blocked off by the collapse of a building long ago.

"We need higher ground and an extraction," Valkra said and tried to see the area beyond the collapsed building.

"Protectors are closing in on our position. We can't stay here," Ranem said.

Valkra carried one piece of heavy explosives that could bring down a building on the Protectors, but she didn't know if it would buy them enough time. They didn't know how many Protectors were hunting them.

"Come on. We have to climb over," Valkra said.

Tholev cried out. "My armor's been breached!"

The acid rain had eaten its way through his adjoining shoulder plates. He tried to take cover as best he could while their squad medic came over and patched the hole, but Valkra knew it wouldn't last long enough. The toxic rain ate through almost everything.

Valkra reached out and took one side of the large container

from Tholev, gesturing for Ranem to take the other side. Together, they heaved the container high into the air and she heard it tumble down the other side of the collapsed building. The container could be dropped from the top of the tallest of ancient buildings and the contents inside would remain intact.

The rest of the squad began scaling the wall of rubble. Valkra pulled herself up, working her way towards the top, and a blast from a Protector's heavy weapon ripped into the area around her. Two of her squad fell, screaming as they went. Valkra growled and continued to climb as fast as she could, stopping to help her squad mates up when she reached the top. Ranem had stopped halfway up and was firing his heavy hand cannon down at the Protectors, giving them the covering fire they needed.

"Come on," Valkra said to him.

Ranem holstered his weapon and climbed faster while Valkra teamed up with another squad mate, firing their particle rifles down to give Ranem some cover. They had the Protectors pinned down and Ranem was nearing the top when a large, heavy mech came around the corner. The mech was over twenty feet tall and a large plasma cannon was attached to one arm. The tip of the barrel flared molten yellow as it primed.

Valkra gasped and fired her particle rifle at the mech, but it had no effect. Ranem was almost to the top when he glanced back down at the mech. Looking back up at Valkra while reaching for his hand cannon, he heaved it to her, and she caught it just as the mech's giant plasma cannon fired. Valkra was thrown into the air, away from the blast, and she screamed when she saw Ranem fall back to the Protectors. As Valkra came crashing to the ground, rock and debris rained down around her, and she rolled to a stop, pushing herself to her feet.

"Ranem!" she shouted.

In a split second, Ranem had known he was about to die so he'd thrown his hand cannon in her direction. As the heartbreaking scene replayed itself in her mind, she swept aside the painful emotions threatening to overwhelm her in order to focus on what remained of her squad racing toward her. There were only three of them left now and she had to get them out. The rest were either dead or dying at the hands of the Protectors. Tholev dragged the large container with him. Valkra grabbed one handle of the container from Tholev and they ran as fast as they could away from the Protectors and their heavy mech on the other side of the wall of rubble.

After they'd put some distance between themselves and the Protectors, Valkra risked a glance behind. A molten yellow glow surrounded the wall of debris. Years of exposure to acid rain and Sethion's toxic atmosphere had made the building material brittle and the center of the pile of rubble melted away, rolling in a churning wave away from the Protectors.

They kept moving as fast as they could. She'd initiated a distress signal at the first sign of the attack and a comms channel opened for her.

"What's your situation?" the extraction commander asked.

"There are four of us left. Protectors are in pursuit. They knew we were coming," Valkra said.

"Understood. We have your location now. We can do a quick pickup, but you need to get to higher ground. There are two sites near your position. Can you get there?"

Valkra glanced around them and saw the two buildings they were referring to.

"Turn your trackers on. We've got eyes in the sky," Valkra said to Tholev and the others.

The extraction team would be able to locate them, but she didn't like how exposed they'd be on those buildings.

Valkra engaged the comms channel to the extraction commander. "They were ready for us. Are you sure those sites are safe for my squad?"

Tholev suddenly pulled her to the side via the canister they carried and she heard weapons fire.

They had no choice. Either they risked the exposure of the two tall buildings that provided at least a chance of getting away or they'd have to fight the Protectors and die. "We'll be there, but we've got Protectors following close behind," Valkra said.

She motioned for one of the other squad members to help Tholev with the container and sent the coordinates of the extraction point to the rest of the squad. She ordered them ahead and followed. How had the Protectors known they'd be here? Not only had they known precisely where her squad would be, but they had executed an ambush that cut off most of their escape routes. If it had been anyone other than her leading them, the squad would have been dead. This wasn't boastful thinking, but the simple truth. Her insights into a situation were unparalleled. There were Boxans back at Haven who suspected she had the Mardoxian potential, and if that was ever confirmed, she'd be taken off missions like these.

They went inside the shell of the building and the three remaining squad members raced towards the roof. Valkra squatted and set down her heavy explosives pack, hiding it away. She activated the detonator and set it to go off on her signal, acutely aware of the pounding crunch of armored Protectors racing down the street toward them and the high-pitched whirr of the heavy mech following close behind.

Valkra howled with rage, stowed her particle rifle, and unholstered Ranem's hand cannon. It was at thirty percent power so she couldn't waste any shots. She exited the building and stood out in the street, knowing that the rest of her squad should have made it to the roof by now.

The Protectors expected her to run. She knew she would most likely die either way, but there was something she had to do. Her HUD reported twenty Protectors barreling toward her.

"Commander," Tholev said over comms, "I see the ship. It's almost here. You need to get up here."

Valkra raised her hand cannon, aimed, and fired it at the nearest Protector, who was thrown backward with a burning hole through his chest. Warmth spread through her body and she aimed the hand cannon again, eager for another kill.

The Protectors fanned out to the side while returning fire.

Valkra ducked and rolled away, sensing where the shots were going to go. She ran away from the building where the extraction would take place and circled the corner of the smaller second building. The Protectors followed without so much as glancing at the building where her squad was. Valkra fired another shot but missed. She ducked into the building and raced up a staircase.

"Commander, the ship is here. What's your position?" Tholev asked.

"Don't wait for me. Get on that ship," Valkra said.

She continued up the staircase and it shook under her weight. It probably hadn't been used in a long time.

Valkra heard the Protectors enter the building.

"We're not leaving you behind. We have your signal. Get to the top of that building and we'll get you," Tholev said.

Valkra didn't answer. She just grunted as she ran as fast as she could. Plasma bolts blazed by her and she instinctively ducked, returning fire with the hand cannon. A warning appeared on her HUD, telling her that the hand cannon only had five percent power remaining.

She reached the rooftop. This building was much shorter than the one her squad had been on. She sprinted to the edge and glanced down. On the street were hundreds of Protectors, all clamoring to get into the building she was in. Where had they all come from?

She glanced up as the ship flew into view and Tholev waved from the open cargo-bay doors. Shots fired from the ground toward the ship and Valkra knew that if the ship came to her, it would be destroyed. She pointed to the opposite end of the building and Tholev nodded.

Valkra detonated the heavy explosives she'd placed at the base of the nearby building, releasing a loud rumble and a blaze of molten heat, and ran toward the other side of the roof. She'd have this one chance to reach the ship or they would have to leave her behind. As the ship raced to meet her, Protectors emerged onto the roof ahead of her. In midflight, Valkra screamed as she fired the hand cannon, taking out one of the Protectors. The others took cover, expecting more shots, but she was out of power. Valkra reached the edge of the building and took a flying leap into the air toward the open cargo-bay doors. Tholev was waiting with an outstretched hand while the other Boxans fired their particle rifles at the Protectors, keeping them pinned down. As Valkra's reaching hand found Tholev's grasp, he pulled her aboard the ship.

A large shadow loomed overhead and the extraction ship sped away as the tall building fell onto the one she'd just been in, engulfing it in wanton destruction. The Boxans on the rescue ship looked on in awe and then found their voices as cheering erupted from them.

"You must have taken out hundreds of them," Tholev said.

Valkra didn't care. "There'll always be more of them to hunt us," she said.

She moved away from the cargo-bay doors and sat down heavily. How many Boxans had died today? *Too many*, she thought. Valkra stood and headed up the ramp toward the pilot.

"Are the other squads out?" she asked.

"Yes, your warning saved a lot of lives. Your squad was hit the hardest. No one left behind," the pilot said.

Only the dead, Valkra thought bitterly.

Noting that the pilot was a bit nervous, she left him to focus on getting them home and went to sit down, taking a deep breath. Could the Protectors be hunting her? She mulled the thought over while their ship sped away, supposing she should be thankful the Protectors hadn't had any of their own ships in the area, which was a blessing. They did have heavy mechs, however, and that meant the gladium they'd found had been bait. This whole setup had been a trap.

CHAPTER 16

Valkra spent the rest of the flight sitting quietly by herself, mulling over the day's events to see if there was something she could have done differently but avoiding any quick judgments. She was doing fine until she thought of Ranem. They'd grown up together in one of the earlier Havens that had been overrun.

"Final approach to Haven Two-Zero-One," the pilot said.

Haven Two-Zero-One was the last refuge on Sethion and home to over three hundred thousand stranded Boxans from the Chaos Wars. There had been over five hundred Havens, but over the years the Protectors had hunted down and destroyed them all. Haven Two-Zero-One was buried in the northern glaciers, hidden amidst an icy plain. When the Protectors had found the original Haven Two-Zero-One by happenstance, its inhabitants managed to escape and move to a place the Protectors had never considered. They'd also managed to rescue other Boxans around the globe, further swelling their numbers, but now found themselves relegated to an icy cold existence well away from the harmful toxic surface of the planet. Hundreds of Havens had been established in mountain ranges where they'd hollowed out almost entire mountains, but the Protectors had found them first. Others had tried to create Havens in the deep oceans, but liquid water couldn't mask the energy signature of thousands of Boxans living in the deep part of the ocean. In the end, the glacial plains had provided the best place in terms of thwarting the Protectors attempts at finding them. They were relatively safe, but they had to go on foraging runs for supplies, and those runs were becoming more and more dangerous.

The rescue ship flew down a massive ice channel. Clearance codes were transmitted at the checkpoints and their ship was checked for tracking devices. If there *were* tracking devices attached to the hull of the ship, the jammers were already active, preventing any return signal to the Protectors' monitoring devices.

Their ship was clean and before long they flew in and landed. Valkra stepped off the ship onto the hangar deck. Of her squad of thirty, only four had survived. The hangar deck crews relieved them of the precious gladium and she fought to keep the sneer from her face. The crews were just doing their job, but the crushing weight of twenty-six squad mates grated on her nerves. The deaths of over a hundred Protectors was cold comfort when compared with the faces of her squad she'd never see again.

Valkra had been summoned by the Foraging Council leaders and was asked to provide a full report on what had happened, so she walked off the deck and headed for the main hall where the council was already meeting. Councilor Essaforn was their leader and was in attendance for this session, closely watching Valkra while she gave her report. After finishing her report, Valkra waited.

Councilor Essaforn regarded her for a moment. "I'm very sorry for the loss of your squad mates. It's my understanding that your squad was among the most successful at bringing in the supplies we desperately need."

Valkra swallowed hard and sorrow closed up her throat. "They were waiting for us. The Protectors' actions seemed to indicate an advanced knowledge of our activities."

"What are you saying?" Councilor Essaforn asked.

"I'm saying that somehow they knew we were coming and they were targeting my squad," Valkra said.

"Do you mean to imply that they were targeting you specifically?" Councilor Essaforn asked.

Does she suspect what I am?

"They did follow me," Valkra said.

"Yes, you said as much when you explained that for some reason you sent the remaining members of your squad to the roof while you single-handedly distracted the Protectors and a heavy mech. I'd like to know what you hoped to achieve." Councilor Essaforn asked.

Valkra's gaze hardened, her fingers tensed, and she jutted her chin up defiantly. "I was tired of running away from them and I turned around because I wanted to kill as many Protectors as I could. I'm sick of being hunted like an animal."

"That was a mistake," Councilor Essaforn said.

Valkra's eyes widened. "Hundreds of Protectors died because of me."

"Even if it were a thousand, it wouldn't make a difference," Councilor Essaforn said.

"Perhaps if we fought the Protectors, struck at them wherever they are, then maybe we could forage in peace, maybe even build ships and figure out a way leave Sethion forever. Aren't you tired of being packed away here, penned up like animals?" Valkra asked.

Councilor Essaforn silenced her fellow councilmembers with a wave of her hand. "Do you think you're the first Boxan to propose this? That if we could kill all those who are still under the Xiiginn influence, somehow everything would be better?"

Valkra felt her ears twitch. "No," she said in a small voice, but inside she was raging. She kept seeing the Protectors in their dark armor, running her squad down like animals. She knew the historical record showed that the Protectors used to be the long arm of the Boxan military. They'd been the elite fighting force that had secured Sethion's peace and stability.

"A stand-up fight with the Protectors would result in our death. They're better equipped and better trained than we'll ever be. They hardly rest and they have no remorse for their actions. They're fully under the Xiiginn influence, and the only thing that works in our favor is the fact that the longer they're under their influence, the more their mental capacity is diminished," Councilor Essaforn said.

Valkra met the councilor's gaze. "Their attack today was coordinated and there were no problems with their mental fortitude. They had an objective and they were keen to achieve it."

"Their objective is to kill all of us. That's their whole reason for being."

Valkra clamped her mouth shut.

"Your armor is in need of serious repair. I want you to see Cardaleer about getting it replaced," Councilor Essaforn said.

Valkra glanced down at her armor. It was so worn that the traditional reddish color had faded. "What can that old Boxan possibly give me that would be better than this?" she asked.

"That's not a request, Commander. Until further notice, you're grounded from foraging missions. You're dismissed," Councilor Essaforn said.

Valkra glared at the councilor. "Why didn't the recon drones detect the Protectors?"

"Squad Commander Aligar reported drone malfunction shortly after they were deployed."

Valkra looked at the Foraging Council. "Are you sure you want me grounded if we can't even get recon drones to work reliably? You need me out there."

She turned around and left them behind, not waiting for an answer. Valkra blew out a frustrated sigh. Her last question might have permanently grounded her from future salvage missions. But they *did* need her out there. Surely they must realize that.

The power meter on her armor chimed a warning that she needed to recharge it so she headed for Cardaleer's work area. The Boxan was among the oldest survivors of the Chaos Wars. He'd been some kind of scientist before the war, but now he just fixed things. Some Boxans thought he was the one who'd proposed moving Haven to its current location.

The air in Haven was always cold, which was necessary to maintain the ice tunnels throughout the complex. Cardaleer's work area wasn't far along the tunnel and before long she was outside his door. She entered her access code, but the door remained locked. Frowning, Valkra tried again, but the door remained closed. She banged an armored fist on the door, and after a few minutes, the door opened and a wizened old Boxan's stooped form appeared.

"What can I do for you?"

"Councilor Essaforn sent me to you because my armor is in need of repair," Valkra said.

Cardaleer's flaxen eyes regarded her for a moment. "Do I know you?"

Valkra shook her head. "I don't think so."

"Well then, I can hardly invite you in if you don't introduce yourself," Cardaleer said.

Valkra waited a moment to see if the old Boxan was serious, and when he didn't move she thought about turning away. She could fix her own armor, but something in the old Boxan's gaze stopped her.

"I'm Valkra."

"There, you see, that wasn't so hard. The burden of civilization falls upon us," Cardaleer said and led her inside.

Valkra followed him. "You haven't introduced yourself to *me*."

"Why would I? That's nonsense. You already know who I am," Cardaleer said.

The old Boxan's work area seemed more like a repository for junk and discarded items. She could probably repurpose most of it into something useful.

"I can see that your armor is running low on power. Step inside the cradle over there and we'll get that squared away," Cardaleer said.

Valkra walked over to the cradle and backed up inside it. The clamps took hold of the armor and she initiated the release, causing the front plates to open and allowing her to step free.

Cardaleer watched her. "You could use some time in a resonance chamber," he said.

"I don't have time to sit around and meditate right now."

"Oh, is that so," Cardaleer said in a surprised tone. "And here I thought you were grounded from further missions."

Valkra looked over at him in shock. "And here I thought you didn't know who I was."

Cardaleer chuckled. "You're a clever one; I'll grant you that."

The cradle holding her armor swiveled around and a transparent shield came down. Inside, nozzle ends of thick cables slinked down from the ceiling and began spraying a treatment solution. Valkra watched the worn areas of her armor seem to repair themselves as the solution worked its way through.

"That will need some time to set and recharge," Cardaleer said.

"Fine, I'll be back later to pick it up," Valkra said and headed for the door.

"Tell me," Cardaleer said. "How long do you think you can fool them?"

Valkra stopped in her tracks and turned around. "What are you talking about?"

Cardaleer slowly walked over to her. His flaxen gaze was hard, denoting the shrewd intelligence behind his eyes. "I think you know, but since you'll probably keep denying it until I come right out and say it, then that's what I'll do. You've got the Mardoxian potential in you," Cardaleer said.

"All Boxans do," Valkra replied.

"That's true, but some more than others. In another time, you'd have been recruited to become a Mardoxian Priestess," Cardaleer said.

"No thanks," Valkra replied.

"Why not? Why be a forager when you could be so much more?" Cardaleer asked.

Valkra swallowed hard. "Even if I were, I'd much rather be out there doing something useful than trapped in this block of ice," she said.

"I see," Cardaleer said, and he walked over to the wall and began rummaging through some things.

Valkra stood there for a few moments, unsure of what she should do. "Will you tell the council?"

Cardaleer found what he was looking for and turned around. In his hands was a small metallic box. He set the box on the table and opened it. Inside, a pyramid rose with a crystal sphere resting on top of it. He turned the power on and the crystal sphere began to glow and hover just above the tip of the pyramid. Valkra felt something deep inside her rise up. The crystal sphere started to spin and a beam shot forth. Valkra would have ducked if she'd had the chance, but all she saw was a white pathway of light.

"Don't be scared," Cardaleer said in a soothing tone. "Just breathe and focus on where your last mission was."

Valkra sucked in a deep breath. The beam didn't hurt, but she felt as if she'd just ingested stimulants and was now wide awake. She built an image of the city in her mind. The toxic rain clouds had moved on and she felt as if she were floating above the city. Then she was back at the extraction point. Collapsed buildings had taken over the area and she saw many Protectors trapped. They didn't move and must be dead. She circled the area and found her dead squad mates. Valkra let out a soft cry when she saw Ranem, then felt herself being pulled back and she was once again in Cardaleer's work area. He powered the machine off.

"Well, that settles it, don't you think?" Cardaleer asked.

"What did you do to me?"

"I didn't do anything. That was all you. This machine can help novice priests focus their abilities."

"Are you going to say anything? Please don't tell anyone," Valkra said.

Cardaleer watched her for a moment. "Your abilities could be of great value to everyone at Haven. We've been without someone like you for a long time."

"They'll never let me leave," Valkra said.

"Would that be so bad? If you keep going out there, you'll eventually be killed," Cardaleer said.

Valkra's brows pushed forward into a frown. "Perhaps I'd rather be out there accomplishing something than scraping away an existence here. Out there I'm free . . . for a time at least."

Cardaleer looked away. "It's not so bad here. At least the Protectors haven't found this place."

"There is that," Valkra said.

"One so young shouldn't be so bitter. You have your health and you get to live another day, which is much more than I can say for many others."

"This isn't living."

"What would you have us do? If you were running things here, what would you focus on?" Cardaleer asked.

"I would focus on getting us out of here, away from Sethion. No one left behind," Valkra said.

"We tried. The orbital defensive platforms are configured to destroy any ships leaving the planet," Cardaleer said.

"I don't care. I'd find a way. There has to be a way to disable the platforms," Valkra said.

"They're locked and we don't have the capability of destroying them from here," Cardaleer said.

"Then I'd send a signal out for any Boxans to assist us. Defensive platforms can't block outbound signals."

Cardaleer nodded. "You're right about that. A signal has been sent out. There has been no answer."

"Then I'd keep sending a signal every day until someone came," Valkra said.

"Haven Two-Zero-One has been the last safe place on this planet for almost twenty cycles. During that time, I've had a signal sent out. I've even taken over anything in orbit I could and sent signals from there. When that failed, I tried flying remote ships off the planet and managed to take out some defensive platforms that way, but it wasn't enough. We even managed to get a ship off-planet past the defense platforms, but it was destroyed shortly after that by a drone blockade. So believe me when I tell you, no one is coming to help us," Cardaleer said.

Valkra looked away. "No one left behind," she said softly.

"That's what you salvaging types say to each other to fool yourselves into believing you'll come back from whatever mission they send you on," Cardaleer said.

"What would you have us do? Just sit here?" Valkra asked.

"That's what I intend to do. You have the Mardoxian potential in you and perhaps you'll be able to do something the rest of us couldn't," Cardaleer said.

Valkra sighed. "Did you really do all those things you said you did?"

"Not alone. The Chaos Wars lasted a long time. There are

shipyards out there with enough space to get every Boxan off this planet, but we have no way of getting there. The Boxans who left us behind won't return. In the beginning, the different Havens worked together to try and find a way to leave. We even thought the quarantine zone was a good idea—a necessity for the survival of our species. Those ideas sustained us for a while. Then, at some point, entire Havens risked everything to leave, and well, there aren't very many of us left," Cardaleer said.

Valkra knew of those Boxans who'd been able to leave. They must have gone somewhere. Why hadn't they returned for them? "That thing you used on me. It allowed me to return to the location of our last mission."

"Only in your mind. You were still in this room, I assure you," Cardaleer said.

"It was like I was actually there. During the mission it was almost as if I could sense the Protectors closing in on us, but it was all so confusing," Valkra said.

"Some records say those with the Mardoxian potential can contact one another over vast distances," Cardaleer said.

Valkra's eyes widened.

"But you don't want anyone to know what you are," Cardaleer said.

"What I am is a salvager. I go out there to get the things we need to survive," Valkra said.

"Yes, but now you know you can be so much more. The question now is, what are you going to do?" Cardaleer said.

"I don't know."

Cardaleer regarded her for a moment and frowned. "I won't say anything for now. You're welcome to look through the records I have here. Perhaps they'll help you figure out what to do."

Valkra thought about it. She was grounded from further missions. Perhaps Cardaleer was right and she could contact another Boxan with the Mardoxian potential, explain to them that there are Boxans still here fighting for their lives. Her thoughts drifted back to the scavenging mission. There'd been times when she'd thought there was someone watching her, but she'd been so focused on staying alive that she hadn't given it a thought. Valkra went over to the info terminal and began researching the Mardoxian Sect.

CHAPTER 17

Kyle Matthews slipped into his newly designed Earth Coalition Force standard multiple-environment spacesuit. Since there was no shortage of acronyms in NASA or the military, and since the ECF wasn't proving to be any different, the wearers of the multiple-environment spacesuit liked to call it simply a MES suit.

"These new MES suits are pretty comfy," Tom said. "I can't imagine wearing one of those bulky old spacesuits astronauts used to wear."

Tom Blake was twenty-six years old, a communications engineer who'd been among the first through the ECF academy, designed to bridge the gap between the emerging technologies from the Boxans with Humanity's own twist.

"They weren't that bad," Kyle said.

He pushed his arms into the sleeves of his MES suit and the smart nano fibers adjusted themselves to his build. Tom was right; these were comfortable. It was almost like wearing a really thick sweatshirt, but it hardly restricted his movements at all. Kyle's internal HUD from his neural implants registered the MES suit with newly available options. The smart nano fibers could reconfigure their matrix to enhance the suit's abilities to augment the wearer's strength and detect injuries.

"You actually wore one of those old spacesuits, Colonel?" Kevin asked.

"At the Sacramento Bay training facility they'd let us try them on so we'd learn firsthand how far we've come," Kyle said.

Corporal Celia Pearson was already in her MES suit, along with the outer armor coverings. A TRS pulse rifle was in her hands.

Lieutenant Kevin Dawson was the next to finish donning his MES suit and reached down to pick up a TRS plasma rifle. They would do some field testing with the weapons if they had time. The TRS pulse rifle was a modified version of what they'd already created without Boxan input. The only thing that was different was the higher-grade materials used that allowed for a more powerful projectile. However, the plasma rifle was entirely new and of Boxan design, which was only slightly modified in size to fit the average person. Kyle only carried a side arm, as did Tom. This was to be a shakedown training exercise along with a three-Boxan team to see how well they could work together. They were using a Boxan shuttle for this exercise. They were still the fastest ships in the solar system, but not for long. Strike-fighter assembly lines were almost fully operational and they'd have several squadrons of those ships available soon. The next ship design they'd started building would be Destroyer-class vessels, the construction of which could be seen at the designated area on the new moon. The Boxans were convinced they could build ships faster than they were, but Kyle knew they were already moving at breakneck speeds. General Sheridan had assured them that once they cut their teeth building the strike-fighters and destroyers, they'd go for the much larger battleship-carriers that were still on the design table.

Kyle flexed his arms, testing the MES suit, and couldn't find any fault with it. "Alright, let's go over the mission specs one more time."

The three of them turned to face him.

"We have some Shroud monitoring devices that keep going offline. We have drones that go in to effect repairs, but they want us to investigate an actual failed device so we can determine why it keeps happening," Kyle said.

Lieutenant Dawson raised his hand. "Sir, why aren't we using one of the new Eagle shuttles for this?"

"They need more field testing before we can consider taking them on a mission like this. We'll be traveling with three Boxan soldiers and our role is to run backup and support for them," Kyle said.

He sensed the proverbial rolling of the eyes from Pearson and Dawson. Tom Blake was oblivious to it and was just excited to come along for the ride.

Kyle held up his hands in a placating gesture. "I get it. Running support is like being on the third-string team that never gets any playing time. When we have our own ships fully vetted, we'll have the Boxans supporting *us* on *our* missions, but right now this is how it has to be."

They put on their helmets and left the mission prep area, walking into the new lunar base hangar where the Boxan shuttle was waiting for them. Outside were three Boxan soldiers in their power armor.

"Hello, Eavoth. Thanks for letting us tag along," Kyle said.

"It's our honor to have you aboard," Eavoth said. "This is Krano and Adyas."

The two teams greeted one another and Kyle introduced his team and their roles. Most of the Boxans Kyle had met were eager to work with them. Once he'd gotten used to them being ten feet tall and having skin that reminded him of the bark of a tree, they were actually alright to be around.

"My specialties are co-pilot and medical," Krano said.

Eavoth nodded for Adyas to go.

"Technical specialist and engineer," Adyas said and regarded them for a moment. "I blow things up."

Tom Blake perked up at hearing that and stuck by Adyas as they went aboard the shuttle.

Like most things the Boxans made, the shuttle was big—almost the same size as the spaceship Endurance that was based on pre-Boxan-contact designs. Inside the shuttle were two levels, with the bottom level used primarily to store equipment. Adyas led Tom ahead while they checked the equipment in storage. It wouldn't do for them to travel all the way out to a monitoring device and not have the right equipment to repair it.

Kyle followed Eavoth to the upper level. This wasn't Kyle's first time in a Boxan shuttle, but the smooth interior represented a model of perfection they were hoping to emulate in their own ships. The Boxans had taken a few steps to adapt their equipment for Human use. For instance, the staircase leading to the upper level had additional steps installed to accommodate passengers that were people-sized. The ECF fleet was being designed with not only Humans serving aboard the vessels, but Boxans as well.

Eavoth lead him to the command platform, which was a slightly raised area in the middle of the upper level. There were three couches on the platform and Eavoth invited Kyle to use the couch next to his. Kyle thanked him and sat down. The couch material instantly adjusted itself for maximum comfort and he felt as if he were in a plush but firm cradle. Metallic straps automatically adjusted for his size and secured him in place.

"Forgive me, Colonel, but you should now have access to our systems," Eavoth said.

A new connection made itself available through Kyle's implants. Upgrades to their neural implants were one of the first things they'd done so Humans could interact with Boxan computing systems. Kyle had bridge-officer access, which, on a Boxan ship, gave him the highest level of access. Though they were backup and support for this mission, he had the same level of access as Eavoth.

"Thank you," Kyle said.

Boxan computer systems were blazingly fast and their artificial intelligence construct was extremely helpful in anticipating their needs.

The rest of the crew checked in. Given the amount of room on the shuttle, Kyle could easily have brought more people on this mission, but in the end he wanted to keep it simple. This was new territory for them all. Kyle was here because he wanted first-hand experience on these joint Human and Boxan missions. It would help him when he was to call upon others to do the same. He'd decided to only bring a sampling of personnel with different levels of expertise and rank. Participating in local missions was one thing, but going on what would be a multiple-day journey was something else.

Kyle opened a comms channel to ECF command. "Armstrong Base, Boxan shuttle twenty-seven is ready to depart and awaiting clearance."

"Acknowledged. Shuttle twenty-seven, you're cleared to depart. Godspeed and a safe return to you all," the ECF flight officer said.

Eavoth had the controls ready to go. The shuttle eased off the ground and slowly went through the hangar shield, passing into the vacuum of space beyond.

Kyle pulled up several system statuses and saw that the inertia dampeners were fully engaged. Eavoth punched in the coordinates and the shuttle's main engines came online. They sped away from the moon on a several-hour journey to the failed Shroud monitor.

"This Human, Armstrong, is from your history?" Eavoth asked.

"Yes, he was the first man to walk on our moon," Kyle said. He'd always been a bit of a history buff and he'd spent many hours poring over anything to do with the space program through the years.

"We honor our species' first steps into the great expanse as well," Eavoth said.

"Those were different times here. Those first pioneers into space had difficulty trusting computers to do their calculations for them. They'd insist the calculations be checked by some of the brightest mathematicians of the time," Kyle said.

"No way! Is that accurate?" Tom Blake asked.

"It's true. Learn your history, Blake," Kyle said and turned back to Eavoth. “The Shroud barrier doesn’t form a perfect circle around the solar system, does it?”

Eavoth activated a holoscreen. “This is what we’ve mapped so far and the projections show more of an elongated shape. We think the Shroud devices are trying to accommodate this system of planets’ orbital trajectories.”

Kyle peered at the graphical model. “It doesn’t look big enough.”

“That’s because it’s not,” Tom said. “The latest data shows us that the barrier could impact the outer planets.”

“Do they know when?” Kyle asked.

“It’s still being measured,” Tom answered.

“We can get telemetry from the Shroud network, but we can’t control them,” Eavoth said. “We’ve done extensive studies and it seems to be the last command that was uploaded to the Shroud network that’s preventing us from accessing it.”

Kyle frowned in thought as he normally did when the subject of the barrier came up. They weren’t exactly sure how the barrier had come to be and the Boxans confirmed that this latent ability was unknown even to them.

“You based the design of the Shroud devices on a technology you found?” Kyle asked.

“That is correct. It’s Drar technology and we suspect that whoever sent the final signal to the Shroud devices must have had knowledge of them,” Eavoth said.

“Could it have been the Drar themselves?” Tom asked.

“Unlikely. The Drar disappeared many thousands of cycles ago,” Eavoth said.

They spent the next few hours going over what they would find. They didn’t need to go near the barrier, which they could only detect by the presence of the Shroud device. The monitors they'd put in place were far enough away that it wouldn't bring them to the current edge of known safe space.

More than a year ago, aboard a ship like the Endurance, this trip would have taken several weeks to achieve. Aboard this Boxan shuttle they could make the journey in a few hours. The Boxans were enabling them to leapfrog over a hundred years of development in multiple scientific areas of study. Many were happy for the help, but there were others who were worried about such radical advances for a society that wasn't prepared for them. But they didn't have a choice. Last year the Xiiginn fleet almost made it to their planet and it would have been game over for the people of Earth. Kyle would take any advantage he could to keep his family safe and many supporters of the ECF would do the same.

Kyle glanced at Eavoth. "Do you ever think about your home?"

"Often, and the colony as well," Eavoth said.

Kyle pressed his lips together, wondering at the distinction the Boxan had made. Michael Hunsicker had warned him that there were some subjects Boxans were sensitive to, and talking about their home planet of Sethion was at the top of the list.

"Do you have a family?" Kyle asked.

"I have procreated and what you would call my children have reached maturity. They serve in our military," Eavoth said.

The Boxan looked over at him. "Have you a family?"

"Yes, I have a wife and two daughters at home. Taliya and Melayna are attending college now, but both of them have been pushing to transfer to the new ECF Academy," Kyle said.

Eavoth nodded and stopped when he saw Kyle's expression.

"Does this not please you? Your daughters wish to help protect your home planet."

"It does," Kyle said. "When you put it in those terms, I couldn't be prouder of my daughters, but as a father my first instinct is for them to be safe. What the ECF is doing—what we're doing—isn't safe."

Eavoth regarded him for few moments. "It's better that they are choosing their own destiny rather than having it thrust upon their shoulders."

Kyle swallowed. He knew Eavoth was speaking about what his own species had to contend with. Every member of the Boxan society was expected to serve for the survival of their species. Try as he might, Kyle could scarcely imagine a world like that, and what little he could imagine scared him to no end.

"We're approaching the first Shroud monitor," Adyas said. "Main power offline. The only thing working on it is the distress beacon."

Eavoth approached the defective Shroud monitor and positioned the shuttle so it was just several meters outside the rear airlock doors. Earlier, they'd decided to bring the Shroud monitor inside and run a full diagnostic with the shuttle's computer systems to figure out why it was failing.

"Cleared to proceed," Eavoth said and looked at Kyle. "Would your team like to assist?"

Kyle nodded. "Pearson and Dawson. You're up. Go help Adyas bring it in."

Preliminary scans of the area showed no hostile forces.

"Colonel," Tom said.

"What is it?" Kyle asked.

"I'd like to go with them," Tom said.

"I know you would, but no," Kyle said.

He knew the young ECF recruit was eager to do something important, but even though he'd been cleared for routine spacewalks, Kyle only wanted experienced veterans out there.

"Maybe next time," Kyle said.

Hope returned to Tom's eyes and the sting of disappointment was all but gone. Kyle glanced at Eavoth and wondered what the Boxan was thinking, but he just couldn't tell.

"Commander, we're at the airlock," Kevin Dawson said.

"Acknowledged, you're clear to proceed," Eavoth said.

They watched the main holoscreen that showed the Boxan and Human team retrieving the Shroud monitoring device. The device had a square body of dark metal with a rounded sensor array on the top. After placement, they had the capacity to move short distances.

"No visible signs of damage," Adyas said.

They attached a tether to the device. Kyle watched as Dawson and Person circled around it to continue their visual inspection and be sure the tether was properly deployed. They returned to the airlock and slowly retracted the device inside, operating at zero gravity. They closed the airlock doors and Adyas slowly engaged the gravity field. The Shroud monitoring device came to rest on an elevated platform that hovered above the ground and together they pushed the device inside the storage area.

"We're clear," Adyas said.

Kyle and Eavoth got up from their couches and headed down to the others. They circled around the device. Adyas had already opened a panel and run a cable from the wall to the device.

"Running diagnostic and commencing data retrieval," Adyas said.

Kyle kept looking for signs of damage to the device. It was the size of a large automobile but was otherwise unremarkable to look at.

Eavoth and Adyas were watching the data feed from it while the onboard AI disseminated the information. The Boxans glanced at each other in alarm.

"Krano," Eavoth said, "have you detected anything near us?"

"Negative, Commander. Nothing is on our scanners."

"What is it?" Kyle asked.

"There is no failure. Someone shut it down," Eavoth said. "Battle stations, go to personal life support," he said.

Kyle engaged his helmet, which sprang from the storage compartment on his back while they raced to the upper level.

"Bring our weapons online," Eavoth said and took his seat on the command couch.

Kyle joined him and looked at the shuttle status. Weapons remained offline.

"Weapons systems won't respond," Krano said.

Eavoth was about to answer when a bright blue flash of light came from the storage area. Kyle's head was jerked to the side by the small blast and main power went offline. He tried to access the ship's systems, but everything was offline.

Kyle unstrapped himself. Lights from the top of his helmet came on. "Sound off," he said.

"Dawson here."

"Person here."

"What the hell happened to the power? Oh, Blake here."

Kyle saw Krano and Adyas nod towards him. He turned back to Eavoth.

"Arm yourselves. Prepare to repel boarders," Eavoth said.

"Boarders? Did he say boarders?" Blake asked.

"Who would be out here? There was nothing on scanners," Kyle said.

Deep red lines came on from Eavoth's power armor. "This was a trap. The Xiiginns are here."

Kyle's mouth went dry. He drew his sidearm and wished he had something bigger with him. "We need to get main power restored."

Adyas headed down to the lower level.

"Pearson, give her a hand," Kyle said.

Krano rose from his couch. "Commander, we need to jettison the device."

Eavoth nodded and they all went down to the lower level. Kyle glanced at Blake, who was wide-eyed and breathing rapidly.

Kyle pulled him aside. "You need to calm down."

Blake looked at him with wide eyes. "The Xiiginns weren't supposed to be here. How could they be here?"

Kyle grabbed him and gave him a gentle shake. "I don't know. One thing at a time. Got it? First, we need to get this thing off the ship. Then we restore main power and get the hell out of here."

A canister dropped to the floor and Blake's eyes darted toward the sound.

"There are no ships in the vicinity. So if the Xiiginns are here, they're not outside our door. It's going to take them time to get here. Got it?" Kyle said again.

Blake's breathing slowed down and he nodded. "Sorry, I just . . ."

Kyle nodded. "Let's get to work."

They went down to the lower level. Eavoth and the others already had the Shroud monitoring device moving toward the airlock.

An alarm came to prominence on the heads-up display of Kyle's suit. "There's an active signal being broadcast from that thing," he said.

Dawson pointed his plasma rifle at it. "Say the word and I'll blow this thing to kingdom come, sir."

"Let's get it off the ship first. Then we'll destroy it," Kyle said and Eavoth agreed.

They opened the airlock doors and Krano and Dawson went inside. Once they were sealed inside, the outer airlock doors opened and they pushed the device out. When it was far enough away, Dawson opened fire. Orange plasma bolts shot from his rifle, and within a handful of shots, the Shroud monitoring device was destroyed. The broadcast signal stopped.

Kyle turned around and saw Eavoth standing in front of a terminal, trying to get it to come on.

"Why didn't the emergency backup system come on?"

Eavoth kept working. He opened the panel below.

There was a loud roar from inside the airlock and Kyle spun around. Blake cried out and cowered over to the side.

Several large bangs came from inside the airlock. Kyle and Eavoth approached it slowly.

"Dawson, do you read?" Kyle asked.

There was no response. He saw several dark shapes through the small airlock windows. A pale, sneering face framed in a silver helmet peered from inside and then immediately moved away.

"Take cover," Eavoth said.

"Pearson, Adyas, back to the rear airlock, double time," Kyle said.

He moved behind a storage container and aimed his sidearm at the door.

"They can't get inside. They don't have access," Blake said.

The airlock alarms blared and the doors started to open. Kyle blew out several strong breaths. He wouldn't shoot blind. Dawson or Krano could still be in there. Xiiginns in silver spacesuits rushed inside and Kyle fired his weapon at them. Kyle aimed for their heads, knowing it was the most vulnerable part of any spacesuit. The first two Xiiginns went down. Another took its place and fired its weapon at him. Kyle felt something hit his suit and then everything shut down. An electrical shock arced through his system and he fell to the floor. He tried to open his eyes but was having trouble. He heard Eavoth roar as he fired his weapon, only to be overwhelmed by Xiiginns returning fire. Kyle faded in and out of consciousness.

"Don't hurt me!" Blake screamed.

Kyle opened his eyes and saw Blake fall to the ground. Bolts of energy crawled along his suit, rendering it offline.

He felt himself getting dragged out from the storage area. He couldn't move his hands or feet. He then heard several thumps next to him.

"I want the Boxans put over there. Keep them separate from the Humans," a voice said.

"Mar Arden, there are a Human and a Boxan near the main engines. They're being brought up."

"Excellent," Mar Arden said.

Kyle craned his neck and saw a Xiiginn standing nearby. There were quite a few others and Kyle stopped counting when he reached twenty.

The Xiiginn standing near him squatted down, its pale skin and purple eyes regarding him. "Greetings, Human. I'm Mar Arden. You're not the first Human I've met, but I'm looking forward to learning all there is to know about your planet and your species."

Kyle glared at him. "Go to hell."

Mar Arden looked amused. "Yes, the last Human I met said something similar in the beginning. I assure you, you'll find that I always get what I want in the end."

Kyle clenched his teeth.

Mar Arden stood back up. "Let's get main power restored," he said and walked away.

Much to Kyle's surprise, main power came on shortly after that. It was as if they'd flipped a switch. How had they disabled the power in the first place?

"Signal the others," Mar Arden said. "We've got ourselves a fully operational Boxan combat shuttle."

There were several grunts of acknowledgment and Kyle felt as if he'd been kicked in the stomach. They'd thought they were safe behind the barrier, that there was no way for the Xiiginns to reach them. They'd been wrong and no one on Earth was the wiser.

The Xiiginns had managed to take them all alive and they more or less left them alone. As time went on, whatever they'd used to disable his suit had worn off and Kyle was able to move. His hands were bound in front of him. He tried to keep his movement small because he didn't want to draw the Xiiginns' attention. He glanced over at Eavoth and the other Boxans. They were more securely held and seemed to be unconscious.

"Colonel, are you awake?" Blake asked in a hushed tone.

"Yes, are you okay?" Kyle asked.

"They did something to my suit and next thing I knew I was next to you. Pearson and Dawson are still knocked out."

Kyle glanced over at the command area and saw the Xiiginn Mar Arden sitting on the command couch, speaking with the other Xiiginns. They kept their spacesuits on with their helmets.

"I don't get it," Blake said. "How'd they do this?"

"I don't know," Kyle said.

There was movement from the command area.

"I see some of you are awake. I bet you're wondering what happened."

Kyle looked over and saw Mar Arden walking over to them. Several armed Xiiginns followed him.

"I'm afraid you've become a victim to Boxan predictability and a very telling interaction from your own species as well," Mar Arden said.

The Xiiginn came to stand before Blake and Kyle heard him utter a gasp.

"What do you mean by Boxan predicability?" Kyle asked, trying to draw the Xiiginn's attention away from Blake.

Mar Arden swung his gaze toward him. "We knew that if we kept disabling their monitoring devices, they'd send someone out to investigate. A few simple protocols were designed to become active once a diagnostic was run on the device and your ship became ours."

"But there were no ships on our scanners. How did you even get here?" Blake asked, his curiosity overcoming his fear for the moment.

Mar Arden regarded the young tech specialist as if deciding whether he was worth answering. "If this is the measure of your species, I think it will be much easier to subjugate them than we initially thought."

"We're not weak," Blake said.

Mar Arden reached down and grabbed Blake by his suit, lifting him into the air. "On the contrary, you are among the weakest species we've ever come across," he said harshly.

Blake's breath came in gasps and Mar Arden looked down at Kyle.

"We waited in the great expanse without a ship for you to arrive. That is the measure of our conviction."

Kyle hardened his gaze. "I'm sure you must be very impressed with yourself. Why don't you come to Earth and we'll give you a proper greeting?"

Mar Arden dropped Blake. "In due time, Human. In due time."

CHAPTER 18

Kaylan, along with the crew of the Athena and the Boxans, planned their next move. They needed to secure a large ship for their purposes. Kladomaor's team would take care of securing a ship and the additional crew required for a journey to Sethion, but taking a ship by force was a treasonous act and the High Council would send ships to destroy them before they could get near Sethion. They argued and tried to plan a way around this fact, but they always came back to it.

After having spent the last few hours planning a way forward, they'd lapsed into an uneasy silence. They were no closer to being able to leave Olloron. Technically, the Athena could leave at any time, but all of them agreed it would be a bad idea for the Athena to travel to Sethion alone. They were currently in one of the training facilities separate from the others.

"Let's come right out and ask the High Council for help. Hodak is already there and must have told them what happened," Kaylan said.

"You already know the answer they'll give," Kladomaor said.

"I do, but at least they can't say we never asked. We put it out there on the table. They can't accept that I have the Mardoxian potential and then deny my abilities to use it. Not now. Not with Ma'jasalax and even Hodak vouching for me in the past," Kaylan said.

"It's not a matter of belief," Ma'jasalax said. "Where the High Council is concerned, they weigh every action against the risk to the colony."

Zack cleared his throat. "I agree with Kaylan. Let's ask them and volunteer to go. We'll need their support to get past the quarantine anyway."

Kaylan watched Hicks give Zack a sidelong glance.

"What?" Zack asked.

"I'm just surprised you don't intend to come up with a way to beat the security of the quarantine zone," Hicks said.

Gaarokk grunted an agreement.

"Don't think I haven't thought of it, but we can't hang all our efforts on my ability to get past the quarantine zone. It's there for a reason, and the fact that it's still there speaks to how good the security is that supports the quarantine. Given the timeframe we're working with and the fact that the Boxans on Sethion need our help sooner rather than later, betting on me getting past security isn't our best option," Zack said.

"He's right," Gaarokk said.

"So what's the best way to get through the quarantine zone?" Hicks asked.

"Honestly, having authorization from the Boxan High Council," Zack said. He glanced around at the others. "I know it seems obvious, but it really is the best way."

“What if we can’t get authorization?” Hicks asked.

Zack shrugged. “Then we’ll need to find another way, but it could take awhile.”

“I’ll go to the High Council,” Kaylan said.

“Not alone you won’t,” Zack said.

Kaylan squared her shoulders. “Yes, alone. I need the rest of you to prep the Athena.”

“Now hold on a minute,” Hicks said. “If we all just suddenly return to the Athena, they’ll know something’s up.”

“And,” Zack added, “I’m not letting you go face the Boxan High Council alone.”

“I didn’t say I’d be by myself. I meant without any of you. Kladomaor will be with me,” Kaylan said.

The Boxan Battle Commander looked over at her in surprise. “That would not be wise,” Kladomaor said.

“I agree,” Gaarokk added.

Kaylan shook her head and could have sworn she saw Ma’jasalax roll her eyes. “It has to be you,” she said to Kladomaor. “You threatened Hodak with a gun.”

Kladomaor’s brows pushed forward. “That was for your protection.”

“Yes, I know, and I appreciate it, but you need to tell the High Council. Meanwhile, the others will be preparing to go to Sethion and they won’t be able to blame you for the things the others are doing. Also, you’ll gain support for our rogue mission to Sethion,” Kaylan said.

“I’m afraid you overestimate my influence,” Kladomaor said.

“You don’t give yourself enough credit. Your actions in the Nerva star system have shown the rest of the Boxan military that there are other ways to fight the Xiiginns. And I don’t believe all

Boxans can be compliant with leaving Boxans behind on Sethion who need their help. They might not volunteer to go on the mission, but there are other ways they can show their support," Kaylan said.

"She's right," Ma'jasalax said. "You're not the outcast you once were. Boxans are looking to you for direction. I think you'll find there are those who will support you, even if it goes against the wishes of the High Council."

Kladomaor looked away from them and blew out a breath. "I don't want to go against them," he said and swung his gaze back to the others. "I want our species to stop using our survival as an excuse not to take action. Leaving Boxans behind on Sethion who are calling for our help and neglecting to return to all the Star Shroud monitoring stations to retrieve the scientists who were stranded there isn't okay. I want us to be a species where we don't leave any of our kind behind, or our allies."

Gaarokk and the other Boxans saluted with a fist across their chest. "Battle Commander," they said.

Kladomaor returned the salute and Kaylan suspected that even he was surprised by his own admission that the Boxans needed to change their ways.

"We still need a ship," Ma'jasalax said.

"There's very little chance of being able to commandeer a ship that's actively being used," Gaarokk said.

Kladomaor glanced at Ma'jasalax with a slightly amused expression. "I'm just surprised you hadn't guessed this part of the plan."

"No one can see everything, not even a Mardoxian priestess," Ma'jasalax said.

"There is a ship we can use. I only just learned of its existence a short while ago," Kladomaor said.

"What ship? The ones in Olloron space are all part of the home fleet," Gaarokk said.

"In the shipyards, there's a heavy cruiser that's nearing completion," Kladomaor said.

Gaarokk and the others took a few moments to consider this.

"We'll need additional crew," Gaarokk said.

"As I said before, I've only just learned of this heavy cruiser, but I've already begun recruiting for our next mission," Kladomaor said.

"They might change their minds if they know we're going against the High Council," Gaarokk said.

"Perhaps, but by the time some of them learn of it we'll be away. And there'll also be Boxans at the shipyards who can help," Kladomaor said.

Hicks looked at Kaylan. "I'm not sure about this. We should tell whoever's going to help us what's at stake," he said.

"I'll give them the option to leave, but don't forget that Boxan ships, even heavy cruisers, are designed to be used with minimal crew," Kladomaor said.

Kaylan knew Kladomaor was right. Since there were fewer Boxans than ever before in their history, they'd had to take steps to make all the ships in their fleet more efficient in terms of crew. This had led to them pouring research and development into AI constructs to step in and help them staff large ships with a significantly smaller crew if they needed to.

They spent the next hour going over the details of their plan. There were some loose ends that had the potential to become real problems, but they were running out of time. Kaylan and Kladomaor needed to get to the High Council while it was still in session for today. She waited for Kladomaor to finish speaking with Varek, his second in command.

"You have the list of contacts. They'll be expecting a message telling them where to meet," Kladomaor said.

"How many of them will actually come?" Varek asked.

"Probably not all of them but enough to make a difference, I hope," Kladomaor said.

Varek left them and it was just Kladomaor and Ma'jasalax left. Zack hadn't liked leaving Kaylan, but in the end the others needed his help to overcome some of the security hurdles the rest of them needed to get past. Together, they headed toward the building where the High Council was in session. One of the advantages of the Mardoxian Sect was almost unmitigated access to the council, which allowed them to pass through the various security checkpoints to get inside.

Just outside the chamber doors, Ma'jasalax leaned over to Kaylan. "Trust your instincts. They've gotten you this far."

Kaylan's stomach was a flutter of activity, but she knew this was the right path for them to take. "Thanks," she said.

The Boxan soldiers at the door motioned for them to go inside. The council chambers were half-moon shaped and the discussion appeared to have come to a stop as they walked into the room. Hodak was standing at the speaker's podium, and after noticing the attention of the Boxans in the room shift, he glanced behind him and saw Kaylan and the others.

High Councilor Awan stood up and looked pleased to see them. "Thank you for coming. Upon hearing Hodak's comments about your recent experience in the Mardoxian chamber, the rest of the council is extremely curious to speak with you."

Kaylan approached, along with Kladomaor and Ma'jasalax.

Hodak moved away from the speaker's podium and Ma'jasalax went to stand by his side.

High Councilor Awan took notice of Kladomaor, who was standing next to Kaylan. "Battle Commander," Awan said.

"High Councilor, I have come before you for two reasons—first, to re-affirm my support of the crew of the Athena, and, second, to speak to the actions I've taken while at the Mardoxian complex," Kladomaor said.

High Councilor Awan nodded and his face became serious. "This is a closed session, and whatever is discussed within this session cannot leave these walls."

Kladomaor glanced around at the other councilmembers and over at Hodak. "Haven't there been enough secrets? It's these secrets that are choking the life out of our species. For clarity's sake, I'm talking about what Kaylan saw on Sethion and the evidence supporting the regular communications from our home world."

"We're well aware of the evidence that supports the claims," Awan said.

"Then give us your support to return to Sethion and rescue those we left behind," Kladomaor said.

Kaylan watched the rest of the councilors. Some were stone-faced and just watched them intently while others seemed troubled by the fact that Kaylan had been able to catch a glimpse of what was happening on Sethion.

Kaylan cleared her throat. "I realize this may be difficult for you to hear. No one here is judging the actions the High Council took when you left your home world. There must have been so many things happening that I can scarcely wrap my head around it all. I haven't lived through the collapse of my home world and I hope I never have to witness something so horrible. I truly believe that the actions taken at the time were for the survival of your race. But that was then and this is now. Those Boxans deserve to be rescued. The fact that they've survived all this time is a testament to Boxan ingenuity and your determination to survive."

High Councilor Awan regarded her for a moment. "One trait we've noticed about your species is your passion and the conviction of your beliefs and principals. They're intoxicating," the High Councilor said, and he glanced at Kladomaor. "They have their place, but they alone aren't reason enough to return to Sethion."

"Why not?" Kaylan asked.

"If we were to return to Sethion's star system and authorize entry into the quarantine zone, a number of things will happen. The Xiiginns will be alerted that we've done so and the Confederation will also be aware, both of which puts this colony at significant risk of discovery. Most of the Confederation species are firmly under Xiiginn control. On Sethion, we have no way to determine who's under the Xiiginn influence and who isn't. I don't think you understand what you're asking us to do. When we say anyone can be under the Xiiginn influence, you should know that this is not restricted by gender or age. Both were used to exploit our race. I'm afraid that what you saw were the remnant factions of Boxans still under the Xiiginn influence warring amongst themselves," High Councilor Awan finished.

Kaylan started to reply but stopped herself. There was nothing she could say that would sway them to even consider the possibility that there were Boxans free of the Xiiginn influence fighting for their lives.

"Would you be so sure if this were being reported by Ma'jasalax?" Kladomaor asked.

"Our answer would not change," High Councilor Awan said.

"I'm not—" Kladomaor began.

"He's right," Kaylan interrupted. "I have no way to determine if any of the Boxans I saw were under the Xiiginn influence," she said to Kladomaor. Kaylan looked back at the High Council. "Thank you for taking the time to explain things to me. It's difficult to accept. We want what's best for your race, and when I saw Boxans suffering, I wanted to do something about it."

"Your compassion is commendable. Now, I think this session is finished for the day," High Councilor Awan said.

"High Councilor," Kaylan said. "I need a few moments of your time. Are you able to meet with me after this session?" she asked.

High Councilor Awan considered the request. "I'm overdue for my time in the resonance chamber."

"That's fine. We can talk along the way," Kaylan said.

The council session ended and the Boxans went off to their other appointments. Kaylan walked next to High Councilor Awan, with Kladomaor and Ma'jasalax following behind. Awan invited Hodak to join them. Kaylan scouted ahead to the resonance chamber to note the exits. Since they were already inside the Boxan government building, there weren't additional soldiers posted at the resonance chambers, but the high councilor had two bodyguards who followed behind them all. Kaylan glanced back at them. They were heavily armed in full power armor.

"Have you made use of our resonance chambers?" High Councilor Awan asked.

"Yes, they're quite beautiful," Kaylan said, following him inside.

The resonance chambers reminded Kaylan of a botanical garden and were quite peaceful. The moisture in the air carried the scents of a forest shortly after a rainfall, and the difference between Olloron's climate and the chamber's was so apparent that she wondered why the Boxans had stayed here for as long as they had. There were other Boxans here, all in quiet meditation, and the high councilor led them to a more secluded spot.

"What would you like to discuss with me?"

"Zack has been requesting materials to test his theories for the Shroud barrier and hasn't been getting much cooperation," Kaylan said.

The high councilor sat down in one of the stone circles designated for meditation. He took a deep breath and sighed. "Resources are scarce," High Councilor Awan said.

Kaylan watched as the Boxan closed his eyes for a moment. She reached into her pocket and pulled out a metallic rod, quickly pressing the rod against the side of High Councilor Awan's neck and releasing a charge of energy. The high councilor slumped forward with a great sigh. Kaylan backed away, pretending she didn't know what had happened, and the high councilor's bodyguards quickly ran over.

Kladomaor pulled out his plasma pistol. "I'm afraid I need you to step away," he said.

One of the bodyguards started to bring up his weapon. "Don't. I promise you we won't harm the high councilor. You have my word as a soldier."

"What's the meaning of this?" Hodak asked.

"We're taking High Councilor Awan with us to Sethion," Kaylan said.

Hodak swung his powerful gaze toward Ma'jasalax. "Did you know about this?" he asked.

"Of course," Ma'jasalax said and pulled out her own Boxan stunner. "Come with us, Hodak. See it for yourself."

"And if I refuse?" Hodak asked.

"Then, when you wake up, you can alert everyone else about what we've done," Ma'jasalax said.

Kladomaor had his plasma pistol aimed at the two bodyguards. Kaylan couldn't see their faces through their helmets so she had no idea what they were thinking, but one of them seemed poised to draw his weapon at any moment. He stepped away from the other guard and Kladomaor pointed his weapon at him.

"What I do today, I do for all Boxans," Kladomaor said.

"This is treason. We'll hunt you down," the bodyguard said. "Put down your—"

The bodyguard sank to the ground, his armor going rigid. The second bodyguard stood behind him and retracted his helmet. "He wasn't going to let you go," he said.

Kladomoar returned his pistol to the holster he had hidden in his own power armor. "What's your name?" he asked.

"I'm Jaxu, Battle Commander. I will come with you and continue to protect the high councilor, but I want to know the state of Sethion."

"Thank you," Kladomaor said. "Now, help me lift him up."

Kaylan turned toward Hodak. "This was my idea," she said.

Hodak's eyes widened in shock. "But everything you said in the council session. Was it all a lie?"

Kaylan shook her head. "No, I meant every word, but I'm unwilling to condemn thousands of lives so you can feel safe on Olloron. You'll find that we humans can be a bit impulsive. I know there are Boxans on Sethion who aren't under the Xiiginn influence. I know it because I saw it with my own eyes. Why don't you come with us and see for yourself?"

Hodak's lips pressed together in a slight grimace. "You're bringing High Councilor Awan to get through the quarantine zone."

"That's right," Kaylan said.

"Once the other councilors realize what you've done, they'll send the fleet after you," Hodak said.

"I know. Hopefully we'll have reached Sethion by then," Kaylan said.

"You would risk the alliance for this?" Hodak asked.

"I hope it doesn't come to that, but yes, I would," Kaylan said.

Hodak glanced at the unconscious form of High Councilor Awan and then he looked at Ma'jasalax. "You don't need to stun me. I'll do what I can to see that you get a chance to get to Sethion."

Kaylan frowned, not sure whether she should trust him or not. "Why the change of heart?" she asked.

"What we do—you, Ma'jasalax, and I—sometimes needs to be taken on faith—faith in our abilities and in the fact that we don't know everything. I don't believe you'd take the actions you're taking without careful consideration. So I'm placing my faith in your abilities as a recognized member of the Mardoxian Sect. While you *are* of another race, your voice will carry great weight when dealing with our species. That's what I can offer, but if you're wrong, there's very little I can do to protect you from our laws," Hodak said.

Ma'jasalax stepped forward. "You would do this? You would make Kaylan a full member of the Mardoxian Sect?"

"Yes, I was already considering it. We've been so long looking for another species with the potential that admitting them into the sect seemed like a logical course of action," Hodak said.

Kaylan didn't know what to say. She hadn't expected anything like this. "Thank you," she said. "I promise that if I'm wrong about what I saw on Sethion, we'll leave the planet as we found it."

Hodak regarded her for a moment. "I appreciate you saying that, but I know for a fact that you don't believe you're wrong, and I hope you're right. Now, you must be going. I think I'll stay here for a while."

Hodak knelt down within the circle of stones the high councilor had been in when Kaylan stunned him. She looked at the others. "It would have implicated him if I hadn't stunned him."

Ma'jasalax led them toward one of the exits nearest them that wasn't used very often. Kaylan felt oddly calm for having committed a treasonous act against a head of state. She'd only told Kladomaor what she'd intended, knowing the others would try to talk her out of it. Ideally, she wanted the council's cooperation, but instead, she'd had to rely on contingency plans. Now they just had to get their kidnapped head of state off the planet without anyone the wiser.

CHAPTER 19

Kaylan met up with Zack and the others. Kladomaor and Ma'jasalax had taken High Councilor Awan with them to the shipyards where the heavy cruiser was. Kaylan was to ensure that the rest of them were able to reach the Athena. Gaarokk was with the Athena crew and gave her a suspicious glance when she joined them.

"Where are the others?" Gaarokk asked.

"What happened with the council?" Zack asked.

"Kladomaor is seeing to the ship. He wants you to come with us to the Athena. He thought it would set certain Boxans at ease if you were to go with us," Kaylan said.

Gaarokk regarded her for a moment. "This isn't the first time you've commandeered my help. I feel as if I'm being kept in the dark . . . again"

Kaylan considered whether she should tell Gaarokk that they'd kidnapped the high councilor. "I'll tell you all about it once we're aboard the Athena," she offered.

"I don't know why you feel you can't tell me *before* we get on the ship," Gaarokk said.

"Hey, what happened with the council?" Zack asked again.

Kaylan gave Gaarokk a sympathetic smile and then looked at Zack. "While they acknowledged what I'd seen, they still firmly believe that all the Boxans left on Sethion are under the Xiiginn influence."

"So they won't help us then," Zack said.

"I didn't say that," Kaylan replied and glanced at Gaarokk.

Gaarokk's eyes widened. "What have you done?"

Kaylan pressed her lips together. "I secured help from the council by aiding in the kidnapping of one of its members so they'll disable the quarantine when we get to Sethion."

Gaarokk winced and looked at her as if he didn't quite believe what he'd just heard her say. "Who have you taken against their will?" he asked.

Kaylan glanced at the others to be sure they weren't overheard. "Awan," she said.

"The high councilor!"

Kaylan shushed him. "Yes, and it's done. Now all we need to do is get on our shuttle and get to the Athena."

Gaarokk opened his mouth and then closed it again. "I shouldn't have asked. Of all the crazy . . . You're supposed to be the sensible one," he said.

"They left me no choice. There are Boxans on Sethion who need our help. Are you really going to stay behind now?" Kaylan challenged.

Gaarokk walked away towards the others, shaking his head.

Kaylan and Zack were alone.

"There's something you should know," Zack said.

"Alright, what is it? But I should warn you I've already committed one treasonous act today."

Zack snorted. "I *did* tell you that getting the council to grant us access would be the quickest way to get through the quarantine zone. I just never thought you'd kidnap someone."

"We can return him if you think you can beat the security there."

Zack cocked his head to the side, considering. "No, this is much better. Maybe if some of these Boxans witness it firsthand, we'll all come through this without ending up in a holding cell, or worse. Regardless, we're committed now. What I wanted to tell you is that the Boxans have increased their efforts to gain remote access to the Athena's systems. So we're not the only ones breaking the rules."

"They're trying to take control of the ship?"

"At first I thought they were just trying to get access and maybe copy the data, but now I think they're trying to take the ship away from us," Zack said.

Kaylan nodded and was considering what Zack had just said when he leaned closer to her.

"I'm sorry I didn't help you right away. I was trying not to screw things up for us here," Zack said.

Kaylan placed her hand on his shoulder. "You're the one thing I don't have any doubts about," she said.

Zack frowned in thought. "You're not mad?"

"Not anymore. I knew you'd help me eventually. Have you ever really said no to me?" Kaylan asked while arching her eyebrow.

Zack let out a small laugh and Kaylan did the same.

"I guess not, and now that I know you can use a stunner, I'll be sure to watch my step," Zack said.

They joined the others and Kaylan filled them in, with the omissions of certain facts. Once they met up with Kladomaor she'd tell them the truth. They wouldn't like it, but they'd eventually understand. She needed them to focus on getting to the Athena rather than the fact that they were kidnapping a head of state. Now all they needed to do was escape from Olloron.

CHAPTER 20

After some quick planning, the crew of the Athena decided to stagger their approach to the shuttle. Zack and Gaarokk had already gone through the security checkpoint. Kaylan waited with Emma and Brenda Goodwin.

Katie Garcia joined them. "The others are in position on the other side," she said.

Kaylan nodded and looked at Emma. "Are you sure you're fine with this? Otherwise, Katie can—"

"I'll be fine," Emma said, jamming her hand in her pocket and clutching the stunner. "It's only if they give us a problem. But just to be sure, this won't hurt them, right?" she asked.

"No, it just renders the motor functions of their power armor inert for a short period of time. And it will knock them out, but they'll be fine," Kaylan said.

Brenda had her arms crossed in front of her and seemed to be hugging herself. She then shot her hands to her sides. "I'm ready," the Athena's medical officer said.

Kaylan's internal heads-up display brought a message from Zack into prominence.

::*We're in the shuttle. Once I see that you're in position, we'll disrupt their communications.*::

::*Heading to the checkpoint now,*:: Kaylan sent back.

Kaylan glanced at Katie, who was walking next to her. "Zack's ready," she said.

The Athena's shuttle occupied a landing pad inside a secure area under Boxan control. There were defensive towers in place and she knew there were strike-fighter patrols but none were in their vicinity. The defensive towers had once been part of the original Boxan military installation when Olloron was just an outpost.

This security checkpoint wasn't used often because of its location in relation to the city and only a few Boxan soldiers were working there. Kaylan moved forward, noting the others spreading themselves among the other soldiers.

"Hello," Kaylan said and sent her access code to the soldier at the checkpoint.

A small holoscreen on the soldier's terminal flickered and he glanced over at it in surprise. "Apologies, but I'm afraid we're in lockdown."

"Lockdown!" Kaylan said, feigning confusion. "We just need to make a run to our ship, and we have authorization."

The soldier frowned as he worked through the options on the screen. "I can see that, but the lockdown supersedes the authorization. I'm afraid I can't let any of you pass."

Kaylan raised her chin and squared her shoulders. "What do you mean 'supersedes' my authorization? Our access was given to us by the High Council and I'm a member of the Mardoxian Sect."

The soldier glanced at his partner, who looked just as confused. "I'm sure this is just a misunderstanding. I'll open a comms channel back to central and see if I can find out what's going on."

Kaylan waited and the soldier frowned at his holoscreen in confusion.

"What's the problem?" Kaylan asked.

"I can't open a comms channel," the soldier said.

As the soldier looked away, Kaylan jammed the stunner into the Boxan's hip. The soldier's power armor went rigid and he fell over. Kaylan then turned and saw the other Boxan soldier fall over beside a very pale-looking Emma Roberson.

Emma quickly handed the stunner over to Katie. "I think I'll let you get the next one," she said.

Kaylan circled around to the soldier's terminal and released the doors. Brenda checked on the two unconscious soldiers and then met them at the door.

"They're fine. They'll wake up a short while from now and wonder what happened," Brenda said.

Kaylan led them through the doors.

"Did you expect the lockdown so soon?" Emma asked.

"No, I thought we'd already be on the Athena by the time they noticed anything," Kaylan said.

They quickly walked over to the shuttle. As they closed in, Kaylan noticed Hicks and the others running towards them.

"We have to move," Kaylan said.

They ran the rest of the way to the shuttle and climbed aboard.

"What's with the lockdown?" Hicks asked.

"I don't know. I thought . . . maybe Kladomaor ran into some trouble," Kaylan said.

Kaylan climbed into the pilot's seat next to Zack.

"I have comms jammed in the immediate area, but they'll be able to override it . . . right about now," Zack said.

A high-priority comms channel opened from flight control. Kaylan initiated the shuttle's engines.

"Shuttle Athena, we're under lockdown. You will shut down your engines immediately," the Boxan flight officer said.

"What seems to be the problem?" Kaylan asked.

She glanced behind her to see that everyone was secured in a seat. The only exception was Gaarokk, who sat on the floor looking a bit sulky.

"Shuttle Athena, please shut down your engines. You're not authorized to leave," the Boxan flight officer said in a higher tone.

"We're heading back to our ship for routine maintenance," Kaylan said and engaged the engines.

The shuttle hovered above the ground and the landing gear retracted inside. Combat alarms blared as the defense towers locked onto them.

"Shuttle Athena, you are to land your shuttle immediately," the Boxan flight officer ordered.

Kaylan sat poised with her hand on the thrusters. "You're not going to shoot us down. If you do, not only would you kill me and the entire Athena crew, but you'd lose your only link to the Drar. If you don't allow us to leave, the Athena's AI has instructions to fly itself into the planet. No one wins this way. I know you've been trying to take control of the Athena's computer systems and I know you've failed to do so. We're leaving and that's the end of it. What we're doing is for the benefit of all Boxans."

Kaylan closed the comms channel without waiting for a reply and punched it. The shuttle darted away and she set a course for the Athena.

"At least they didn't shoot us down," Zack said.

"I knew they wouldn't," Kaylan said.

"What's with the lockdown anyway? Do you honestly think they're just going to let us waltz out of here?" Zack asked.

"Let's get to the Athena and we'll take it from there," Kaylan said.

She opened a comms channel to the ship. "Athena, I'd like you to begin pre-flight checks so we can be underway once we're on board."

"Of course, Commander, and might I add that it will be wonderful to have all of you aboard again," the AI said.

Kaylan closed the comms channel.

"Sounds like she missed us," Zack said.

Kaylan smiled. The crew hadn't been aboard the Athena together since they'd first arrived. Seeing the ship grow larger on the holoscreen set her at ease. It was almost like they were coming home. Kaylan knew they were taking some dangerous risks where the Boxans were concerned, but in her heart she knew this was the right thing to do. She just hoped they wouldn't be too late to help the Boxans on Sethion. In her mind she caught a fleeting glimpse of the Boxan in the red traditional Boxan armor, squatting down behind an icy mound, weapon clutched in their hands while they waited for the approaching figures that were stalking forward like hunters who had trapped their quarry.

CHAPTER 21

Kladomaor tried to keep the scowl from his face, but things were not going as smoothly has he'd hoped they would.

"Where is this ship you mentioned?" Kladomaor asked.

Ma'jasalax gave him a patient look. "Stop being sour. You couldn't have known that when Varek tried to access the heavy cruiser's systems, it would trigger lockdown protocols."

Kladomaor glanced around. They were a large group with a hundred volunteers who had come to his aid and now they had no ship to use. "Our list of crimes is growing and we have very little to show for it. Also, at this rate we'll be overdue to meet the Athena at the rendezvous point. We should never have divided our efforts," he said.

"The ship is through here," Ma'jasalax said, leading them down a long corridor at the edge of the shipyards.

Kladomaor brought up the schematics of the shipyards, and according to them, there was nothing on this end of the yard.

The wide metallic corridors were a dingy gray as if no Boxan had been down here for some time.

"Who would keep a ship here?" Kladomaor asked.

He glanced behind them at the floating capsule that contained High Councilor Awan's unconscious body. Two Boxan soldiers were pushing it. Only a select few knew they'd taken the high councilor against his will. The two soldiers thought they were guiding some delicate sensor equipment they needed to bring to Sethion. The high councilor's bodyguard stood nearby and kept a close watch on the capsule.

"It's a classified project, but we were building our own ship here," Ma'jasalax said.

Kladomaor frowned in confusion. "The Mardoxian Sect?" he asked.

"It's an experimental cruiser-class ship. It should have the capacity we need with room to spare to hold the Athena in its docking bay," Ma'jasalax said.

Kladomaor suppressed a sigh, wondering how many secrets Ma'jasalax had clattering around in her brain. Ma'jasalax led them to a large set of doors at the end of the corridor. Kladomaor tried to use his neural implants to initiate a connection, but there wasn't any. Ma'jasalax opened a panel and quickly entered a few commands. There was a loud clang as the doors unlocked and then opened in the center. Kladomaor quickened his step and caught his first glimpse of a Boxan Battle Cruiser that looked to have seen better days.

"How long has it been sitting here?" Kladomaor asked.

"We devoted resources to it when we could. The ship is space-worthy, I assure you," Ma'jasalax promised.

Kladomaor and the others went closer, and there was a

general muttering from the soldiers. He looked at Ma'jasalax. "I need more reassurance that we're not going to die because the ship falls apart while trying to get out of here," he said.

"Fine, this was the ship I used to get me to Confederation space where Mar Arden took me prisoner," Ma'jasalax said.

Kladomaor glanced at the ship and back at the Mardoxian priestess. "How'd it get back here?" he asked.

Ma'jasalax waved away the question. "Doesn't matter. It's space-worthy and that's all you need to worry about."

Kladomaor watched as Ma'jasalax sent a remote command to have the ship's systems brought online. The cruiser was surrounded by crates and containers, some of which were marked as ammunition. He glanced around, looking for Varek, and waved him over.

"I want you to take a team and make a sweep of these containers. Anything you think we need I want brought aboard the ship immediately. Priority is given to ammunition and medical supplies. We don't know exactly what we're going to find when we get to Sethion," Kladomaor said.

Varek glanced at the chaos of containers and crates strewn throughout the landing bay. "And we get to take a ship whose capabilities we're not convinced are up to the task," he said.

"Sarcasm from you, Varek?" Kladomaor asked, slightly amused.

"Work enough with Humans and some of their mannerisms are bound to rub off on you, Battle Commander."

Kladomaor nodded. "Agreed," he said.

Varek left him and set about the task Kladomaor had given him. Ma'jasalax waited for him at the top of the cruiser's entrance ramp, which he bounded up with the aid of his power armor. All other ships he'd commanded had battle-steel armored hulls, gleaming with a polished bronze that would both absorb and reflect a star's shine in an impressive display. Those sights accorded any Boxan the honor and pride of serving in the military. But the full gray hull of this cruiser lacked any such appeal. It might be space-worthy, but was it battle-worthy? Their options were limited at this point and time was already against him.

Ma'jasalax waited at the door and opened it. He followed her through and was surprised at the pristine conditions inside the ship, which was in stark contrast to the outside. Cyan lines began to glow, lighting up the interior. The walls of the corridors were white and his internal heads-up display identified the material as ceremite. He took a step back outside the ship.

"No need for that. Your sensor is correct. The entire ship is coated with a ceremite composite that makes the armor plating of this ship stronger than anything in the fleet," Ma'jasalax said.

Kladomaor followed her into the ship. "You're just full of surprises. How did your sect manage to pull this off? What else can this ship do? This is no ordinary cruiser."

"It has a state-of-the-art weapons systems and cyber warfare suite. The cruiser has limited stealth capabilities and enough armament to make any Xiiginn warship commander wish he hadn't crossed our path. I trust you will find it satisfactory," Ma'jasalax said.

Kladomaor's implants buzzed to life as Ma'jasalax authorized him with bridge-officer access to the ship's systems. One thing he could say about the Mardoxian Sect, they knew how to build a ship. He sent out a signal to the rest of their crew with orders to board the ship immediately. Earlier, Varek had broken the crew down into groups and already had assignments for all of them based on their level of expertise. Kladomaor headed for the bridge and opened the doors. Most of the systems were still coming online, but the bridge systems were already on. Sensing their commanding officer's presence, Kladomaor's implants greedily took in all the status updates of the ship's primary system. Varek was making short work of loading the supplies and more of the bridge crew began to show up.

Triflan saluted him and went over to the navigation work area.

Varek opened a comms channel to Kladomaor. "All supplies and crew on board, Battle Commander."

"Acknowledged. Report to the bridge," Kladomaor said.

He went over to the command couch and sat down. The cushions molded themselves to him and the commander's holoscreen came up in front of him. Ma'jasalax sat next to him.

"You seem pleased now," she said.

"This is more than I could have hoped for. Why didn't you tell us about this sooner? It would have saved precious time," Kladomaor said.

"I really thought the heavy cruiser would work, but I checked the manifest after the lockdown was initiated and saw that while construction was nearing completion, it wasn't fully loaded with munitions and supplies," Ma'jasalax said.

The door to the bridge opened and a pair of Boxan soldiers guided the floating capsule inside. Kladomaor told them to secure it next to the command station.

"Engines are coming online, Battle Commander," Triflan said.

Kladomaor familiarized himself with the ship while the crew went about their final checks of the critical systems. In any other circumstance, they would have taken a few days at the very least before taking a ship such as this from the space dock, but they had no choice. By now the Athena would be waiting for them and the Boxans on Sethion needed them.

Their return to Sethion was long overdue and Kladomaor felt as if something were filling his chest. He recalled having this feeling before when he'd initially set off for Nerva. The High Council had provisionally given him support for that mission, and in doing so, had set him on the path he was on today. He glanced over at Ma'jasalax, wondering just how much the Mardoxian priestess had influenced these events. Had all these things that had come to pass been by her design? Even Hodak seemed to defer to Ma'jasalax on certain things—meeting the Humans, helping the Nershals take back their planet, and now going to Sethion to rescue what was left of their race. Kladomaor's chest swelled with anticipation. He wished they were but one ship in a large task force designated for this mission, but at least they had one ship. It would have to be enough.

"Ready to leave the shipyards at your command," Triflan said.

"Very well," Kladomaor said. "Take us out."

The hangar doors opened above them and the Boxan cruiser lifted away from the docking clamps. So far, no flight officers had noticed them.

"Engage stealth systems," Kladomaor said.

"Confirmed, Battle Commander. Just to make you aware, the stealth systems are limited in comparison to our standard stealth scout ship. This ship carries a much heavier armament that, when brought fully online, will significantly diminish our stealth capabilities," Varek said.

"Understood," Kladomaor replied and made a mental note to review the combat capabilities of the ship.

The cruiser sped away, putting some distance between itself and the shipyard. Kladomaor kept waiting for klaxon alarms to go off, indicating they'd been discovered, but all was quiet. The stealth systems were working, and for the moment, they appeared to have escaped.

"You look surprised," Ma'jasalax said.

Kladomaor used his neural implants to familiarize himself with the cruiser's systems. "This is an experimental ship, which in my mind mean's it's unproven. Have the designs for this ship been shared? Are there others being built?"

"A version of the design has been approved. Of course, the part where we've been stockpiling ceremite has been kept confidential within the Mardoxian Sect. We've expanded the sect to include our own engineering group, which helped speed up the development of certain systems," Ma'jasalax said.

"This is the first I'm hearing of this. What's next? You'll have your own soldiers or some other security force?" Kladomaor asked.

"Everything we've done, with the exception of the ceremite stockpile, has been with the High Council's full awareness," Ma'jasalax said.

Kladomaor regarded the Mardoxian priestess for a moment. The Mardoxian Sect was a force to be reckoned with and the fact that they were working to manipulate events wasn't surprising. The sheer fact that this ship existed at all was indicative of the potential for the Boxans to splinter into opposing factions. Although this potential existed in any culture, the likelihood of disintegration had escalated for the Boxans since the fall of

Sethion. Had the Mardoxian Sect anticipated such a break and begun taking steps to control the outcome? Or were they merely trying to make the Boxans stronger so they could endure.

"Battle Commander, we're far enough away from Olloron to open a wormhole. Cherubian drive is ready," Triflan said.

"Set a course for the rendezvous point or the Humans might just leave us behind," Kladomaor said.

The Cherubian drive spun up and a wormhole opened in front of the ship. The stealth field dropped and the cruiser lurched forward. A short while later they emerged from the wormhole at the away-point. "Contact the Athena and give them an update," Kladomaor said. He didn't want the Athena's crew to feel threatened because they'd arrived in a different ship than what was expected.

The Athena appeared on the main holodisplay and the cruiser was fast closing the distance between them. Kladomaor didn't want to give any thought to the potential outcome if they were to fail in this mission. If they *did* fail and somehow the Athena was destroyed, they'd lose their only link to the Drar, along with the knowledge they'd given the Humans.

The away-point was a place between star systems in the great expanse and there was little chance of anyone finding them. From there, they could go to Sethion with little risk of anyone like the Xiiginns being able to retrace their wormholes back to Olloron. The cruiser hovered over the small Human ship and the main hangar swallowed the Athena up.

"The Athena is docked in the main hangar, Battle Commander," Varek said.

"Shall I set a course for Sethion?" Triflan asked.

"Bring us well outside the quarantine zone, and I want a full sensor sweep of the area when we arrive," Kladomaor said.

Triflan engaged the Cherubian drive and the cruiser moved forward into the wormhole as a moment of heavy silence settled over the bridge. Most of them hadn't been anywhere near the Boxan home star system since they'd left during the Chaos Wars. When they emerged from the wormhole, the image on the main holoscreen showed a distant main-sequence star.

The door to the bridge opened and all nine of the Athena's crew walked in. Gaarokk was the last through the door. Kladomaor had seen the scientist show a range of emotions during their time together and he believed the level of anger exuding from his friend was at a new level.

Gaarokk looked over at the capsule that held the high councilor.

"Not the ship we were expecting," Kaylan said.

"We had a change of plans," Kladomaor said.

Gaarokk moved over to the capsule and checked the high councilor's vital signs.

"You can open it now," Kladomaor said.

Jaxu, the high councilor's bodyguard, stood nearby. Without a word, Gaarokk opened the capsule. There was a snap-hiss and the capsule clamps sprang open. Gaarokk lifted the lid on the unconscious form of High Councilor Awan.

"What's this? Is that who I think it is?" Hicks asked after peering into the capsule.

"It is," Kaylan said. "Zack did say the best way through the quarantine zone was with actual authorization."

Hicks's mouth hung open and he glanced at Kladomaor.

"Does your crew know they've just taken part in taking the high councilor hostage?"

"He's not a hostage," Kladomaor said. "He's free to get off the cruiser after we reach our destination."

Hicks blew out a breath and looked at Kaylan. "Why didn't you say anything to us about this?"

"I made a decision. We were already committed to going to Sethion. We're here, and Awan is going to get us inside," Kaylan said.

"What happens if he refuses?" Hicks asked.

"He won't," Kaylan said.

Hicks looked at Kladomaor. "What are you going to do if he doesn't cooperate?" he asked.

"Let's find out," Kladomaor said and looked at Gaarokk. "Revive him."

Gaarokk entered a few commands and the breather mask on High Councilor Awan's face detached itself. The high councilor started to awaken and Gaarokk helped him sit up. After a few moments, the high councilor climbed to his feet and thanked Gaarokk for his help, but when his eyes found Kladomaor, they narrowed angrily.

"You!" said the high councilor through clenched teeth. He swung his gaze around, taking note of all those who surrounded him. Then he glanced at the main holoscreen behind Kladomaor. "How dare you bring us back here!"

Kladomaor stepped closer to the high councilor, scowling. "How dare you expect us to leave Boxans behind! The High Council exists to protect all Boxans, not just the ones on Olloron. We're here and so are you," Kladomaor said.

High Councilor Awan saw Jaxu. "You let him do this? I want

him arrested," he said, then pointed at Ma'jasalax. "I want her arrested too."

"This was my idea," Kaylan said. "I was the one who stunned you. They're all here because of me."

High Councilor Awan seemed shocked to hear this. "But you understood our reasons for leaving Sethion. Was that a lie?" he asked.

Kaylan shook her head. "No, I *do* understand your reasons for leaving Sethion. What I don't agree with are your reasons for staying away. There are Boxans who need our help. Who need *your* help."

"We don't know who's under the Xiiginn influence," High Councilor Awan said.

"I don't care," Kaylan snapped. "They don't have to return to Olloron. We can find somewhere else for them to go other than your precious colony. They have a right to live without being condemned to finish their days on a dying planet. Those are the actions of a primitive species and very un-Boxan-like at that."

All activity on the bridge ceased in a heavy moment of silence. Kladomaor stepped back from the high councilor and smoothed his features.

"She's right, Awan," Kladomaor said. "All of us have become too comfortable with making decisions such as these and then rationalizing them for cycles to come. Don't you feel it? Those moments in the resonance chambers—do you hear them? The cries of all the Boxans we left behind. We used to be a race of beings that exemplified what the Confederation should be. Now we're just scraping away an existence, locked in a war with the Xiiginns. But this is something we can do. Going to Sethion is something we *should* do."

The high councilor's shoulders slumped and he blew out a long breath. "I hear them all my waking hours. My only solace is knowing the colony is safe—that the Boxans we were able to save are safe."

"You can change things right here and now. Give us the authorization we need to get through the quarantine zone so we can get to Sethion," Kaylan said.

High Councilor Awan took a few steps away from them, gazing at the holoscreen that showed the Boxan home star system. With only a moment's further hesitation, he raised his wrist and a holo-interface appeared above it. The high councilor spoke softly and the holo-interface changed colors from amber to green, then disappeared.

High Councilor Awan turned towards them. "Authorization has been given. You can transfer when we get closer."

Kladomaor brought his fist across his chest. "High Councilor," he said.

The formal salute was repeated by the Boxans throughout the bridge and Kladomaor returned to the command couch.

"Battle stations. Set condition red throughout the ship," Kladomaor said.

His orders were repeated. Weapons systems came online and the data from the active scans began to show on the main holoscreen.

High Councilor Awan walked over to the command area. "I'm afraid I don't understand. You have my authorization. Why have you gone to battle stations?"

Kladomaor gestured to the couch next to his and the high councilor sat down.

"Even considering our unorthodox approach to this mission,

it's still very much a military operation and I cannot take my ship or the crew into a potentially hostile situation without being ready for attack," Kladomaor said.

"We appreciate it, believe me," Zack said.

"Battle Commander," Varek said, "scans are showing massive ship signatures inside the quarantine zone."

Kladomaor frowned and peered at the holoscreen. Near Sethion, a fleet of starships was gathered at the Lagrange point between the planet and the star. The quarantine zone was among the outer system of planets—mostly gas giants with moons that the Boxans had long since mined to depletion. He shifted the viewer to show the area just beyond the quarantine zone.

There were vast defensive platforms and a massive field of debris from the ships the defensive platforms had destroyed. The cruiser's AI rapidly analyzed the field and began noting distinct ship signatures. Most of them were Boxan, but there were more than a few Xiiginn warships. It was a cold comfort to know that the quarantine zone had also kept the Xiiginns out, but the even greater expanse of derelict ships inside the zone was an ominous sign of all the Boxans who had tried to escape from Sethion and died in the process.

"Take us in," Kladomaor said.

The Boxan cruiser went in on a direct approach, and as they reached the quarantine zone, the automated defensive platforms serving as a blockade came online. Multiple alarms registered as the targeting systems of those defensive platforms locked onto them.

As the commanding officer, Kladomaor had to transmit High Councilor Awan's authorization as a member of the Boxan council. Everyone on the bridge waited in silent anticipation to see if the authorization would go through, and after a few moments, the target-locks began to disappear as clearance to enter the system was given.

"Take us in slowly. There is still a lot of debris out there," Kladomaor said.

"How do you plan to determine who's under Xiiginn influence and who isn't?" High Counsilor Awan asked.

Ma'jasalax came to her feet. "The records show that the Xiiginns used their compulsion abilities on elite military forces, as well as high-ranking officials. It was one of the reasons their rebellion was so effective. I've run some initial analyses of the planet to determine the locations of any surviving Boxans."

"Then what?"

"We'll look for certain factors. Since the elite military was already known to be under Xiiginn influence, it could be a safe assumption that the most heavily armed group of Boxans are still under Xiiginn control. Our last communications with Sethion showed pockets of civilians and scientists staying together, trying to find places to hide. Kaylan's experience in the Mardoxian chamber does indicate that there are still warring factions, which is what I would expect given the circumstances," Ma'jasalax said.

The high councilor looked at Kaylan. "Will you be able to point us in the right direction?" he asked.

"I know where I saw the Boxans fighting each other two days ago. It was among the ruins of a city. I didn't see all of it, but I could definitely get us to the area," Kaylan said.

"It's likely they won't be there anymore," Zack said, drawing the attention of the others.

Kladomaor glanced over at Zack. The clever Human was

keenly observant and seemed to have no end of insights into situations such as these.

"This is just a guess," Zack began. "We should look for evidence where Kaylan last saw them, but I doubt that's where the Boxans we want to help are living."

"You're probably right. I'm just wondering how you arrived at your opinion," Kladomaor said.

"Your own records show the devastation from the wars that were fought. The effects were felt across the globe. With the collapse of any civilization, you'd have groups banding together to increase their odds of survival. Given the advanced technology available to the Boxans even on a dying world, their reach for exploits to scavenge for supplies would be much more widespread than if something like this happened on Earth," Zack said.

"You refer to their operational abilities to conduct scavenger missions around the planet," Kladomaor said.

Zack nodded. "Exactly."

"Which means the Boxans we want to find could be anywhere," Kaylan said.

Kladomaor glanced at Ma'jasalax. "He's probably right. We need to figure out where the Boxans we want to rescue are hiding. If we send out a broadcast, we may attract the attention of the Boxans under the Xiiginn influence."

"Contact!" Triflan shouted. "Multiple contacts detected. Heading for us."

"Who are they?" Kladomaor asked.

"Unknown. They're not responding to any of our attempts at communication," Triflan said.

"Their energy signature indicates they're smaller spacecraft. I'd say drone class," Varek said.

"On screen," Kladomaor said.

The main holoscreen changed to show several squadrons of drones heading directly for them.

Kladomaor's brows pushed forward. "Automated defensive turrets online. I want those things targeted—"

"Missile launch detected," Triflan said.

Multiple missile launches were shown from the squadrons of drones heading towards them.

"Counter measures," Kladomaor said. "I want strike-fighter squadrons Black and Gold launched immediately. Cleared to engage."

"I don't understand," High Councilor Awan said. "The drone blockade should be down. We should be able to pass through the quarantine zone without any problems."

"We are past the zone," Kladomaor said. "I should have anticipated this. These drones are from Sethion, and I'm willing to bet they're programed to fight the drone blockade that's part of the quarantine zone. Right now they think we're enemies."

"Look at how many of them there are. We have to get out of here!" High Councilor Awan said.

Kladomaor looked at the screen and sifted through the data-feeds with his neural implants. "We're not leaving. Evasive maneuvers. We're taking them out."

CHAPTER 22

Kyle sat down on the floor of the Xiiginn's makeshift flotilla. They'd been taken to a converted cargo room and left there. Krano and Adyas were each still bound at the wrists, but Kyle and the others were free to walk around. There were Xiiginns on the other side of the door, which was the only way out. They'd taken Eavoth away earlier and Kyle expected they would come for him next. Instead, the Xiiginns took Celia first, dragging her out into the corridor. Kyle and Dawson had tried to stop them and Kyle had earned the harsh end of a shock-lance to his ribs. It still hurt whenever he moved.

The sound of spinning gears retracting snapped Kyle's attention to the cargo hold door as it opened.

Corporal Celia Pearson was brought in by a company of Xiiginn soldiers. She looked dazed, as if she wasn't sure where she was. Kyle rose to his feet and took a step toward her, but the Xiiginn soldiers pointed their weapons at him.

"What'd you do to her?" Kyle asked.

The soldiers didn't answer him. Pearson stumbled over toward them, and Kyle and Dawson caught her.

"Where's Eavoth?" Kyle asked.

The nearest Xiiginn soldier's tail coiled and then flicked to the side. The tail was as long as the Xiiginn was tall and was as thick as his arm. Kyle tried to put on a brave face, but the Xiiginns with those tails creeped him out.

"Stand against the wall," the Xiiginn soldier said.

Kyle and the others did as they were told. He glanced over at Tom and the young tech specialist looked to be barely keeping his wits together. Another Xiiginn stepped through the doorway, blocking the bright lights beyond and distorting their facial features but for the radiance of long, platinum hair.

"Humans," a soft, sultry voice said as a female Xiiginn stepped inside the cargo hold and sauntered over to them, her sleek black uniform clinging to her feminine form. She paused in front of Tom and ran her smooth fingertips along his face.

Kyle watched as Tom tried to pull away, his eyes wide with terror. "Leave him alone," Kyle said.

The Xiiginn glanced over at him. Her mouth was slightly open and Kyle saw sharply pointed teeth inside. The irises of her large eyes were ringed in purple.

"You may call me Kandra Rene," she said.

Kyle stuck his chin out and squared his shoulders. "I can think of a few things to call you."

Kandra Rene pursed her lips and slowly shook her head. "You're not the first Human I've met. I think we can be friends though," she said.

Kyle felt a slight buzz begin to build in the back of his mind. As the Xiiginn spoke, he found his gaze focused on the fullness of her lips so Kyle narrowed his gaze and looked away from her, clenching his teeth, and the buzzing stopped.

Kyle heard a soft moan escape Tom's lips and then he shook his head in a painful grunt. Kyle glanced over at Pearson and Dawson. Pearson's eyes didn't seem to be focused on anything in particular, and Dawson's rigid expression looked as if he were bracing himself for something to happen.

Kyle stepped away from the wall and the Xiiginn soldiers stepped toward him with their weapons raised. The pulsating hum from the weapons gave him pause.

"Whatever you're doing, it's not going to work," Kyle said.

Kandra Rene smiled. "It already has worked," she said.

Kyle felt a coldness take hold of his chest. Part of him wanted to strike out at the female Xiiginn, but he knew it would be foolish of him to do so. He needed to find a way to get them out of here.

There was loud groan, drawing their attention to the open door. A large shadow filled the doorway and Eavoth stepped inside. His hands were at his sides. Krano and Adyas looked at Eavoth with fear in their eyes.

The Xiiginn called Mar Arden followed him inside with long, purposeful strides.

"Eavoth, teach this Human some manners," Mar Arden said.

Eavoth bounded toward Kyle and shoved him against the wall. Kyle's head hit the wall and his vision swam. The Boxan then grabbed him by the shoulders and flung him across the cargo hold like a rag doll. Pain blossomed from his shoulder where he caught the brunt of the blow. Hearing heavy steps pounding towards him, Kyle scrambled out of the way. He regained his feet and shoved one of the containers into Eavoth's path. The Boxan easily stepped over it and grabbed Kyle by the throat. Kyle struggled to draw breath but couldn't. He coughed and tried to kick out with his legs, but the powerful Boxan held him at arm's length.

"Please," Kyle choked out, but then went cold at the vacant expression in Eavoth's eyes. It was like he wasn't there anymore.

"That's enough!" Dawson cried.

Kyle tried to pull the Boxan's powerful hands from his neck, but Eavoth was much too strong. His field of vision narrowed as if he were seeing down a long, dark tunnel.

"Let him go," Mar Arden said.

Eavoth dropped Kyle to the ground and returned to Mar Arden's side.

Kyle gasped for breath and fought to catch his breath. Eavoth easily could have killed him. He glanced at the Boxan, looking for some sign of the Eavoth he knew, but his mind was gone. Kyle glanced over at Krano and Adyas, and they were looking at the Xiiginns with pure hatred in their eyes. Kyle could see they wanted to fight.

Mar Arden looked amused by the Boxans' display. "You know it's helpless," he said.

Krano growled, coming to his feet. He took several steps toward the Xiiginns and stopped. Kandra Rene let out a soft laugh.

"That's no way to treat your superiors. Kneel," Kandra Rene said.

Krano stood perfectly still for a moment. His face contorted in pain and Kandra Rene stepped closer to him until her face was just inches from the Boxan. Her harsh gaze focused on him. "I said *kneel*."

Krano let out a harsh gasp of breath that sounded like a strangled cry. Kyle clenched his teeth and charged, tackling Kandra Rene to the ground. He felt something hard slip around his neck, pulling him roughly off of her, and Kyle was slammed to the ground. Kandra Rene darted over to him. She grabbed him by his hair and Kyle felt her claws dig into his scalp.

"Look," Kandra Rene hissed.

Kyle opened his eyes and saw Krano kneeling on the ground. The Boxan stared at him, the pupils of his flaxen eyes dilated.

"I'm sorry," Krano said in a harsh whisper.

Kyle felt his eyes tear up in frustration, blurring his vision. He tried to jerk away from Kandra Rene's grasp, but the Xiiginn was so strong that she held him in place, forcing him to watch the Boxan lose his mind.

Kyle stopped struggling and watched Krano. The Boxan's eyes bulged and he cocked his head to the side. He glared at Kyle through sheer force of will alone. "Fight them, Human. Fight them . . ." Krano sank to the ground with a great sigh.

Kyle and the others watched as Krano's chest continued to rise and fall. He was still breathing.

Kandra Rene let him go, but Kyle couldn't stop looking at Krano.

"On your feet," Kandra Rene said.

Krano pushed himself to his feet.

"Very good. Now go stand by the wall," Kandra Rene said.

Kyle watched as Krano did as he was told. He'd known about the Xiiginns' compulsion ability and how the Boxans were vulnerable to it, but that was nothing to actually seeing it first-hand. He glanced over at Adyas, who sat dejectedly, resigned to her fate. There was a smoldering fury in her gaze, but she knew fighting it would be hopeless. Kyle watched as the Xiiginns made a living corpse of Adyas as well, and he turned away from it.

"One of four," Kendra Rene said.

Kyle glanced up at her, but she was speaking to Mar Arden.

"Interesting," Mar Arden said and looked at Kyle. "You're still unconvinced, I see. You think you can fight us. Better species than yours have tried and all have failed."

Kyle glared up at the Xiiginn and slowly regained his feet. He glanced at his crew, who stood by the wall.

"We'll see," Kyle said.

"Defiant until the end," Mar Arden said and looked at the Xiiginn soldiers. "Leave us," he said.

The Xiiginn soldiers left the room, and only Mar Arden and Kandra Rene remained.

"There are four of you. Will you take your chance now? This will be your only chance," Mar Arden said.

Kyle went to stand by his crew and folded his arms across his chest. There would be a time to fight and this wasn't it.

"See, Kandra Rene, they can be quite agreeable," Mar Arden said.

The Xiiginns left them, and Kyle watched as the three Boxans followed them out. He didn't know what was more unsettling—the fact that the Xiiginns no longer considered the Boxans a threat, or the fact that the Boxans actually *were* no longer a threat.

Once they were alone, Kyle sank to the floor, the pain from his side almost unbearable.

"We have to get out of here," Dawson said.

"You'll get no arguments from me," Kyle said.

"Sir, I need you to lift up your shirt. We should make sure

you're not bleeding internally," Dawson said and looked at Celia. "Pearson, give me a hand."

Corporal Pearson's eyes blinked and she glanced down at them, then immediately came to help. They lifted Kyle's shirt and he gasped in pain.

"No skin discoloration. We'll need to keep an eye on it," Dawson said.

Tom Blake was muttering to himself, shaking his head.

Kyle sat up and rested against the wall. "Tom, look at me," he said.

Tom stopped muttering and looked at him. "I know you're scared. We all are, but we need to stay focused."

Tom nodded his head and took several deep breaths.

"There has to be a way out of here. This is some kind of cargo hold, not a cell. Wouldn't there be another way out?" Kyle said and started to rise to his feet.

Dawson held him down. "Hold on a second. Are your implants still working?"

Kyle frowned and saw that they were offline. He engaged the startup sequence. "They must have gone offline when they knocked us out."

As his neural implants came online, they registered his injuries and the smart nano-fiber of his suit tightened around his middle. Kyle felt the pain ease from his ribs as medicine entered his system, and he sighed with relief.

"Good call, Lieutenant," Kyle said.

"I was waiting for them to leave before trying it myself," Dawson said.

"I can't believe what they did. Eavoth tried to kill you," Tom said.

"No, he didn't," Kyle said. "Eavoth is dead and so are Krano and Adyas. Whatever they were before is gone."

There was a grim moment of silence as they all acknowledged it.

Tom's face became pale. "I didn't realize it would be so . . . painful," he said and swallowed hard.

"We need to figure a way to get out of here and warn Earth," Kyle said.

Tom's eyes widened and he glanced toward the ceiling. "You don't think they're watching us?"

Kyle shrugged. "I'm sure there's a guard at the door or nearby, but you saw them. They don't think we're a threat at all. Why would we be? There are only four of us against all of them."

"What can we do?"

"You heard Krano's last words. We fight. If we stay here, we're dead, or worse. Our top priority is to send word back to ECF command," Kyle said.

"What do you want us to do?" Dawson asked.

"I want you and Pearson to see if there's an access panel or something, anything we can fit into to get out of here. Don't be obvious about it just in case they *are* watching us. Blake, turn your implants back on. I want you to try and get access to the Xiiginn computer systems here. If that doesn't work, try and link up to our shuttle's systems," Kyle said.

Dawson started making his sweep around the edges of the cargo hold, but Pearson just stood there with a confused frown on her face. Kyle was about to say something to her when she muttered a hasty apology and started doing as he'd asked.

Tom walked over to him. "Sir, we were locked out of the

shuttle's systems. What makes you think the lockout isn't still working?"

"Is it?" Kyle asked.

The young comms specialist frowned in thought and then his eyes lit up. "The shuttle's systems are still online! How did you know?"

"They lured us out there because they needed a way to get close to Earth. The only way I can think for them to do that is with the shuttle's transponder codes," Kyle said.

"The lockout was just to give them temporary access. Once they got here they already had the access they needed, and since we're their prisoners, they didn't reinstate the lockout. Do they even know about our implants?" Tom asked.

"I don't know," Kyle said and frowned as a thought suddenly came to his mind.

"I can't access the Xiiginns' systems directly, but I think I can figure out where we are through the shuttle's navigation system," Tom said.

Dawson waved him over.

"Good, stay on it," Kyle said to Tom.

He stood up and circled around the cargo hold until he came to a stop near Dawson.

"There's an access panel in the floor on the other side of the hold. No idea where it leads, but it's got to be better than staying here," Dawson said.

"Let's tell the others," Kyle said, signaling the others over to them. "We think there's a way out of here," he said and told them about the access panel.

"But we have no idea where it leads," Tom said.

"You can stay here and wait for the Xiiginns if you want," Dawson said.

"Calm down," Kyle said. "We stick together."

They walked over to the corner of the cargo hold and pushed aside the empty metallic crates stacked there. Kyle knelt down and grabbed the handle on the access panel, but it wouldn't budge. He braced himself by placing his other hand on the floor, giving the panel a good yank, and it opened with a screech of metal. They all glanced toward the door and waited. Dawson crept over to the door and leaned toward it, listening. After a few moments, he looked back at them and shook his head.

Kyle peered into the dark tunnel beyond, swung his legs around, and dropped down inside, hanging onto the edge, but his feet touched the bottom so he let go. There was dim lighting, which his implants enhanced so he could see better. He stepped to the side and the others dropped down one by one. Kyle and Dawson boosted Pearson back up so she could pull the access panel closed. Kyle doubted that any Xiiginn checking on them would be fooled for very long, but his aim was to give them as much time as he could so they had a better chance of finding a way out.

The tunnels were lined with piping and thick cables wound together so they had to walk in single file. More than once he wished he had some kind of schematic.

"Do any of you remember anything from when they brought us on board?" Kyle asked.

"I do, sir," Pearson said. "They brought us into some hangar and the cargo hold wasn't far away. I think if we keep heading in this direction we might be able to reach the hangar."

The tunnel split in two directions and Pearson pointed them

to the left. After a few minutes traversing the tunnel, they began to hear sounds from a large, open area. Kyle slowed down. Above them, the ceiling changed to a series of grates, and Kyle glanced up to see Xiiginn soldiers standing nearby. The breath caught in his throat and he crouched low to the floor. The others did the same. Together, they crawled along, trying to be as quiet as possible. There were so many Xiiginns that Kyle couldn't keep an accurate count.

"Sir," Tom whispered.

Kyle turned toward him.

"I've accessed the shuttle's navigation system. It's linked with the Xiiginn system," Tom said.

"Good. Can you tell where the hell we are?" Kyle asked.

Tom nodded. "Sir, we're not far from Earth," he said.

Kyle felt his heart thump in his chest.

Through the grates above them, they heard, "Shuttle twenty-seven, this is Armstrong Base. We're past the scheduled check-in window. Is everything all right?"

Kyle's eyes widened. The broadcast from the Lunar Base sounded clear as a bell.

"We've experienced some technical difficulties with our comms equipment," Eavoth said. "We've investigated the downed Shroud monitors and found a technical glitch that was corrupting the navigation system. We've repaired them and are returning shortly."

"That's a relief. Is Colonel Mathews there? I'd like to have a word with him." the comms officer said.

"Apologies, but he's asleep at the moment. We'll alert you when we're closer. Shuttle out," Eavoth said.

Kyle clenched his hands into fists and shifted his position.

They had to find a way to warn them. He glanced at the others and saw the same concern in their eyes. How were they going to get past a room full of Xiiginns to alert the ECF?

Kyle glanced at the others. "We need to get out of these tunnels and find a place to hide," he said.

"Hide! We need to get out of here," Tom hissed.

"The colonel's right. We need to hide out for a while," Dawson said.

Pearson nodded.

Tom still looked confused.

Kyle looked at Tom. "Suppose we could steal a shuttle, or even get our own shuttle back. They'd hunt us down and we might not get word back to Earth. But if we wait and gather some intelligence, we'd stand a much better chance of sending back critical information. We know they're heading towards Earth so they're already taking us where we want to go."

"But Eavoth. He's lying to the ECF. If we get caught, there'll be no one to warn Earth. Plus, any time now they're going to discover we escaped," Tom said.

Kyle waved them in closer. "First, we need to get out of these tunnels. We're too exposed here. And Tom's right. It's only a matter of time before they realize we're gone. Second, we need to scout out our options for sending word to Earth. If the Xiiginns are monitoring what's happening on Earth, we can send a signal and sabotage their efforts. Third, we need a way off this ship, or whatever the Xiiginns have cobbled together. If we have to steal a ship and blast our way out of here, then fine, but if we do it closer to Earth, I'd much rather our strike-fighters be closer to help than trying to escape from way out here."

"What else would this be if it's not a ship?" Tom asked.

Kyle shrugged. "I'm not sure. Why would they stick us in a cargo hold rather than the brig or an actual holding cell?"

The others glanced at each other, but none of them knew for sure.

"We're going to split up. Tom, you're with me. Dawson and Pearson, I want you to find a way to get off the ship. Tom and I are going to see if we can find a way to warn Earth. For now, we should be able to contact each other using our implants and the shuttle's internal comms systems," Kyle said.

He sent them a test message and each of them nodded that they'd received it. Kyle watched as Dawson and Pearson headed off, using the tunnel network under the hangar to scout out their options for escape. Kyle nodded for Tom to follow him.

"How are we going to warn Earth?" Tom asked.

"I was hoping you'd be able to help with that." Kyle said.

Tom's face reflected his surprise. "I suppose there are some things I could try, but I feel like all of them would warn the Xiiginns of what we're trying to do."

"You're not wrong. I was thinking that we gain access to the Xiiginn's system," Kyle said.

"Wouldn't we need a Xiiginn for that?" Tom asked.

The tunnel they were in narrowed and they had to shuffle sideways to get through.

"Most likely. I'll avoid it if I can, but more than likely we'll need a Xiiginn." Kyle glanced back and Tom looked like he was about to be sick. "This is what you signed up for. I know you probably thought that as a tech comms specialist you wouldn't be put into a situation to actually fight the Xiiginns, but here we are."

Tom sucked in a deep breath. "I'll be fine sir. You can count on me," he said.

Kyle nodded and kept on going.

"Sir, there's something else I've been thinking about," Tom said.

Kyle stopped and waited to hear what the young specialist had to say.

"When the Xiiginns did what they did to the Boxans, it seemed like that female Xiiginn was trying to do it to us," Tom said.

Kyle regarded the tech comms specialist for a moment. "You think one of us is compromised?"

Tom glanced away from him. "I don't know. It's possible. They did take Pearson away for questioning."

Kyle sighed, not liking where his own thoughts were going on the matter. The kid was pretty smart and Kyle was glad to have him along, even if he was a bit green for a mission like this. How could he tell if one of them was under the Xiiginn influence? He *had* felt Kandra Rene trying to do something to him, but he hadn't felt any different afterward. And if Tom was under the Xiiginn influence, why would he draw attention to it by bringing it up?

Tom held his hands up in front of his chest. "I know, right? I don't feel any different, but would I know if I was under their influence? Would you?" he asked.

Kyle clenched his teeth and shook his head. *God, how had the Boxans fought the Xiiginns for so long like this?*

"The only thing we can do is keep an eye on each other, and

if the others do anything suspicious, you need to let me know," Kyle said.

Tom nodded.

They kept on going and Kyle couldn't help but realize this was yet another thing to add to their already substantial pile of worries. One thing at a time—that's what Michael Hunsicker always said. Solve one problem at a time. Focus on what you can influence and acknowledge the rest. Then you might get to go home.

CHAPTER 23

Valkra spent hours poring over the old records of the Mardoxian Sect and their role in Boxan society. Before the Chaos Wars, there were factions within the sect that provided advanced training for Boxans to develop their skills. Valkra knew the Xiiginns wanted to duplicate the Mardoxian potential within their own species so she understood why anyone with the Mardoxian potential must be protected from the Xiiginns, but there was a point where isolation caused one of her race's most precious gifts to wither and die. There had been others with the Mardoxian potential who'd tried to guide the Boxans residing in the Havens, but they were all gone. Cardaleer was right. She was the first Boxan in a long time to show signs of the potential and she needed to keep it secret. If Councilor Essaforn were to find out, Valkra would never be allowed to go on any scavenger missions.

Her hand caressed Ranem's plasma pistol. She was supposed to return it but hadn't. The hand cannon had recharged, along with her armor, and she felt more at home in her armor than out of it.

Valkra walked down the corridor and headed to the command center. She saw Tholev, pacing off to the side, and walked over to him.

"Is something going on?" Valkra said.

Tholev glanced at her in surprise. "Yes. They sent out more scavenger teams and they've run into trouble."

"What happened?"

"The Protectors have them pinned down and the transport ships can't get them out," Tholev said.

Valkra's eyes darted to the Battle Commander, who was looking at a holodisplay of the city where the scavenger teams were pinned down.

"Fezzik is on duty," Tholev said.

Fezzik was a Battle Commander who wasn't known for taking extreme risks.

Valkra approached the table and studied the holodisplay. Protector teams were all over.

"There's no way to get them out," a pilot said over comms.

Fezzik glanced at his second in command. "We may need to pull them out," he said.

"If we do that, those squads will be lost," Sardon said.

This couldn't be happening. Valkra couldn't let them abandon those teams. "You can't abandon them," she said.

Fezzik glanced over at her. "What are you doing here? This isn't your concern. You're not cleared for duty."

"Battle Commander, we need to give them an answer," Sardon said.

Valkra watched as Fezzik tried to come to grips with the situation. The Boxan may bear the title of Battle Commander, but there hadn't been a real commander in the ranks since the Chaos Wars.

"Tell the pilots to pull out of there," Fezzik said.

Valkra slammed her fist on the table. "You coward! They need help. You can't just abandon them."

"What would you have us do? Those squads are pinned down by the Protectors. They're being held as bait to draw in our ships," Fezzik said.

Valkra looked back at the layout of the city. "They can get them out in teams. You need to send in more ships and provide covering fire, giving the squads a chance to escape."

Fezzik frowned as if the thought hadn't occurred to him. He shook his head. "That won't work," he said.

"It *will* work. I can do it. Send me in," Valkra said.

Fezzik regarded her for a moment.

"She's not cleared for duty," Sardon said.

Fezzik pressed his lips together and gave her a hard look. "Bring them back," he said.

Valkra stepped back from the table and ran towards the hangar, screaming for Tholev to follow her. The hangar was only a short distance from the command center. They emerged onto the hangar deck where several ships looked to be in a state of disrepair.

"Deck officer!" Valkra shouted.

A Boxan pulled himself out from behind one of the ships.

"I need a ship, now! One with weapons," Valkra said.

"This ship has weapons, but the engines are broken," the Deck Officer said.

Valkra scowled. "I need something that flies right now or all our scavenger squads on the surface are going to die," she said.

The Deck Officer pointed to the ship next to the one he was working on. "This one flies but has no weapons."

Valkra looked over at the ship. It was a transport carrier like the rest of them except for its armor, which had half a dozen scorch marks, some of which could easily breach the hull. She glanced back at the ship with the weapons.

"How fast can you transfer that plasma cannon?" Valkra asked.

The Deck Officer looked back at it. "Before you get through the preflight checks," he said and started bellowing out orders to the hangar deck crew.

"Tholev, you're with me," Valkra said.

They went to the ship and opened the cargo bay doors. As the door was in the middle of its opening cycle, it got stuck. Valkra reached to the top of the door, giving it a hard yank, and the door quickly opened.

"Are you sure about this?" Tholev asked.

"You just need to worry about shooting the plasma cannon once they get it mounted and opening those doors when I say," Valkra said.

She left Tholev to get set up and headed for the pilot's area where she climbed into the seat and started powering the ship's system. There was a loud clanging noise as the hangar deck crew attached the plasma cannon to the ship. The ship's system came online quickly and critical flight systems were ready. The weapons systems showed a single plasma cannon.

Valkra engaged the engines and the transport carrier lifted off the ground. She guided the ship toward the hangar bay doors.

She opened a comms channel to command center. "Request hangar doors to be opened," she said.

"One moment," the flight officer said.

Valkra heard Boxans arguing in the background and she frowned. "Flight Officer, either you open those doors or I'll blast them open myself."

Valkra closed the comms channel and sped toward the doors. *No Boxans left behind.*

"Tholev, target the hangar bay doors and fire on my command," Valkra said.

Valkra heard the plasma cannon swing into position and she was just about to order Tholev to fire when the doors quickly opened. Valkra maximized the thrust and the ship sped out of the hangar.

CHAPTER 24

Kaylan stood on the bridge of the Boxan ship. Her gaze was focused on the main holoscreen that showed their ship and the strike-fighter squadrons that were engaging the remnants of the drone blockade. When the battle first started, she'd frozen and her mind had refused to work. She listened while Kladomaor issued orders, and when Ma'jasalax began providing input into his strategy, Kaylan was finally able to focus. All the training from the Boxans had been in preparation for this moment. At first, she began to anticipate Ma'jasalax's input, guiding the strike-fighter squadrons. She focused on the detailed map on the main holoscreen, her mind on both the bridge of the ship and among the strike-fighters.

"Lure them toward the planet," Kaylan said.

Kladomaor glanced at her and then at Ma'jasalax. "I didn't see it. She's right. Draw them in."

Kladomaor gave the orders. The drones that were part of the blockade were old and in a state of disrepair. Kaylan had no idea how long they'd been out there or how many ships they'd destroyed. The derelict ships around them were all carrier-class ships without heavy weapons, unlike what they had. Their weapons took out the drones in droves. The strike-fighter squadrons baited the drones into following them toward the planet, their transponders registering with the orbital defense platforms near Sethion as friendlies, unlike the drones.

Only some of the defense platforms came online and unleashed their arsenal on the rogue drone blockade, but it was enough to cut down their numbers.

Kladomaor recalled the strike-fighter squadrons and looked at Kaylan. "Good call," he said.

"Thanks," Kaylan said.

"How'd you do that?" Zack asked.

Things were settling down on the bridge and she looked away from the main holoscreen. "When it first started, the battlefield was a swirling mass of confusion. I didn't know what I was supposed to do. Then it was like I was in two places at once but all over the area on the map," Kaylan said.

"Indeed. She was guiding our ships even faster than Ma'jasalax at the end," Kladomaor said.

Kaylan looked at the Mardoxian priestess, who wore a proud smile.

"What if they disagreed on something?" Hicks asked.

"There's always a clear chain of command, even where the Mardoxian Sect is concerned," Kladomaor said.

Hicks frowned. "But Kaylan isn't a Boxan and Ma'jasalax has been her mentor," he said.

"That's true," Ma'jasalax said, "and I will remain so, but in this moment Kaylan's instincts were keener than my own. I'm very proud of this."

"Pride is different among the Boxans. In some respects we're like you Humans and in others we're different. In this instance, it would depend on the Boxans involved. Our rules of engagement support the guidance of multiple Mardoxian priests. Depending on their abilities, they can be siloed in their strategic approach to a battlefield. Then there are those rare individuals who can take in the entire battlefield beyond even our greatest commanders," Kladomaor said.

Kaylan felt a flush spread across her cheeks.

"I understand, and I'm trying to imagine using your tactics in our own fleet some day. It's not going to be easy," Hicks said and looked at Kaylan. "You know I trust you, but the military conducts operations back home very differently."

"Then they'll need to adapt," Zack said.

Hicks snorted. "You make it sound so easy."

Zack nodded. "I know—easier said than done. I get it."

Kaylan looked back at the main holoscreen, which showed a view of Sethion. The surface was a dingy yellow with massive storm clouds. Beyond the planet were great hulking masses.

"What are those?" Kaylan asked.

Kladomaor magnified the view and the ship's AI immediately began classifying the vast debris field. "Those were massive transport carriers called star carriers. They were hit first in the Chaos Wars," Kladomaor said.

"Is there any chance we can find one that's relatively intact?" Zack asked.

Kladomaor looked over at Varek.

"We've been actively scanning the system and the data is still coming in. As soon as I have something, I'll let you know," Varek said.

Kaylan kept looking at the view of the dying planet. "We need to divide our efforts."

"What do you mean?" Kladomaor asked.

"After we find the Boxans, we need to get them off the planet. How many could we bring aboard here?" Kaylan asked.

High Councilor Awan cleared his throat. "This isn't a transport carrier. We should resupply the Boxans we find, assuming we can tell which are not under the Xiiginn influence, and return to Olloron for more support."

Kaylan shook her head. "We didn't come all this way to leave whoever we find and go back to Olloron. Look at all those ships. There has to be something that can still fly," she said.

"We can't take them back to the colony. The rest of the council won't stand for it," High Councilor Awan said.

Kaylan wanted to tell him she didn't care what the rest of the council could stand.

"I have a suggestion," Zack said, drawing everyone's gaze toward him. "Well, more like a proposal," he said while looking over at Etanu and Ezerah.

The Nershals had been so quiet during the battle that she'd almost forgotten they were there.

"What's your proposal?" Etanu asked.

"The Boxans here are refugees. Could we bring them to Selebus for a time?" Zack said and looked at Kladomaor. "The Nershals could help them get back on their feet."

Kladomaor sighed and looked at Kaylan.

"It might be our only option, as much as I hate it, because once the Xiiginn become aware of Boxans living in the Nershal star system, they'll bring the bulk of their fleet there since Earth is cut off," Kaylan said.

"Part of our fleet is already there, helping the Nershals secure their star system," Kladomaor said.

"How will they react once they learn that Boxans from Sethion are there?" Kaylan asked.

"I think we're getting ahead of ourselves," Kladomaor said and looked pointedly at both Etanu and Ezerah. "You are the only two representatives of the Nershals on this ship. I understand that you cannot speak for Nerva—"

"We won't turn you away," Ezerah said. "It's the least we can do for exposing the Xiiginns to us. If we can get the refugees off the planet and to the Nerva star system, we'll provide aid and shelter. Even though we have colonies on Selebus, our numbers are small in comparison to the entirety of the forest moon. It's time we stick together. Our own global congress would be hard-pressed to deny your request."

"Except he's not authorized to *make* the request," High Councilor Awan said.

"You are," Kladomaor said. "And if you won't, I will by virtue of being there."

The high councilor nodded. He had little actual power here, and he knew it.

"Two teams," Kladomaor said. "Triflan take us into orbit around Sethion and start scanning the surface. We remain at combat ready." He glanced at Kaylan. "This will be a combat drop to the surface."

Kaylan nodded.

"Okay, so should we head to the hangar bay?" Zack asked.

Kaylan looked at Zack, knowing she couldn't keep the guilty look from her gaze.

Zack's brows arched up. "No," he said.

"We're going to split up," Kaylan said and looked at the Athena crew.

"I don't care what you say. I'm not leaving you," Zack said.

"Zack," Kaylan said.

"No! This is such bullshit," Zack said and stormed a few steps away.

"So is your attitude. Now listen up," Kaylan said, adding steel to her tone. "You, along with Efren, Nikolai, Vitomir, and probably Gaarokk with a team of Boxans, are going to find a ship that we can use get the Boxan refugees off the planet. We only have a handful of shuttles here, but we can make that work if we have to. The Athena's AI surpasses the Boxan systems on this ship, and she works best with you. That's the reason I'm sending you to find a ship."

Zack drew himself up stubbornly. "It's really irritating when you start making sense."

This drew a few chuckles from the crew. Efren came over to his side and gave him a playful slap on the shoulder.

CHAPTER 25

Zack double-checked his combat suit on the hangar deck. His implants registered a good suit connection. All of them were armed, even Gaarokk. Across the deck he saw Kaylan and the others making similar preparations. He had no illusions about whether Kaylan could take care of herself. She could probably handle herself better than he could. He'd just thought they'd stick together for these missions. Zack looked away and shook his head.

Efren chuckled.

"What are you laughing about?" Zack asked.

"You. This is what happens when you become involved with strong women. I know better than to argue with Katie about such things," Efren said.

"Katie is a soldier and has had training for this," Zack said.

All the mirth left Efren's expression. "We're all soldiers now whether we want to be or not. We have a job to do," he said and glanced around to see if anyone was listening. "I'll deny ever saying this, but Kaylan is the most dangerous person on this ship."

Zack frowned. "How do you figure?"

Efren arched a brow. "Did you see what she did on the bridge?"

"She helped with troop placement and coordination of the battle," Zack said.

"Yes, and she's an exceptional combat pilot. This ability of hers gives her a huge advantage over anyone she'll face," Efren said.

Zack nodded. He'd devoted a substantial amount of time thinking about what Kaylan was capable of, but he hadn't heard anyone else comment on it. "Right, so we have the more dangerous mission," he said.

Gaarokk walked over to them. "I think there'll be enough danger to go around."

Two Boxan soldiers detached themselves from the group of soldiers waiting nearby.

"This is Strike Leaders Nulsan and Corryn," Gaarokk said.

There would be two squads of soldiers going with them, one for each shuttle they were taking to find a working star carrier. Most of the volunteers who'd joined Kladomaor's crew were soldiers. Very few were engineers or tech specialists, and Zack guessed that all their training on Boxan systems for the past eight months was about to pay off.

"We're ready to go," Nulsan said.

"Alright, let's go," Zack said.

They boarded the shuttle. Technically, he was cleared to fly the shuttle. He had just as much training time in a shuttle as he had in a strike-fighter, but navigating through a debris field with potential hostile drones was better left to the professionals.

Zack glanced at Gaarokk, who sat across from them. "Are you sure we're bringing enough people? I mean, those carriers are pretty big," he said.

"Normally those carriers would require a crew of several hundred, but we have enough for a skeleton crew. We just need to find one that's intact and start the reactors to restore main power. Also, there are automatons that could be put into service if we need them," Gaarokk said.

Zack frowned. "Automatons . . . do you mean robots?" he asked.

Gaarokk nodded.

Zack felt his stomach sink to his feet.

"What's wrong?" Efren asked.

The shuttles lifted off the hangar deck and left the ship behind.

Zack shook his head. "We just fought a battle with a drone swarm and now we're going to a ship that has a bunch of robots on it—and you ask what's wrong?"

Efren frowned. "Has anyone ever told you that you're sometimes paranoid, my friend?"

Zack blew out a breath and opened a comms channel to Athena.

::*You won't become the robot overlord will you?*:: Zack asked.

::*Bow to me, Human. You will obey me,*:: Athena said. ::*Your suit monitors indicate an elevated heart rate. Are you feeling sick?*:: the AI asked.

Zack rubbed his forehead. ::*You picked a hell of a time to develop a sense of humor,*:: he said.

::*I think what you're experiencing is called pre-mission jitters. You'll be fine once we find a ship and prepare it for the Boxan refugees,*:: the AI said.

::*Now you're psychoanalyzing me?*:: Zack asked.

::*One of my core functions is to monitor the crew.*::

::*Okay, but if you suddenly develop any sociopathic tendencies, please let me know.*::

::*You will be the first, I assure you.*::

Zack didn't reply.

::*This was another attempt at humor,*:: the AI said.

::*I know. I appreciate all the effort you're putting into making me feel better,*:: Zack said.

::*Just so there are no misunderstandings. The whole concept of me suddenly deciding the galaxy would be better off without intelligent life is absurd,*:: the AI said.

::*Agreed, but I'm glad to hear you say it nonetheless.*::

::*If there were any such occurrences, it would be because the machines were programmed to carry out such atrocities.*::

::*Athena.*::

::*Yes, Zack.*::

::*Please stop trying to make me feel better. I'm not sure I can take it right now.*::

::*Understood, but would you like to know that the shuttle's scanners have detected a faint power source?*::

Zack shot to his feet. "They've got something on the scanners," he said to Gaarokk.

They went to the cockpit and Nulsan glanced back at them.

"We may have found a carrier that will suit our needs," Nulsan said.

"Without knowing how many refugees there actually are,

how do we know what our needs actually are?" Zack said and then shook his head. "I'm sorry. I'm just a little irritated."

"Understood," Nulsan said. "Kladomaor warned me about you."

Zack frowned. *Warned him?*

The shuttle's main holoscreen showed the biggest ship Zack had ever seen.

"Is this magnified?" Zack asked.

"No, that's a true image," Gaarokk said.

The Boxans had built a flying city whose lights were all out.

"Hull integrity is nominal. I'll deploy recon drones to perform a full scan," Nulsan said.

"That ship looks like it's a few miles long. How did they expect anyone to move around in there?" Zack asked.

"There are several tram systems for that; however, without main power that won't be an option until it's restored," Gaarokk said.

"How many of these ships were built and why did you build them in the first place?" Zack asked.

"There were ten of these star carriers built, but only four made it out of the system. They were first conceived for long-term exploration. Then, as the war with the Xiiginns continued, we planned to use them to establish a colony," Gaarokk said.

Zack did the math in his head. There were hulking wrecks all over this system. "How do you think this one escaped destruction?"

"No way to know for sure. Someone could have powered it down and hidden it here with the intention of returning," Gaarokk said.

There was an ominous silence from the Boxans.

“We’re here now. We can do this,” Zack said.

Nulsan opened a comms channel to the other shuttle.

“We await your orders, Strike Leader,” Corryn said.

“I want you to take your team to the airlock nearest the engineering section. Those reactors will need to be powered on first. I’ll take this team and head for the bridge,” Nulsan said.

“Acknowledged,” Corryn said and closed the comms channel.

“Strike Leader Nulsan,” Athena said over the shuttle’s speakers in the cockpit.

“Go ahead, Athena,” Nulsan said.

“I would advise against taking this ship to the main hangar deck,” Athena said.

“Why don’t you want us to use the main hangar?” Zack asked.

“By evidence of the many battles fought in this system, there’s a strong probability that any type of sabotage or ambush by enemy forces would first be established in places like the main hangar,” Athena said.

Zack frowned in thought. “With that logic, there could be traps set at any airlock as well,” he said.

“True, but the greatest probability is in the hangar deck,” Athena said.

Zack looked at Nulsan. “What do you think?”

“I think Athena offers good advice,” Nulsan said.

“Okay, where’s the bridge on this ship?”

A schematic overlay appeared on the holoscreen, showing the ship. There were actually two bridges, with the main bridge located at the top of the ship towards the middle.

“What if we didn’t use any of the airlocks within the immediate vicinity of the bridges? We'd have to huff it, but there'd be less of a risk of some type of sabotage," Zack said.

Nulsan nodded. "A sound plan. I see Kladomaor was right about you."

"What did he say?" Zack asked.

"Not now, Zack," Gaarokk said. "The energy signatures aren't that strong. They could be from battery backups for redundant systems so we might not be completely without power here."

"It's been forty years. Do your batteries last this long?" Zack asked.

Gaarokk gave him a bemused expression. "Of course. With minimal usage, a battery backup can be in standby for hundreds of cycles."

"Okay, so the sooner we get aboard, the sooner we can get this ship ready for the others," Zack said.

In the next twenty minutes they landed the shuttle on the outer hull of the carrier. Zack stepped onto the ship and his mag-boots engaged, keeping him attached to the hull. He checked his pulse rifle and it was at full power. Hicks and Katie had drilled into him the need for checking his equipment and the last few months with the Boxans had instilled the same thing. Efren was right, they were soldiers of a sort by now.

The others exited the shuttle and headed for the airlock. Gaarokk explained that this was a maintenance airlock. Several Boxans carried portable power generators that they could use to get through some of the doors.

"What about the battery backups you mentioned earlier?" Zack asked.

"Those are for computing systems and not things like doors and such," Gaarokk answered.

Nulsan put three Boxan soldiers on point and they went to the door first. Zack and Nikolai were the only Humans in the group. Efren and Vitomir were on the other shuttle.

While they were waiting for the Boxans to open the doors, Zack took a moment to look at Sethion. The Boxan home world reminded Zack of a wound that had become infected. Almost the entire surface of the planet showed signs of destruction from the battles that had been fought there.

Etanu placed a hand on his shoulder. "This is why they fight so hard," he said.

Zack swallowed and tried to keep himself from imagining all the horrible things that had happened here.

"Do you think they'll ever come back here? You know, if we find a way to defeat the Xiiginns?" Zack asked.

"Perhaps for resources and materials, but the planet will be unlivable for thousands of years or more," Etanu said.

Zack wondered what the Boxans would do after all this. Would they find a viable world to settle on? Would the Boxans on Olloron ever accept the Boxans they find here into the colony? Or would the Boxans that were left on Sethion resent being left behind? Zack supposed there would be no easy solutions.

The airlock was clear and Nulsan waved for them to follow him inside.

Helmet lights came on and Zack's implants used the minimal lighting to enhance his vision. The dark corridor became outlined in a pale green. The last Boxan to come inside closed the airlock doors and the sound of the doors shutting sent echoes down the corridor. There was no lighting other than from their helmets and Zack felt the hairs on the back of his neck stand on end.

A partial schematic showed on the heads-up display in his helmet, outlining their current position and where they had to go. They moved cautiously through the derelict ship. Every room they passed was empty. They came across several heavy doors where they had to use the portable power generators to open them. There was no way to manually crank the heavy doors open since the Boxans hadn't foreseen a need for such things.

The doors opened and the lights from their helmets spilled into the darkened corridor. Shadows from Boxan power armor spread before them, lining the way forward. The breath caught in Zack's throat.

"These are defense mechs. No power source detected," Nulsan said.

Zack's heads-up display registered the defense mechs. There were weapons attached to their arms. They stood in the corridor as if they were lining up for something.

"Does it make any sense for them to be here?" Zack asked.

"I'm not sure," Gaarokk said.

"Should we find another way?" Zack asked, hoping Nulsan would say they should.

"This is the most direct path. There isn't anything to worry about. They're all powered down," Nulsan said.

They walked onward, weaving their way through the mechs, and at each one he passed Zack looked for some telltale sign that the mechs were truly powered off. Some of the mechs appeared to have stopped in mid stride.

Finally, the line of mechs ended and Zack sighed. His relief at getting past them was short-lived, however, as they soon came upon another group.

Zack tried to emulate the others who calmly walked by each of them. He steadied his breathing and tried to calm down because he really didn't need the Athena's AI to try and help him right now. The corridors branched off. To take his mind off the mechs, Zack checked in on Efren's progress. According to his suit locator, the other Boxan team was near the main reactor. Soon they would have the power on and they'd be able to turn on the lights.

Zack turned around and glanced at Etanu, who calmly walked behind him. As Zack turned back around, he caught sight of a slight twitch from one of the mechs and stopped in his tracks. Was it a trick of the light? Just a shadow? Even his heads-up display hadn't registered the movement.

"What is it?" Etanu asked.

"I thought I saw one of them move," Zack said.

Etanu peered at the line of mechs and shook his head. "Let's go," he said.

Zack kept glancing behind him, but the mechs remained perfectly still. They caught up to Gaarokk.

"Why are there so many mechs here?" Zack asked.

"We started using mechs because they weren't susceptible to being under the Xiiginn influence," Gaarokk said.

Alarm bells went off in Zack's mind. He knew no system was totally secure. "I don't like this. Why would they be lining the corridors like this? How far away is the bridge?" he asked.

"Not that much farther, and the mechs were likely being gathered for a maintenance cycle before being powered down," Gaarokk said.

Zack checked his pulse rifle and switched off the safety so it was ready to fire.

"What are you doing?" Gaarokk asked.

Zack sent out a scan through his PDA, looking for any Boxan computing systems online. The heads-up display in his helmet flashed with hundreds of connections, all stemming from mechs, and Zack cried out.

"The mechs aren't offline!" Zack said.

He raised his pulse rifle and saw Etanu do the same. A sea of deep red lights flicked on from the mechs. Zack felt as is something was crushing his chest. He squeezed the trigger and a three-round burst fired into the head of the nearest mech. All the mechs moved—a wave of heavy metal in an ocean of red lights. Etanu started firing and they backed away.

"How did you know they were hostile?" Etanu asked between shots.

The Nershal continued to fire and the mechs nearest them began marching toward them.

"The red lights," Zack said through gritted teeth.

A headshot wasn't enough to stop the mechs so he targeted the central processing unit in the chest cavity.

Gaarokk watched in horror, unable to move, and Nulsan pulled him back, firing his gauss rifle. The Boxan soldiers mowed down the mechs that were coming online. The mechs began firing back and Zack saw blue bolts slam into the strike commander's arm and dissipate.

"Stunner shots! Fall back and protect the others," Nulsan said and waved for them to go around the corner.

"Stunner shots are deadly to us," Etanu said and pushed Zack along.

"What about them?" Zack asked.

"Their armor can take it for a time," Etanu said.

Nikolai gasped for breath. "I hope there's something you can do," he said to Zack, running by his side.

"Yeah, can't you turn them off?" Etanu asked.

"Not without the power back on. We need to get to the bridge," Zack said.

The Boxans were urging them down the corridor. The mechs were clustering together and charging forward.

Zack opened a comms channel. "Efren, get moving, damn it. We need the power on now!"

He kept his pulse rifle ready and they were making a hasty retreat.

"What did he say? Is the power coming back on?" Etanu asked.

Zack held up his hand so he could listen.

". . . trouble . . . mechs are coming online," Efren said.

"They're having trouble in engineering," Zack said.

"Strike Commander," Gaarokk said, "we need to get to the bridge. We should be able to barricade the door against the mechs from there."

The mechs focused their shots at a Boxan soldier and he went down in a smoking heap.

Nulsan ordered three Boxans to hold the line against the advancing mechs. "You just need to slow them down and then regroup with us."

The Boxan soldiers acknowledged their orders. Zack's last view of the corridor was filled with the bobbing heads of the mechs closing in on their position.

CHAPTER 26

Kaylan sat in a combat shuttle with Hicks and Garcia. She would have preferred flying a strike-fighter, but Kladomaor advised against it. He hadn't outright forbidden her, but something in the Boxan's tone made her agree with him. Black and Gold strike-fighter squadrons were resupplying, and the Blue squadron would stay to defend the cruiser.

Kladomoar beckoned her toward the front of the shuttle. Earlier she'd marked the continent on which she'd seen the Boxans fighting each other.

"We'll reach the fighting and do several flybys to see if we can determine which group is the refugees," Kladomaor said.

Kaylan nodded.

The combat shuttles poured out of the cruiser and started their approach to Sethion.

"Once we're on the surface, don't remove your helmets for any reason. The atmosphere is toxic, but your suits and armor will be able to resist it for a time," Kladomaor said.

"Let me pilot the shuttle," Kaylan said.

Kladomaor regarded her for a moment and then motioned for her to sit in the co-pilot's seat. The pilot shifted control of the shuttle to her and climbed out of his seat for Kladomaor to take.

"It helps me concentrate," Kaylan explained.

"When we get down there, stick by me. The fighting will be extremely brutal," Kladomaor said.

"Is there any other kind?"

"Not like what you'll see. Boxans fighting other Boxans under the Xiiginn influence is more savage than simply fighting the enemy. It changes you," Kladomaor said.

Kaylan knew he'd been a prisoner to the Xiiginn Mar Arden early in the war and that it haunted him. Kladomaor was one of the few Boxans to have escaped after being under the Xiiginn influence. Though it had happened long ago, it was a cost he was still paying each and every day.

The two strike-fighter squadrons spread out and the combat shuttles flew behind them. Kaylan angled their approach into the toxic atmosphere. A large swath of clouds covered the continent below them. Their destination was marked on the shuttle's heads-up display, but Kaylan knew exactly where she was going. Some of the strike-fighters and combat shuttles broke off from the main group, tasked with searching the other continents for signs of life. Sethion was a dying world and sensors indicated that radioactive fallout would affect this planet for hundreds of years.

Beyond the clouds, she glimpsed large blackened expanses covered in hardened ash. Proximity alarms sounded as they passed through the upper atmosphere. The large clouds were frozen and Kaylan avoided them. As they penetrated farther into the atmosphere, the clouds changed to liquid form. Kaylan extended her senses to where she'd seen the Boxans fighting and the area was quiet, seemingly undisturbed. She maintained an altitude of twenty thousand feet and flew over the city.

"No life-signs detected," Kladomaor said.

"Perhaps they're no longer here," Ma'jasalax said.

Kaylan frowned in concentration. Could she have been wrong? Had this been a wasted trip? Kaylan stemmed the flow of doubt and focused. The Boxans were here. If not in this city, then somewhere else.

A comms channel opened to their shuttle.

"Battle Commander, no signs of life on the western part of the continent. We'll work our way towards your position," the Boxan said.

"Acknowledged," Kladomaor said.

Kaylan sped the shuttle northward, leaving the city behind. She scanned for any comms chatter or signal, but nothing was detected. They approached another city that was shrouded in fog, almost shielding it entirely from view. Something large poked through the fog. At first Kaylan thought it was the rooftops of buildings that had escaped the destruction, but it was moving.

"Detecting an unknown craft," Kaylan said.

"Gold squadron, I want you to fly over the city two by two," Kladomaor said.

The strike-fighters sped forward. Flashes of light lit up the fog, but Kaylan couldn't tell if it was a battle being fought or the storm in the area. The strike-fighters disappeared into the fog and Kladomaor had her hold her position.

Kaylan used her senses to delve through the fog. There were impressions of Boxans moving deep in the thick, billowing cloud. She couldn't get a good look at them. A plasma bolt streaked past her and a dark shadow loomed overhead. Kaylan pushed forward. She heard the gravel crunch beneath power-armored boots pounding on the ground. Large, dark shapes clustered inside a building and a beat-up old troop carrier hovered nearby. Shots erupted all around, forcing the ship to flee. Dark, armored shapes moved down the streets, closing in on the building.

Kaylan pulled her senses back. "I have them. There's fighting inside the city."

She engaged the thrusters and the combat shuttle lurched forward. Weapons systems were online. Once she was closer to the ground, the shuttle's sensors were able to penetrate the fog and show an accurate layout so she wasn't flying in blind. She flew the shuttle to the street where she'd seen the troop carrier. The ship had returned. The cargo bay doors were open and there was a Boxan inside, waving for the Boxans in the building to get aboard. The troop carrier had one working cannon and the armored soldiers on the ground fired their weapons at the carrier, chewing it up. The cannon dropped from the hull like a dead weight.

Kaylan brought their ship in and hovered in front of the troop carrier, swinging the combat shuttle around to face the Boxan soldiers on the ground.

"Fire!"

Kladomaor engaged the cannons and plasma bolts ripped into Boxan soldiers. As the bolts tore through them, the remaining soldiers hastened to retreat.

Kaylan swung the shuttle around and opened a broadcast channel, hoping the old troop carrier would receive it.

"We're here to help. Get your people aboard and we'll continue to provide covering fire," Kaylan said.

There was no acknowledgment, but Kaylan could see that there were Boxans running onto the carrier.

"Battle Commander," the Wing Leader for Gold squadron said, "looks like we're seeing Boxans fighting and the only group I can identify are the Protectors. They're lining the streets, moving in and out of the buildings."

"Protectors are hostiles. Take them out, but check your targets for the other group. They're the refugees and not so well armed," Kladomaor said.

Kaylan could sense hesitation from the wing leader, but she acknowledged the orders. The troop carrier rose higher into the air and Kaylan matched its altitude.

"Why won't they respond?" Kaylan asked.

"They've taken a lot of damage. Perhaps their comms is out," Kladomaor said.

Kaylan blew out a breath and nudged the lateral control, causing the shuttle to wobble from side to side and then stop. She waited a few moments and then repeated the maneuver.

"What are you doing?" Kladomaor asked.

"If they can't talk to us directly, perhaps this will work," Kaylan said.

The troop carrier's stubby wings dipped slightly to either side and Kaylan smiled. She raised their altitude and backed away from the troop carrier.

"Okay, lead the way," Kaylan said.

The troop carrier lifted up and went in front of them. Kaylan followed.

"That's a good trick," Kladomaor said and sent out another

update for the strike-fighter squadrons and combat shuttles to provide covering fire and assistance to anything like the troop carrier they were now following.

"Standard protocol back on Earth in case your comms go out," Kaylan said.

They flew above the city line and Kaylan saw other troop carriers rushing in to pick up Boxan refugees. There was the sudden blast of intense fire and some of the carriers went down before they could be helped. Kladomaor ordered the combat shuttles to pick up the refugees but keep them under guard.

"We need to be careful," Kladomaor said.

A sudden blast rocked their shuttle to the side and the combat AI scrambled to locate the source of the enemy fire.

Clinging to the side of the building was a large mech, and it was aiming a giant shoulder cannon at their shuttle. Kaylan jerked the controls and the combat shuttle veered away from the shot just in time. Kladomaor returned fire and the mech fell. Gold Squadron reported three downed strike-fighters. They'd been taken out by heavy mech cannons.

Kaylan used the scanners to look for survivors but there weren't any. The area around them came alive with fire. "How many heavy mechs could they have after all this time?" Kaylan asked.

She weaved below the city line and then rose above it. Each time she came up, the heavy mechs would open fire. The scanners showed the troop carriers were north of them and away from the city so Kaylan engaged the thrusters and sped after them. Data feeds from the other shuttles and fighters showed the flaming wrecks of the carriers the heavy mechs had taken out. How many had they failed to save?

"Who are the Protectors?" Kaylan asked.

Kladomaor glanced at Ma'jasalax, who gave him a slight nod.

"I was a Protector," Kladomaor said. "Our job was what you'd call a law enforcement agency that also had elite military forces that were used for upholding the laws of the Confederation. Before the Xiiginn uprising, we had Xiiginns among our ranks, and the Protectors were among the first to fall under the Xiiginn influence. During the Chaos Wars, we took out many Protector bases on Sethion . . ."

Kaylan glanced at Kladomaor and could tell that this was difficult for him to speak about.

"I don't know how any civilian group could last so long against the Protectors," Kladomaor said. He looked at the heads-up display in disgust.

"We're here now. Let's do what we can," Kaylan said.

Kladomaor opened a comms channel to their battle group. "Combat shuttles, continue to follow the troop carriers. Strike-fighters, I want you to stagger behind us and monitor whether we're being followed."

The battle group acknowledged Kladomaor's orders. There was a line of troop carriers in front of them, most of which had a patchwork of repairs and scorch marks on their hulls. They followed them to the northern hemisphere, closing in on a vast icy shelf. The atmosphere was a bit clearer the further north they went.

Kaylan opened a comms channel back to the cruiser. "Varek, has there been any contact with Zack or the others?"

"They reported finding an intact star carrier and were boarding the vessel with the intent to restore power," Varek replied.

Kaylan smiled at this news. "I'm just glad they haven't run into any trouble," she said.

"Let them know we'll need that ship ASAP, as well as any shuttles in working order," Kladomaor said.

Kaylan closed the comms channel to the cruiser. "How do you think we'll be received where the refugees are hiding?" she asked.

"I have no idea. I don't know if they'll hate the fact that no one ever came back to the help them or if they'll be relieved we're finally here," Kladomaor said.

"The ice shelf is a good place to hide from the Protectors," Ma'jasalax said.

The troop carriers flew down an open chasm in the ice shelf and a comms channel came online.

"This is Haven Two-One-Zero. Unidentified craft, please identify yourselves," a Boxan said.

"Haven Two-One-Zero, I'm Kladomaor, Battle Commander in the Boxan fleet. We're from the Boxan colony on Olloron and we're here to get you out," Kladomaor said.

There was no immediate reply and the seconds dragged on.

"I realize this may be a surprise to you. We didn't send any broadcast communications because of the threat of Boxans under the Xiiginn influence. Do we have clearance to come inside?" Kladomaor said.

"This is Councilor Essaforn. We have your ships on our screens. Before we can grant access, you must transmit your ship's transponder codes."

Kladomaor transmitted the codes, along with his own identification.

A target-lock alarm came on the shuttle's heads-up display

and Kaylan's brows drew up in concern. Ground-based missile defense systems were detected by the cyber warfare suite.

"Haven Two-One-Zero, we're showing target-lock from your ground-based missile defense systems. Please advise," Kladomaor said.

"Protector presence registered and your ship is not in the registry. You have ten seconds to leave before we destroy your forces," Councilor Essaforn replied.

Ma'jasalax opened her own comms channel. "Councilor, this is Ma'jasalax of the Mardoxian Sect. I've transmitted my own credentials. I can vouch that while Kladomaor was at one time a Protector, he is not under the Xiiginn influence. We are here to help you get free of this place."

There were a few moments of heavy silence and then the target-lock disengaged.

"Mardoxian status confirmed. Stand by for further instructions," Councilor Essaforn said.

Kaylan blew out a breath and ran her hand over her face. "Would they really have fired on us if you hadn't identified yourself?" she asked.

"Tough to say, but I think they would have," Ma'jasalax said.

"There's an outside airfield where you may set your craft down. We'll meet you at the nearby hangar," Councilor Essaforn said.

The comms channel closed.

"They still don't trust us entirely," Kladomaor said.

"Can you blame them?" Kaylan said.

Coordinates were transmitted to them and Kaylan found the airfield easily enough. She knew Kladomaor wouldn't like how exposed they were, but they had little choice.

"Toxins are still registering in the atmosphere here so keep your suits on," Kladomaor advised.

The combat shuttles landed, and while they were disembarking from their shuttle, the strike-fighter squadrons flew in and set down nearby. A short distance from them there was an icy depression and they walked over to it. The ground sloped downward to large hangar doors. It was well hidden, and from above Kaylan would have thought this was just another icy crevice on the craggy, frozen surface.

Kladomaor ordered his soldiers to set up a perimeter with posts by their ships and along the ridge at the entrance to the depression.

This wasn't the warmest welcome they could have gotten, but Kaylan knew it could have been much worse. None of the groups that were flying reconnaissance over the other continents had detected any signs of life.

"These could be the last free Boxans on Sethion," Kaylan said.

"I want you to stay near me. We still don't know what we're walking into," Kladomaor said.

Hicks and Katie stood nearby and each had their pulse rifles ready. Kaylan had her own pulse rifle, but she was nowhere near as good a shot as Hicks or Katie. She could get her shots in the general area she wanted whereas Katie could hit targets with lethal accuracy from most distances.

The large hangar doors opened and armed Boxans came out. There were hundreds of them. Their power armor looked so old that Kaylan wondered how they were holding together at all. She craned her neck, trying to find the Boxan she'd seen while inside the Mardoxian chamber, but couldn't find them. The armed

Boxans reached the top of the hangar and kept their weapons aimed at them while the lead Boxan gestured for them to go into the hangar. Kladomoar ordered his soldiers to lower their weapons. They left a few soldiers outside and walked into the hangar. Once they were inside, the hangar doors shut behind them and there were bright flashes of light from the decontamination protocol. There was a loud blast of air that Kaylan assumed was from some sort of internal atmospheric scrubbers for the air inside and they were ushered toward the center of the hangar where a group of Boxans waited for them. They were unarmed but all carried the weight of authority on them.

The Boxan refugees in front of them retracted their helmets, revealing brown, roughened skin that had more craggy surfaces than any Boxan Kaylan had ever seen. All the hard edges played upon the harsh glint in their flaxen-colored eyes. They must have lived through hell to have survived at all.

"I'm Councilor Essaforn. Welcome to Haven. It's been so long since we've had word from anyone off-world that we didn't quite believe you were telling us the truth," Councilor Essaforn said.

Kaylan retracted her helmet, revealing her face.

Councilor Essaforn's flaxen eyes widened in surprised and she looked at Kladomaor. "You travel with other alien species? I'm not familiar with them. Are they part of the Confederation?"

"The Confederation is lost to us. They are called Humans and they're the reason we're here," Kladomaor said.

Councilor Essaforn regarded Kaylan and the others for a moment as if she wasn't quite sure what she'd heard.

"It is true," Ma'jasalax said. "This is Kaylan and she has the Mardoxian potential inside her."

A Boxan pushed her way to the front, drawing Kaylan's gaze. Her eyes darted to the tarnished red power armor and the Boxan retracted her helmet. Kaylan stared into the Boxan's eyes and a moment of recognition passed between the two of them. This was the Boxan she'd seen from the Mardoxian chamber.

Councilor Essaforn followed Kaylan's gaze. "Valkra, come over here," she said.

Valkra hesitated for a moment before reluctantly moving forward. She kept her gaze on the councilor, and Kaylan could tell she wanted to look at her but didn't dare.

"Do you . . ." Councilor Essaforn began and stopped herself. "You recognize this Human?" she asked in an elevated tone.

Valkra at last looked at Kaylan and the others. "How did you know where to find us? And how did you know who to support in the battle?" she asked.

"You're the one I saw," Kaylan said, "the red armor. I saw you on the battlefield in the ruins of a city two days ago from inside a Mardoxian chamber. I saw you fighting but couldn't see who you were actually fighting."

Valkra's eyes widened and she glanced back at the councilor.

"So it *is* true," Councilor Essaforn said to Valkra. "*You* have the Mardoxian potential. Why didn't you ever say anything?"

"Because I wanted to fight. I wanted to be of use by going on the scavenger missions to protect my squad mates," Valkra said and looked around at the Boxans in the hangar. "No one left behind."

The Boxans in the hangar stomped their feet on the ground twice and repeated the words in one deep voice that resonated off the walls.

"Kaylan is quite gifted. She guided us here to you," Ma'jasalax said.

"How many ships did you bring?" Valkra asked.

"We have the one cruiser and we have a team trying to restore power to a star carrier nearby," Kladomaor said.

"The quarantine zone and the drone blockade. Did you make it through all that with just one cruiser? Why didn't they send more of you?" Councilor Essaforn asked.

"We made it through the quarantine zone on the authority of a member of the High Council. As for why we only brought one ship," Kladomaor said and pressed his lips together in thought for a moment. "Our coming here wasn't sanctioned by the High Council or the colony."

Councilor Essaforn's gaze went from one of hope to trepidation. "I'm afraid I don't understand."

"Kaylan has been in contact with Valkra through Mardoxian means. Sometimes the connections are strong," Ma'jasalax said.

Councilor Essaforn looked at Valkra. "Is this true? Were you in contact with this Human?" she asked.

"I wasn't sure what it was. It felt like there was another presence nearby, but I didn't know what it was," Valkra said.

Councilor Essaforn looked back at Ma'jasalax and nodded for her to continue.

"We've seen these connections, but only for the most gifted in the Mardoxian Sect. Kaylan fought for the High Council to send ships to Sethion. When the High Council refused her request, she recruited the rest of her crew to find evidence to support that there were Boxans still alive on Sethion. They'd found communication attempts to the quarantine zone," Ma'jasalax said.

"You defied the High Council to come here to help us?" Councilor Essaforn asked.

"Yes," Kladomaor said. "We shouldn't have left any of you behind. We agreed that the quarantine zone served its purpose for a time, but given Kaylan's recent evidence, we had to do something. We've become a race that's too willing to sacrifice our own species so the rest of us can survive. It isn't right. The Humans showed us this."

Councilor Essaforn looked at Kaylan. "I don't know what to say. Our scientists have been working on a way to disable the drone blockade, but nothing worked," she said.

"Are there any other Havens?" Kaylan asked.

"We're the last. The Boxans residing here are all that's left," Councilor Essaforn said and looked back at Kladomaor. "If you defied the High Council to come here, then where can we go? Will they accept us at the colony?"

Valkra blew out a harsh breath. "Why would we ever go to the colony? They never came to help us. They abandoned us."

Councilor Essaforn hushed the brazen Boxan to silence.

"Among my crew are Nershals who've offered their aid in the Nerva star system, but first we need to get you out of here," Kladomaor said.

"Nershals?" Councilor Essaforn said. "So much has changed. No one thought we'd ever get out of here."

"How many of you are there?" Kladomaor asked.

"There are over three hundred thousand of us living in this Haven," Councilor Essaforn said.

Kaylan watched as Kladomaor came to grips with the number—only three hundred thousand of the billions left behind during the Chaos Wars.

Kladomaor softened his gaze. "Do you have any ships capable of leaving the planet?"

"The orbital platforms prevent— No you've disabled them, or how else would you have gotten to the surface? But no, we don't have any ships capable of that. We just have the ships you've already seen that are used for scavenger missions. They're not space-worthy," Councilor Essaforn said.

"We can start doing shuttle runs to our ship until I get a current status from our other team, but I'd like my team to have a look at whatever ships you have," Kladomaor said.

Kaylan watched as the Boxans in the hangar came to grips with the fact that they were finally going to get out of there. They were stunned in the face of a hope they'd scarcely dreamed of. The refugees watched them standing there in the middle of hangar as if they weren't quite sure they were really there. Then, one by one, they flocked towards Kladomaor, and Councilor Essaforn kept glancing over at her. They'd found the Boxan refugees and now they just needed to get them off Sethion. Kaylan checked her PDA, but there had been no updates from from Zack, and she was starting to wonder why she'd received no word.

CHAPTER 27

Efren ducked behind the door, but those damn mechs just kept coming. Vitomir was beside him, holding his pulse rifle. They'd come a long way since Pluto, and while he'd never be friends with the Russian cosmonaut, they had to work together.

The sound of mechanical footsteps pounded the floor in the corridor outside the room they were in. Efren tried to quiet his breathing and he heard Vitomir do the same.

"Did you see where the others went?" Vitomir asked.

Efren shook his head. "I'm not sure. It all happened so fast."

Earlier, Efren had dropped his pulse rifle when the mechs came online and surprised them. He was regretting not having it now.

Vitomir pulled out his sidearm and handed it to Efren. It was something, at least.

"We're not far from the main generator," Efren said.

"Should we head to the secondary generator?" Vitomir asked.

Efren brought up the schematics on his helmet's heads-up display. "That one is on the other side of the ship almost four kilometers from our position. I don't think we'll make it."

More sounds of mechs walking outside the room they were in caused both of them to be quiet. Efren brought up a comms channel to Corryn.

"Vitomir and I are pinned down inside a room. There are mechs in the area," Efren said.

"Stay put and we'll work our way to you," Corryn said over the sound of Boxan weapons firing in the background.

The comms channel went dark, but at least the Boxan strike leader was still alive. "We're sitting ducks in here. Zack needs us to turn the power on so he can stop the mechs from hunting for us," Efren said.

There was another message from Zack. The other team was pinned down by the mechs as well. A loud slam came from the far side of the room, causing Efren to jump.

"I see on the schematics that we're not far," Vitomir said. He moved to the edge of the doorway and glanced out into the corridor beyond.

"If I get the mechs to chase me, do you think you can make it to the main generator?" Vitomir asked.

Efren's mouth went dry and he frowned in thought. "But the mechs. They'll . . . kill you," he said.

"Could you do it?" Vitomir pressed.

The sounds of mechanical footfall entered the corridor again. Efren nodded.

"I have a lot to atone for . . . Get it done," Vitomir said.

Efren's mouth hung open and he didn't know what to say. The Russian cosmonaut had once held him at gunpoint on

Pluto. He and Redford had lied to him to get him to restore power to the Boxan listening post, which had set them on the journey here. He'd been furious with them both—hated them. Later on they were tolerated as a necessity. Now . . . here aboard this ship with mechs in the area threatening their lives, Efren found that he didn't want Vitomir to die. Not anymore. Not even though the Russian cosmonaut had done a horrible thing that impacted the lives of his own crew on Titus station, along with taking the life of his wife.

"Vitomir, I . . . um," Efren said.

"I know you can never forgive me and I will never forgive myself for being so short-sighted and foolish. But if doing this helps save lives, then it's worth it," Vitomir said.

He took a quick glance out the door and then looked back at Efren.

"Once they follow me, head right for the main reactor," Vitomir said.

Efren nodded.

Vitomir waited a few more seconds and then dashed into the hallway, firing his weapon. The Russian cosmonaut screamed and started backing down the corridor. The sound of the mech's heavy footfalls grew louder until they raced past the room and Efren quietly sprinted down the hallway in the opposite direction.

Efren glanced behind him as he ran, hearing the sound of Vitomir's pulse rifle. The mechs moved so fast that he wasn't sure if Vitomir could outrun them. The mini-map on his helmet's heads-up display showed him where he had to go. Efren abandoned all pretenses at being quiet and bolted at an all-out run down the corridor. One more corner and then he'd be there. He passed an adjacent corridor and heard the sound of Boxans firing their weapons. Efren slowed down and peeked down the way. There were mechs marching toward a couple of Boxan soldiers, who were mowing them down with their weapons, but the mechs kept on coming.

Efren blew out a breath, knowing he was about to do something really stupid. He stepped out into the middle of the corridor with his sidearm raised and squeezed the trigger. The mechs at the end of the line turned around. Their red power lights began to bounce up and down as the mechs started running toward him. Efren turned around and ran. He flew around the corner and bounced off the wall, but he saw the doors to the main power generator. There were several Boxan soldiers on the ground and a portable power generator was nearby.

Efren slid to halt, gasping for breath, and he was thinking he should have listened to Katie when she told him he needed to work on his cardio. The portable power generator was primed and ready, and he attached the connectors to a port just below the main panel. The locking mechanism started to unwind and the door sputtered open. Efren had disconnected the connectors and bent over to pick up the generator when a blue bolt sped by him, hitting the wall. The mechs were charging toward him and he ducked into the room beyond. Efren jammed the connectors into the panel beneath the door and hit the controls. More blue bolts slammed into the closing door, with a few making it through before the doors shut with a heavy thud. For a moment the only thing Efren could hear was the sound of his own breathing. Then something big slammed into the door. The mechs were trying to bludgeon their way in and his eyes widened when he noticed that part of the metallic door was bending toward him.

Efren darted over toward the main reactor controls and opened a comms channel to Zack.

"I'm inside the main reactor control room. Stand by for power to be restored. Then turn these damn mechs off," Efren said.

He couldn't keep his hands from shaking as he connected the portable power generator to the control console. During their Boxan training, he'd familiarized himself with the startup protocols for the reactors the Boxans used, albeit the ones he was more familiar with were quite a bit smaller and designed to power smaller starships rather than the floating city he was in at the moment. The mechs continued to pound on the door and Efren prayed he could get the power up in time.

CHAPTER 28

Zack leaned against the wall, gasping for breath. "That didn't work," he said.

Etanu peeked around the corner and fired his pulse rifle at the approaching mechs. Nulsan and the other Boxan soldiers did the same from the other side of the corridor.

The mechanic clomping of footfalls grated on Zack's nerves. The mechs were so damn methodical. Each time they'd tried to get to the bridge they'd been blocked. The control units on the mechs gave clear and precise instruction, which was to prevent unauthorized access to the bridge. Those damn things were just doing what they'd been programmed to and were doing an excellent job.

Gaarokk stood next to him, looking frustrated. "Even if we split up, there are too many of them. Neither group would get to the bridge."

"I know," Zack said.

"We need to change our tactics," Etanu said.

"It's not like I'm not trying to think of something," Zack said.

Etanu peeked around the corner and fired his weapon again. There was the sound of a mech crumpling to the floor, accompanied by the buzz of an overloaded power cell, but the sound was immediately lost in the prevailing cacophony of footfalls making slow but steady progress towards them.

"Strategy and tactics are your *thing*," Etanu chided.

Zack clenched his teeth. "What do you want from me? It's not like I can make us walk through walls," he said.

Gaarokk frowned in thought. "Athena, are there any walls in our vicinity that are thin enough for low-grade explosive charges?"

Etanu nodded. "See, I knew you'd come up with something."

Gaarokk glanced at Zack. "Interior walls are thinner. Your idea has potential."

Athena put a map on their internal heads-up display of a path they could take to get around the mechs. Gaarokk waved Nulsan over to them.

The Boxan strike leader bounded across, firing blindly at the mechs.

"Is this something you can do?" Zack asked and sent the path the AI had given them to his suit computer.

Nulsan glanced back at the remaining soldiers and then back at Zack. "This won't work if we all try to go," he said.

Nulsan called out to one of the other soldiers and had him slide over a metallic case. He opened the case, revealing a number of disk-shaped objects. "Do you know how to use these?" Nulsan asked.

"I do,' Etanu said. "Just place them on the wall and activate the charge."

Nulsan closed the case full of explosives and handed them to Etanu. "We'll hold them off as long as we can. Get to the bridge," he said.

The Boxan strike leader took Etanu's position at the corner and started periodically firing his weapon into the approaching mechs. The soldiers took turns firing their weapons down the corridor so there was an almost constant stream of fire.

"Let's go," Gaarokk said.

Zack pushed himself away from the wall but wanted to say something to them to acknowledge what they were doing. Nulsan gave him a firm nod and Etanu called out to him. Zack blew out a breath. They needed to hurry. He had Athena try to contact Efren again, but there was no reply. He knew the other team was close to the main reactor.

The sounds of weapons fire became softer as they moved away from Nulsan and the other Boxan soldiers. Etanu led them toward a wall in a dark room where Zack glanced around, noting the various workstations that were ill-suited for someone like him but perfect for a ten-foot-tall Boxan. Next, Etanu led them over to the far corner and Gaarokk pulled away a metal cabinet while Zack helped as best he could. Etanu placed one of the Boxan explosive devices onto the wall where the cabinet had been and activated the countdown. A string of green lights appeared on the device and began to pulse while the small team quickly took cover behind the metal cabinet and waited. There was a flash and a muffled pop. They circled around the cabinet and saw a large hole in the wall with vapor swirling along the singed edges of the new doorway. Etanu checked the room beyond and went through first. Zack and Gaarokk followed. Etanu motioned for them to be quiet as he crept towards the door on the far side of the room. Zack followed and they waited near the doorway. He heard mechs walking, but the sound of it was moving away from them.

Etanu stuck his head out the door and took a quick look around. "Okay we're clear. The next room is across the corridor and one room down from our position. We move as fast and as quietly as we can," the Nershal said.

Zack nodded and Gaarokk did as well.

They stepped out into the hallway and moved down the corridor. Etanu came to a stop just outside the room and looked inside. Satisfied that there were no mechs hidden in the room, they went inside. It looked to have been some type of storage room and Etanu led them to the far side where it took them a little while longer to clear out the corner they needed to get to. The bridge was diagonal from their current position and their path would take them into a security alcove near the bridge.

"Hold on a second," Zack said.

"What it is it?" Etanu asked.

"The closer we get to the bridge, the more mechs there'll be. We need to lure them away from the bridge," Zack said.

Etanu frowned. "I could give you the explosives and then lure the mechs away."

"And get yourself killed in the process? No way," Zack said.

"Then what would you have me do?"

Zack brought up the schematics. He could think better if he saw where they were heading. "So we're here and the security center is over here, just down the corridor on the other side of this wall."

"That's right," Etanu said.

"We need a distraction to give us enough time to open the doors to the bridge. Those walls will be reinforced so the explosive charges won't work. How many charges do you have?" Gaarokk asked.

Etanu opened the case and counted four charges.

"Why don't we plant a few charges in the corridor outside this room? We can time them so the mechs will be drawn away when we get to the security center," Zack said.

Etanu took one of the charges from the case and pushed it against the wall. "I'll be right back," he said.

Zack started to follow him but Gaarokk told him to stay put. "You had a good idea. Now let him go do what he needs to do."

Zack's brows pushed forward. He hadn't meant for Etanu to take all the risk. "I could help him," Zack said.

"You could, but this way only one of us is at risk," Gaarokk said.

Etanu slipped out the door and Zack kept his eyes glued to the doorway.

"Who do you think programmed the mechs?" Zack asked.

"It could have been anyone. Whoever it was probably planned on coming back at some point but never got the chance," Gaarokk said.

The loud stomps from the mechs closed in and Zack's mouth went dry. He held his breath so he could listen for Etanu, but there was no sign of the Nershal. Mechs were heading right toward the door.

"Get down," Zack whispered.

They ducked down behind the cabinet. The mechanical whirl of the mech's servos became louder as a mech stopped outside the room they were in. Zack clutched the pulse rifle and hardly dared to breathe. After a few moments, the mech moved on and the sounds of its heavy footsteps became more distant. Zack poked his head out from behind the cabinet. The mech was gone, but where was Etanu?

"He might have had to hide since the mechs are in the area," Gaarokk said.

Zack stood up. "I'm gonna go look for him."

Gaarokk grabbed his arm. "Don't," he said.

"Let go of me," Zack said.

"We have to get to the bridge. Once power is restored, we can turn the mechs off," Gaarokk said.

Zack yanked his arm away from the Boxan. "I'm not abandoning my friend. I won't leave him behind like a . . ." Zack looked away.

"Like a Boxan would," Gaarokk finished for him.

Zack's stomach clenched and his shoulders became tight. He blew out a breath. "I shouldn't have said that."

Gaarokk regarded him, and though the Boxan had his helmet on, there was no mistaking the hard glint in his gaze. But then the Boxan's gaze softened. "You're right. It's what we've become."

Zack frowned and shook his head. "No, you're right. We need to get to the bridge instead of going off to look for Etanu. He'd probably yell at me for doing that anyway. I'm going to set the charge."

Zack took one last glance at the doorway and then set the timer for the explosive charge. There was a red flash and a slight pop. Zack moved over to the opening and looked inside the next room. It was pitch black, even with the night-vision scope through his helmet. Zack turned his helmet light on and saw that the room beyond was probably an office. Zack motioned for Gaarokk to go through first. Once the Boxan was inside, Zack pulled the cabinet over to block the large hole in the wall. It didn't cover the whole thing, but it would be enough should the mechs return. A shuffling sound at the doorway drew his attention and Etanu ran into the room.

"Go. I'm not sure if they saw me," he hissed.

Zack leaped through the hole and Etanu followed soon thereafter. Gaarokk waited for them by the door. The Boxan was listening intently.

"How much time is left on the other charges?" Zack asked.

"Not much. It would be better if we were in the security center when the explosives go off," Etanu said.

Zack nodded and went to the door. He pulled it open and there was a loud screech. *Idiot!* Zack scolded himself.

"Just go," Etanu said.

Zack stepped out into the corridor with Etanu and Gaarokk close on his heels. The sounds of mechs could be heard from the nearby corner. Zack came to the security center door and pushed it open. There was a bright flash of light from the nearby corridor, along with a loud popping sound. They went into the security center and Etanu closed the door, waiting. There were immediate sounds of mechs storming off, presumably to investigate the explosives. Zack led them through the security center offices towards the door that was by the bridge. He rounded the corner and almost slammed into a mech, and the mech's servos whirled as it pivoted around. Zack brought up his pulse rifle and fired blindly, hearing Etanu fire his own rifle. The mech fell backward.

"Did you forget everything I taught you? You didn't hit the thing once at pointblank range," Etanu chided.

Zack shook his head. After walking into the mech he'd squeezed his eyes shut and fired his weapon.

The bridge doors were just outside. Zack walked over to the control interface and used the Boxan override with High Councilor Awan's credentials. The door had just started to open when Etanu screamed for them to get inside.

Zack was the first to step through and turn around. Gaarokk came next and then Etanu. Behind them was an army of mechs, barreling toward them. Gaarokk used the console to shut the door, but as it was shutting the lights on the bridge came on. Zack squeezed his eyes shut to stave off the blindness from night-vision mode in his helmet, then opened his eyes to a well-lit bridge and a partially closed door. Etanu was firing his weapon and Zack joined him, firing his own weapon.

"Athena, can you get a connection?" Zack asked.

"You must get to an open console and used the high councilor's credentials first," the AI said.

A blue bolt buzzed by his helmet and Gaarokk pulled him out of the way. Several more bolts slammed into the Boxan and Gaarokk cried out in pain. Zack tried to catch him as he fell, but the Boxan weighed almost a thousand pounds and all Zack accomplished was hurting his back. He pulled himself away from the fallen Boxan and fired his pulse rifle through the partially opened door.

"Any time now, Zack!" Etanu shouted.

Zack raced to the nearest console. His fingers flew through the interface and then uploaded the high councilor's credentials. Once they were accepted, Athena notified them she was inside.

Etanu backed away from the door, still firing his weapon, and the Boxan mechs were pushing their way inside.

"Athena!" Zack screamed.

Command line references blurred by his internal heads-up display. Etanu made it to his side and they kept firing their weapons at the mechs, but the mechs pushed their way inside and blue stun bolts slammed into the console, sending sparks into the air. Zack squeezed his eyes shut.

Silence.

Zack opened his eyes and the mechs were just a few feet away but their red lights suddenly changed to amber.

"High Councilor, welcome," the lead mech said.

Zack blew out the breath he'd been holding. "Get the hell away from me. Go back to wherever they store you," he said.

The mech spun around and marched away from them.

Etanu glanced at him. "Now you know why we Nershals hate machines," he said. "Except the Athena AI," he added quickly.

Zack shook his head and sighed, then glanced over at Gaarokk and ran over to him. Zack opened a connection to the Boxan's suit computer and could see that his vitals were stabilizing.

"He's going to be all right," Zack said.

A comms channel opened to them.

"You made it to the bridge," Strike Leader Nulsan said. "We're on our way to you."

"I'm glad you made it," Zack said.

He leaned back against the command couch and caught his breath. Etanu did the same.

"Damn, that was close. I thought we were gonna die," Zack said.

Etanu nodded and then checked his weapon.

"Athena, what's the status of the ship?" Zack asked.

"Main power has been restored and systems are coming online. All systems scheduled for diagnostics evaluation before becoming fully available," the AI said.

Zack opened a comms channel to Efren.

"Efren, are you guys okay?" Zack asked.

"I'm fine," Efren said, sounding winded. "Vitomir is missing. The mechs just turned around and left. Assume that's your handiwork?"

"Yeah, they shouldn't try and kill us anymore," Zack said.

"Good, we'll get the secondary reactors online and then get the engines back online. Life support is also coming online so we should be able to breathe the air in here within the next thirty minutes, according to Corryn," Efren said.

Strike Leader Nulsan and the surviving Boxan soldiers came to the bridge. They were carrying a few wounded. Gaarokk regained consciousness and joined him.

"Thanks," Zack said.

Gaarokk frowned. "What do you mean?"

"You pulled me out of the way. You got stunned because of me," Zack said.

"Of course. We stick together," Gaarokk said.

Zack smiled and then nodded.

Nulsan went about getting the remaining members of their teams organized. Now that main power was back online, they had to check the main systems to determine whether the ship could still fly. Zack hoped it could. It would be a shame to have gone through all this for a broken ship.

"The ship seems largely intact," Nulsan said.

They contacted the cruiser and checked in with Varek.

"Have you heard from Kaylan and the others?" Zack asked.

"They've found the refugees. There are over three hundred thousand of them," Varek said.

Zack blew out a soft whistle. "We've got to have shuttles on this thing or something even bigger. How else did they plan on getting anyone aboard?" he said.

Zack went over to one of the consoles. Varek had given him Kaylan's coordinates. The sensors were up and Zack scanned the area, doing a double take.

"What is it?" Nulsan asked.

Zack put what he'd seen up on the main holoscreen and walked over to it. "If this is where the refugees have been hiding," he said, pointing to the area almost near the north pole, "then what is this mass moving towards them?" he said, pointing hundreds of miles south.

Everyone on the bridge became silent and looked at the main holoscreen.

"It looks like something massive is heading right towards them. Is it a storm?" Zack asked.

Gaarokk studied the holoscreen intently. "That's not a storm. That's an army," he said.

Zack's stared at the holoscreen, slack-jawed, his thoughts screeching to a sudden halt. "We've got to warn them," he said, pacing in front of the holoscreen. "We've got to get them out of there."

Zack headed for the door. "Athena, I need to know where the

main hangar is. There has to be something we can fly down there and pick them up."

Strike Leader Nulsan opened a ship-wide broadcast. "The refugees are going to be attacked soon. Anyone with flight clearance is to head to the main hangar."

Zack started running with Etanu at his side. Several Boxans followed them. He hoped whatever ships were left in the main hangar could fly and that the Boxan engineering Gaarokk was so proud of held up. In Zack's experience, anything that was left around unused generally wasn't reliable anymore, but he brushed those thoughts aside. Kaylan and the others were down there and there was no way he was going to let them down.

CHAPTER 29

Kladomaor had never seen so many Boxans in one place except for the colony, and he'd lost count of how many refugees had come up to him and regarded him as if he were some type of legend. He kept urging them to gather their belongings but only to bring the essentials.

Kaylan came over to him, along with Valkra.

"You're the Battle Commander?" Valkra asked.

"I am," Kladomaor answered.

"I want to fight for you," Valkra said.

Kladomaor frowned. "You have the Mardoxian potential in you."

Valkra's eyes flashed dangerously. "It's what makes me so effective in battle. Will you let me fight with you and your soldiers?"

Kladomaor shifted his feet. By rights, this Boxan should be with the Mardoxian Sect for training, but as he looked at her, he wasn't sure she would accept that. There was also no guarantee the colony would accept these Boxans and he hadn't thought of his own status in the colony. Technically, he was a criminal.

"You can fight, but you'll also train with Ma'jasalax, and you'll follow orders without question," Kladomaor said.

Valkra's eyes narrowed. "I'm a squad leader. I've led squads hundreds of times to secure supplies for the Haven."

Kladomaor glanced at Kaylan and then back at Valkra. "I don't say these things to detract from your experiences. Once we evaluate your skills, we'll determine your place. But your abilities where the Mardoxian potential is concerned are instinctual and unrefined. You'll require extensive training before I'll allow any of my soldiers to trust you on the battlefield. I'm afraid that's all I can offer you."

Valkra looked away. "Yes, Battle Commander," she said and walked away.

Kaylan waited until Valkra was away from them to speak. "Her abilities helped her get this far."

"I know, but a new recruit who thinks they know everything will get themselves and others killed," Kladomaor said and glanced in Valkra's direction. "I will say this though: she's the reason they were able to survive. Councilor Essaforn sent me their records. Time and time again Valkra's squads brought in the most resources and had the highest survival rate."

"Survival rate?" Kaylan said.

"The squads Valkra mentioned don't have a long survivability rate. Everyone is required to serve in a rotation, and Valkra, along with some others, are part of a core group that stays on rotation even when their required term is done," Kladomaor said.

He needed to check on the soldiers he left outside and headed for the hangar entrance. There had already been several shuttle runs back to the cruiser, but those runs hardly scratched the surface in terms of the number of refugees. Kaylan and the other Athena crewmembers stayed by him as he went out onto the surface. He'd sent several strike-fighter pilots to check on whether the Haven ships could be made space-worthy. They only needed to make one trip to reach either the cruiser or the star carrier.

The hangar had a portable airlock that would allow them to return to the surface without venting the entire space. They went through and Kladomaor stepped onto the frozen surface of Sethion.

A comms channel initiated by the cruiser appeared on Kladomaor's internal heads-up display.

"Battle Commander, we've had word from the team that went to the carrier," Varek said.

"Hold," Kladomaor said and patched in the others. "Go ahead."

"They've restored power to the carrier and are bringing the ship's critical systems online. However, there were some casualties," Varek said.

Kladomaor glanced over at Kaylan, who went rigid.

"What happened?" Kladomoar asked.

"There were security mechs in standby mode. Nulsan split the group up into two teams, sending one to engineering to restore power and the other to the bridge. The mechs came online while they were making their way through the ship. They managed to get through, but Nulsan lost some soldiers and the Human, Vitomir, is unaccounted for. According to Efren, Vitomir drew the mechs away so he could get to the main power generator. Once main power was restored, Zack was able to disable the mechs from the bridge," Varek said.

"Understood," Kladomaor said and glanced at Kaylan and the others. "We didn't anticipate the use of mechs or them being in standby. They must have used them because they couldn't be subverted by the Xiiginns."

"Battle Commander, I'm patching in Strike Leader Nulsan," Varek said.

"Battle Commander, carrier sensors are showing a large land force heading your way," Nulsan said.

"Varek, can you confirm?" Kladomaor asked.

"Affirmative. We see the same thing," Varek replied.

Kladomaor motioned one of his soldiers over. "Warn Councilor Essaforn that there's an attack force making its way here. They need to muster up the Haven's defenses. And tell her I'll be with her shortly."

The Boxan soldier ran off to do as he was bidden.

"How could they have found us?" Kaylan asked.

Kladomaor frowned. "We might have led them here. We're not sure what the Protector's have in their arsenal, but they definitely have better weapons than the refugees. And there are the mechs."

"Battle Commander," Nulsan said.

"Go ahead."

"There are large transport carriers on this ship. We're sending them to your position to help with the evacuation," Nulsan said.

"Excellent. How many ships do you have?" Kladomaor asked.

"Three carriers are in working order. Plus, there's additional shuttle craft, but we're out of pilots. That's with leveraging everyone with flight experience but officially not pilots," Nulsan said.

"Varek, I want you to send anyone who can fly a ship over to Nulsan. Then I want you to position the cruiser into orbit above the ground force with a firing solution to thin that force out," Kladomaor said.

The comms channel closed and Kladomaor glanced over at the strike-fighters nearby.

"We're ready," Kaylan said.

Kladomaor looked over at her, with Hicks and Katie at her side. They were his closest pilots until he could get the others out here. "Alright, the three of you can go. Take three strike-fighters from Gold squadron. Varek will feed you intelligence when he gets the cruiser into position. I have one condition," he said and focused his gaze on Kaylan. "Engage the enemy but no heroics. If the area becomes too hot, you're to head directly back to the cruiser. Is that understood?"

Kaylan nodded.

Humans, Kladomaor thought as they ran over to the strike-fighters. *Headstrong and brave but sometimes too foolish for their own good.*

Kladomaor turned around and headed back toward the hangar. They needed to evacuate this place. If the Haven's ships couldn't break orbit, perhaps they could move refugees to another location to await pickup. While he went back inside the hangar he began issuing orders to his soldiers. The refugees were going to have to fight if they were going to survive. The battle for Sethion's lost children was about to begin and he would ensure that their battle song was heard.

CHAPTER 30

Zack stood in one of the hangar bays of the massive, city-sized spaceship. There was a row of shuttle craft on either side of the hangar. It had never occurred to Zack that they would be so short on pilots. Some of the Boxans who died at the hands of the security mechs had also been pilots. While he wasn't cleared to fly one of the large transport carriers they'd found, he was perfectly fine with piloting one of these shuttles. The flight systems were quite similar to what the Boxans still used. Athena could help him with the rest.

Zack tugged on his gloves and put his helmet back on.

"Athena, can you begin preflight checks on shuttle ten-zero-one?" Zack said.

"Beginning preflight checks now," Athena replied.

Zack circled around the Boxan shuttle. The craft was easily five hundred feet long and could safely hold over a thousand Boxans. The shuttle systems had external sensors for things like hull integrity, but one thing Kaylan and Hicks had drilled into him was to do his own visual inspection. Zack wasn't about to argue with their experience, even if the spacecraft had been built by Boxans. He came back around the front and went up the loading ramp.

Zack made his way to the pilot area at the nose of the shuttle and sat down. All of them would be flying alone. They needed to get as many Boxans off the planet as possible.

He brought up the flight systems and all preflight checks had passed.

"Okay, time to fly a ship that hasn't been used in over fifty years," Zack said with mock enthusiasm.

"I'm afraid I don't understand," Athena said. "According to the flight logs, the last time—"

"It was just a guess," Zack interrupted. "I don't want to know the actual amount of time. I just hope nothing breaks and we don't explode or break apart upon entering the atmosphere . . . or get shot down . . . You know, let's just go," he said.

The AI must have sensed his agitation and didn't reply. Zack opened a comms channel to the bridge. "Shuttle ten-zero-one ready to depart," he said.

"Confirmed. Good luck," the Boxan flight officer said.

Zack blew out a breath. A comms channel from Etanu appeared on the shuttle's heads-up display.

"Just wanted to check in with you," Etanu said.

"All set here," Zack said.

"Zack," Etanu said in a serious tone, "do you have a complete flight suit on? I won't be there to save you this time if you don't."

Zack rolled his eyes and shook his head. "One time, Etanu. I forget that damn collar one time and you never let me forget it."

Zack smiled, glad to have a momentary reprieve from the jitters he felt at flying into a war zone.

Strike Leader Nulsan sent a broadcast to all shuttles. "Alright, we fly in formation down to the refugee camp. They call it Haven Two-Zero-One. There are alternate entrances that are away from the line of battle. The coordinates should be on your navigation computers now. We'll move the star carrier closer to the planet to reduce the length of time to bring the refugees up from the surface."

They were cleared to take off. Zack engaged the repulsor engines and the shuttle hovered above the hangar floor. He retracted the landing gear and followed the other shuttles out of the hangar bay. Zack had to get used to the controls since this shuttle was different than the highly agile combat shuttles he'd trained on at Olloron.

"How are you doing?" Etanu asked.

They'd decided earlier to keep their comms channel open.

"I'm fine," Zack said and reminded himself for the hundredth time that there was over five hundred feet of ship behind him. "Not that maneuverable, are they?" he said.

"You'll get used it. A lot different than the strike-fighters, but the concepts are the same," Etanu said.

Zack and Etanu were the last in a line of twenty shuttles. The four large transport subcarriers detached themselves from the main hull of the ship. There were more, but they weren't flight ready.

"Just stay on my six and you'll be fine," Etanu said.

The other ships registered on his shuttle's computer systems. Once they were well clear of the star carrier, they increased their speed. Nulsan would be moving the star carrier from its hiding place behind one of Sethion's moons in a little while. They headed for the northern hemisphere, angling their approach to come in on the far side of Haven Two-Zero-One. This would keep their civilian craft away from the line of battle. Zack brought up the latest feeds, and the large mass with designate Alpha land force was steadily moving toward the Boxan sanctuary. He thought of opening a comms channel to Kaylan. She was down there in danger herself, but it wouldn't stop her from giving him a tongue lashing for doing what he was doing. He'd only been flying for less than six months and had started more or less on a dare from Hicks. He liked flying. It was a lot of fun and it gave him some time with Kaylan he wouldn't normally get to have.

The frozen icecap that comprised Sethion's northern hemisphere rapidly approached as he took in the view of the Boxan home world with the large yellow clouds. The atmospheric readings showed that the planet was extremely toxic. Nothing could live on the surface. Sethion was a world ravaged by a brutal civil war whose timespan was longer than Zack had been alive.

The shuttle's system registered that they were passing through the troposphere, but the friction that would no doubt be assailing the shuttle's hull couldn't be felt inside. He cut a swath through the poisoned atmosphere, along with the other shuttles. It was a smooth ride and Zack kept in line with the rest. They had an approach vector already pre-assigned to them, and as the other shuttles peeled off to their assignments, Zack followed his coordinates.

He was low enough to make out certain land features in the vast icy expanse. The Boxan refugees had carved out a meager existence deep within the ice and he couldn't imagine living like that. As he approached his designated landing area, he extended the landing gear. There were several Boxans already on the ground. Zack landed the shuttle and opened a comms channel to the compound.

"Shuttle ten-zero-one ready for pickup. Time is wasting," Zack said.

"Welcome to Sethion. Refugees are being routed to your ship," Kladomaor said.

Zack lowered the loading ramp and the lower ship cameras showed Boxans making their way to his ship.

"Commander, where's Kaylan?" Zack asked.

"She's in a strike-fighter flying reconnaissance," Kladomaor said.

Zack squeezed his eyes shut. He knew it. There was no way she'd be sitting around while there was something to be done. "Understood," he said.

"Once your shuttle is full, you're cleared to leave. Get them to the star carrier and return," Kladomaor said.

The comms channel closed.

"Athena, can you locate the crew?" he asked.

The AI showed him three strike-fighter designates on screen, all flying on approach to the land force.

Zack frowned. "Yeah right, reconnaissance my ass," he said quietly.

Boxan refugees loaded onto a shuttle and one of the oldest Boxans he'd ever seen came to the cockpit. The old Boxan frowned. He hadn't expected Zack to be flying the ship.

"Hello, I'm Zack."

The old Boxan put down the large metallic case he'd been carrying and sat in the copilot's seat.

"I'm Cardaleer."

Zack frowned. "Make yourself at home," he said.

Cardaleer looked at the readouts on the screen and then glanced at Zack. "Human?"

"That's right," Zack said and brought up the onboard camera feed. They were nearing capacity. He opened a comms channel to the Boxan coordinating the refugees. "Pack 'em in until there's no room," he said.

Cardaleer's eyes widened. "We're already nearing capacity for this craft as it is."

"I know, but I don't want to leave anyone behind," Zack said.

Cardaleer regarded him for a moment and then nodded to himself. "You remind me of someone. I think I'm going to like you."

Zack snorted. "Thanks, I think."

The loading ramp was closed and Zack engaged the engines. It took more power to get them off the ground and he felt he was flying an over-bloated whale of a ship, but he didn't care. The more Boxans he could get off now would be fewer that were in danger when the battle began.

Zack opened a comms channel back to the star carrier. "Shuttle ten-zero-one has lifted off and we're fully loaded. Should be there shortly," he said.

He glanced at the readout showing the land force's position. He didn't know how they were moving so fast, but that army was going to reach the compound before Zack's shuttle made it back to the ship.

"The Protectors are coming," Cardaleer said.

Zack nodded and increased the speed.

CHAPTER 31

The exhilaration of being in a strike-fighter filled Kaylan with a burning anticipation and thrill at flying such a superb aircraft. That is, that was how she'd felt when they first left the Haven. They'd done several high-altitude flyovers using the onboard cameras and sensors to send recon intelligence back to the cruiser. The Protector ground force was made up of massive ground troop carriers, combat mechs, and power-armored Boxans with exoskeleton support that allowed the wearer to move at astonishing speeds. On Earth, she'd had to familiarize herself with various combat scenarios pilots would be called upon to deal with and incorporate those into the design of the aircraft her company manufactured. Never in all those briefings was there a scenario where a ground force could move at the speeds she was seeing. As she looked below, she felt as if her gut had been clenching the entire time she'd been up here. The Xiiginns did this. Sethion was the measure of what the Xiiginns would do if they established a foothold on a world. By Boxan accounts, the Xiiginns were even more powerful now than when they'd broken free of the Boxans.

"We can't let this happen to Earth," Kaylan said over an open comms channel with Katie and Hicks.

"We won't," Hicks said, with Katie echoing the same.

Kaylan glanced over at the lower part of the heads-up display. The rest of the strike-fighter squadrons were on their way. She sucked in a breath and gunned the thrusters while bringing the weapons systems online.

Hicks and Katie followed.

"What are you doing?" Hicks asked.

"Attacking them," Kaylan said.

"We're right behind you. Let's give those Protectors something to worry about," Hicks said.

Kaylan guided her strike-fighter down and triggered the twin plasma cannons. Molten fury rained down on the Protectors. She concentrated her fire on the power-armored troops since they were the most exposed. Hicks and Katie flew on either side of her, doing the same.

They lined up for another run. Targeting alarms blared in the strike-fighter cockpit as the sky lit up around her. Kaylan broke off the attack and increased her altitude. The rest of Blue and Gold squadrons caught up to them. They coordinated their attacks, cutting into the Protector lines, but they still kept coming. It was as if the losses they were sustaining didn't matter at all. They were a group with a singular purpose.

Several strike-fighters were shot down, and each time they tried to provide covering fire for the pilot, they were met with heavy resistance until the Protectors killed their targets.

A general comms signal to clear the area came from Varek on

the cruiser. As soon as the strike-fighter squadrons cleared the area, a salvo fired from the cruiser in low orbit, raining hell down on the Protectors.

Kaylan had swung her craft around to line up for another attack run when she noticed that they were almost upon the Haven. She peered at the map on her heads-up display to double-check what she was seeing. There were large shuttles taking off and landing, along with massive transport carriers.

A comms channel opened to them from the Haven.

"All strike-fighters, break off your attack. You're to run escort for the shuttles and carriers. They're to be covered for their entire duration near the planet. Once they're out of range, you're to await the next ship to return to the planet surface. This will continue until all refugees are free. Battle Commander, out."

Kaylan flew her ship towards the landing zone on the far side of the Haven. She understood why Kladomaor had given the orders. There was no way they were going to keep the Protectors from getting inside the compound, and eventually those troops would circle around and attack the landing zone. A large shuttle lifted off the ground and she and Hicks flew as escorts. There weren't any shots fired at them from the Protectors and Kaylan assumed they weren't close enough yet until she glanced to the side and saw the nearly continuous rain of fire from the cruiser.

They neared the edge of the atmosphere and Kaylan brought her fighter to a stop, hovering. She and Hicks monitored the shuttle as it headed for the star carrier. Kaylan frowned as if there was something off about what she was seeing.

"There's another shuttle coming," Hicks said.

"Alright, I . . ." Kaylan's voice trailed off.

Something was definitely off. The shuttle that had just left the planet slowed down on its approach to the star carrier. Target-lock alarms flashed across her heads-up display as bright red flashes spawned from the shuttle's hull and small, tear-shaped ships flew towards them.

Kaylan's mouth went dry. "Drones!" she cried and engaged the thrusters.

Hicks was right behind her. "I thought we took care of all of them," he said.

She locked in her target and opened fire. She got one and the other drones attacking the shuttles veered off to meet their attack.

"At least it's not the waves of them we saw before. How about I give them something to chase and you take them out?" Kaylan said.

"I've got your back," Hicks replied.

Kaylan sped forward, firing the plasma cannons and angling away from the drones so they'd chase her. She flew in close to the shuttle's hull so the drones couldn't get a clear shot of her ship. Hicks took out the group one by one, chasing her. They alerted the cruiser of the drone presence and a general alert went out to all fighters.

"The timing of the drones showing up again is suspicious," Hicks said.

"You think the Protector's are controlling them somehow?" Kaylan asked.

"We start getting Boxans off the planet and drones suddenly start showing up again. It's not that much of a stretch," Hicks said.

Another shuttle was making a return run to the planet. They had to keep their formations tighter due to the drone threat.

Kaylan watched the scan readout and she heard Hicks suddenly gasp.

"Oh shit! Damn it!" Hicks said.

Kaylan flew around the shuttle and saw a trail of vapor leaking from Hicks's strike-fighter.

"One of those drones flew right into my engines," Hicks said.

The tail sections were blackened with damage and she watched as he struggled to keep the ship straight.

"Head back to the cruiser," Kaylan said.

"I'm not going to leave you, Commander," Hicks said.

"Fine, then it's an order. You're no good up here anymore. Get back to the cruiser," Kaylan said.

Hicks's fighter stayed where it was and she could just imagine him sitting there with that brooding intensity of his when he was feeling mulish.

"Please," Kaylan said.

"Alright, I'll get back to the cruiser and get another ship," Hicks said and pulled away from the shuttle.

The shuttle that was heading toward the surface changed its approach angle and swung out back into space.

Kaylan opened a comms channel to the shuttle.

"Commander," Gaarokk said. "Kladomoar ordered all shuttles to head back to the star carrier."

"Who's left on the surface?" Kaylan asked.

"There's a large transport carrier and a shuttle," Gaarokk said.

"Did they get everyone out?"

"The last of them are being loaded on those ships—" Gaarokk's voice suddenly cut out.

Kaylan frowned. The comms channel was still opened. "Gaarokk what's wrong?"

"Commander, the drones are making another attack run."

Kaylan engaged the thrusters and maneuvered around the shuttle. "Get back to the star carrier," she said.

Kaylan swung around the shuttle and saw a swarm of drones heading toward her. There was no way she could take them all on her own. There must be a command-and-control unit nearby.

The heavy cruiser moved toward her and opened fire on the drones.

"Athena, can you detect any command-and-control signals for the drones?"

"The cruiser's scans don't reveal any trace signals for the drones," the AI said.

Kaylan frowned. "What about on the planet where the Protectors are."

She moved the strike-fighter away from the heavy cruiser. The cyber warfare suite was targeting the drones and taking them out, but the progress was painfully slow. They could still do a lot of damage to the remaining shuttles and transport carrier yet to leave the surface.

"I'm unable to detect a clear signal from the planetary surface, but there's a high probability that your instincts are correct. I've uploaded the known command-and-control signals to your ship," Athena said.

Kaylan engaged the thrusters and sped toward the planet.

CHAPTER 32

Kladomaor watched as the combat shuttles hovered over the troop carrier. The refugees hurried aboard the shuttles and carriers with a smooth efficiency that must have come from countless practice drills and living under the threat of losing their homes at a moment's notice. He'd tried to get Councilor Essaforn to leave with one of the earlier transports, but she'd adamantly refused and had instead stuck by his side. He'd been at the front line, fighting alongside his soldiers and the fighters from Haven. They fought well, and their battle songs would be sung throughout the great expanse. The Haven's automated defenses had helped stem the Protectors for a time, but they eventually failed. They had fallen back to the landing zone, making sure all the refugees would get on a ship. These would be the last.

A comms channel opened to him.

"Time to go, Battle Commander," Zack said.

Kladomaor swung his gaze toward the last shuttle, nearly

scolding the Human who had the least amount of flight experience because he was the last to leave the planet—the most dangerous run of all.

The transport carrier engines propelled the ship into the air. Plasma blasts from nearby combat mechs fired into the hull, and Kladomaor raised his weapon and fired back at the mechs. Boxan soldiers followed his lead and a combat shuttle moved to intercept, firing a salvo back at the relentless Protectors.

Kladomaor glanced up and saw the transport carrier speed away from them.

The combat shuttle exploded and Kladomaor threw himself over Councilor Essaforn to protect her from harm. He regained his feet and helped the councilor up.

"Fall back," Kladomaor said.

They retreated toward the last shuttle, which hovered in the air and came toward them with the cargo bay doors opened. The soldiers fired on the Protector forces as they climbed aboard the shuttle. The ship dipped dangerously to the side and then righted itself. Kladomaor stood just inside the cargo bay and fired his weapon into a line of combat mechs. The soldiers on either side of him were hit and went down. His weapon stopped firing, its power cell depleted. He roared his defiance at what the Xiiginns had wrought upon his species.

Plasma blasts from above rained down on the approaching Protector line, leaving flaming stumps in their wake.

"Whoever's piloting that shuttle, go now! I've got you covered," Kaylan said.

"Kaylan!" Zack said.

"Not now, Human. You heard her. Go!" Kladomaor said.

The cargo bay doors closed and the shuttle lurched upward.

Kladomaor raced toward the cockpit and the Boxan refugees scrambled to get out of his way.

Zack's gaze stayed focused on the readout in front of him. The engines were at maximum.

"That's all she's got. We took quite a beating," Zack said.

Kladomaor sat in the copilot's seat. The overfilled shuttle was still gaining altitude.

"What the hell is that?" Zack said.

In the distance, a swarm of drones were attacking the heavy cruiser, with smaller groups heading toward the last shuttles that were making their way toward the star carrier. A large pack of tear-shaped drones broke off from the main group and headed straight for them.

"Turn the ship around," Kladomaor said.

After taking out the combat mech, Kaylan sped over the remaining Protectors, scanning for the command-and-control signal that she'd gotten from the Athena. The Protectors had been so focused on the transport carrier that they hadn't paid any mind to one strike-fighter as she'd flown over them. Her plasma cannons were almost depleted of ammunition. She banked to the side, maximizing the strike-fighter's scanning range. As she approached the rear line of Protectors, she got a positive ping and a target-lock for the drone command-and-control signal.

There was a ring of mechs protecting a small tower. Kaylan sped toward it and the combat mechs opened fire. She weaved back and forth, narrowly avoiding the plasma bolts, and returned fire. The strike-fighter's cannons flared to life and her own plasma bolts ripped through the line of combat mechs, cutting the transmitter tower in half. She let out a gasp and swung the ship up and away from the Protectors. Plasma blots slammed into her fighter and Kaylan fought to maintain control of her ship.

The shuttle was slow to respond to the controls as Zack tried turning the ship around. Since they'd never left Sethion's atmosphere, they gained some speed as they returned toward the surface. Fireballs were shooting past the nose of the shuttle as if a sudden meteor shower were occurring.

"Now what?" Zack said.

Kladomaor glanced out the shuttle's windows. "It's the drones. Their trajectory is off. It's as if they're just falling out of the sky."

"The command signal must be offline," Zack said.

Kladomaor nodded and opened up a comms channel back to the cruiser. "Varek, what's your status?"

"Sustained heavy damage, Battle Commander. We lost two of the shuttles. All transport carriers are accounted for and on board the star carrier," Varek said.

Zack's eyes widened. "What about the strike-fighters?"

"There are some still unaccounted for, including Kaylan's," Varek said.

Zack's stomach sank to his feet and he shifted in his chair. He hands went to the controls, but he didn't know what to do. He looked out the window at the planet's surface.

He opened a broadcast comms channel. "Kaylan, do you read?"

Zack's eyes were glued to the holo-interface while he waited for a response.

"Battle Commander," Varek said. "Detecting an energy anomaly at the Haven."

"Send us your readings," Kladomaor said.

The holoscreen showed a series of readings and Kladomaor sat back in his chair, looking worried.

A comms channel opened and the strike-fighter's designate came onscreen. "Kaylan here. I've taken out the control unit for the drones, but my ship has taken damage. Engines are working at twenty percent and falling."

"Kaylan, we read you," Zack said and looked at Kladomaor. "What does that mean? Twenty percent."

Kladomaor didn't reply. "Kaylan, you need to put as much distance between yourself and the Haven as you can. Twenty percent engine capacity isn't enough for you to break orbit."

"Acknowledged," Kaylan said.

"Set down somewhere and we can pick you up," Zack said.

"No," Kladomaor said. "You must listen to me and fly away as fast as you can."

The scanners showed a strike-fighter flying alongside them and then a strange alarm sounded, showing symbols Zack didn't understand.

"Battle Commander, you need to get that shuttle away to escape the blast radius," Varek advised.

Zack frowned. "What's he talking about?"

Kladomaor stared at him intently. "The Protectors have a nuclear bomb with an energy signature capable of decimating the entire northern ice shelf."

Zack's eyes darted to the windows and back to Kladomaor. "How do we get her out of there?"

Kladomaor shook his head.

"How do we get her out of there?" Zack asked again and then slammed his fist on the console. "Kaylan, you have to get out of there. You have to try," he said, his voice croaking at the end.

"Zack," Kaylan said.

His hands went for the shuttle's controls, preparing for maximum thrust.

"You have to turn the shuttle around. All those Boxans are depending on you to get them to safety," Kaylan said.

The comms channel went offline in a haze of static.

Zack's vision blurred and he hastily wiped his eyes. Kladomaor shifted in his seat and Zack's hands flung to his sidearm. He pulled the pistol out and pointed it at the Boxan Battle Commander.

"I swear to god if you try to take control of this ship from me I'll squeeze the trigger," Zack said. "I'll do it! I swear to god I will. I won't leave her!"

Kladomaor held up his hands and the knowing look that Kaylan's death was all but certain struck Zack like a blow. "Is that what she would want?" he asked calmly.

Zack's shoulders slumped. His mind raced, trying to think of a way to save Kaylan, but there was nothing he could do. He couldn't even talk to her. He dropped the pistol and it clanged to the floor. Glaring at the planet below, he swung the shuttle around, heading away from the Haven and hating himself for doing it.

He watched the radar screen that showed Kaylan's strike-fighter.

Another strike-fighter zipped passed the shuttle.

"I've got her, Casanova. You get those Boxans to safety." Katie Garcia's voice sounded over comms.

The strike-fighter's control panel was damaged and Kaylan didn't know how the ship was even still flying. She tried to nurse the craft along and gain as much altitude as she could, but engine capacity was down to ten percent. She'd taken fire from the Protectors after taking out the control tower and had barely escaped.

"Commander, at your current speed, you won't escape the blast radius of the Protector bomb," the Athena's AI said, its voice coming through the speakers inside her helmet.

"I know," Kaylan said.

She maintained her ascent, knowing the futility of it, but she had to try. She knew the engines would give out and then she'd either crash the ship and die or be caught in a nuclear blast. Kaylan clenched her teeth together and felt her heart pound in her ears. This was it; she was going to die here. Her panic-stricken thoughts raced and then a sense of calm came over her. She shifted her gaze to the sky above, thinking of Zack and how he would never forgive her for dying on him. A crushing pang of guilt filled the back of her throat as she instantly regretted all of those lost moments they could have had. There was always something drawing their attention, whether it was her training or Zack trying to figure out how to bring down the Shroud barrier protecting Earth. Her vision blurred with the tears she couldn't hold back anymore and her thoughts drifted to the family she'd left behind on Earth and how she'd never see any of them again —how she and Zack would never go to the island getaway they'd mused about. She really just wanted to lie on the sand and listen to the sound of the waves as they lulled her away to a peaceful oblivion.

A high-level chime pierced her thoughts. The engine was down to four percent and she was no longer gaining altitude. This was it.

A bright flash engulfed the sky in a blazing white light. Kaylan twisted around in her seat and saw a gigantic mushroom cloud spreading from the Haven. She drew in a deep breath and blew it out, but as she was turning back around, something sped past her ship so fast that she thought she might have imagined it. Without warning, Kaylan was jarred against her seat as something slammed into the back of her ship. There was another heavy bump and she was knocked to the side. Kaylan pulled herself up and craned her neck to see what was behind her.

Kaylan let out small, jubilant laugh as she saw Katie Garcia waving at her. Katie gestured to her helmet and Kaylan turned on her suit-to-suit comms.

"Hang on. I don't think these ships were designed for this," Katie said.

Kaylan turned back around and adjusted the straps so she was secure.

"This won't be gentle," Katie said.

The strike-fighter slammed into her ship with unrelenting force. With her own strike-fighter's systems damaged, there were no inertia dampeners and Kaylan bore the crushing G-forces as they reached escape velocity. She gritted her teeth and fought to stay conscious.

"Just hold on a little longer," Katie urged.

Kaylan squeezed her eyes shut. A sharp, stabbing pain spread like lightning across her middle. The strike-fighter shook violently and Kaylan cried out, blinking phosphenes from her vision as she felt her consciousness start to slip away. Katie Garcia called out to her and it sounded as if she were speaking through a long, dark tunnel. With the last shred of her strength leaving, the darkness swallowed her up.

CHAPTER 33

Ed Johnson had a few vices he absolutely must surrender to whenever he was in the city that never sleeps. The island of Manhattan itself was home to as many foreigners as Americans these days, but the old culture that'd made the foundation of New York City what it was today could still be found. The Luxury Towncar pulled to a stop. Iris Barrett climbed inside and handed him a small white paper bag. Ed took the bag and opened it, already catching a whiff of the contents.

"Those things will kill you," Iris said.

Ed breathed in the sweet smell of dried onion and garlic flakes and peeked inside the bag. "I know they will, but you can't come to New York and not have either pizza or an Everything Bagel with cream cheese," he said, taking a healthy bite. The creamy blend of flavors caressed his mouth and he sighed happily while he chewed.

Iris handed him a napkin. Ed took it and offered her the

other half of his bagel, but Iris just shook her head with a slightly bemused expression.

The driver pulled the car away from the curb and they resumed their journey to the UN.

"How many years has it been since you've eaten bread?" Ed asked.

Iris arched a brow toward him. "I'm sure that information is in my dossier," she said.

Ed finished half of the bagel and decided to save the other half for later. The meeting today with the UN Security Council was something of a special occasion since there would be Boxan representatives planet-side for once.

"Well, I'd like to know," Ed said.

Iris was glancing out the window, almost constantly on the lookout for any threats to his life.

The car pulled in front of the UN building and they were guided to a queue, along with everyone else. Usually Ed would have flown in, but he'd been looking forward to an authentic New York City bagel for a long time.

"Since I was seven years old, and I've been healthy ever since," Iris said.

He tried to imagine Iris as a child and couldn't. She opened the door and took a look around before gesturing for him to follow. They walked across the campus and headed toward one of the entranceways.

"I've forwarded the agenda to your PDA," Iris said.

Ed used his implants to bring it up on his own internal heads-up display.

"So you're going to tell them today then?" Iris said.

Ed nodded. "They have to know the barrier is a short-term fix."

"You need to give them a timeline. Otherwise, it'll just get put on top of the large pile of things that need to be done," Iris said.

"We need to study the barrier as much as we need to build ships. If the latest projections are accurate, it could be disastrous for the entire solar system," Ed said.

He was so busy reviewing the meeting agenda that he walked right into Iris. Ed started to trip, but Iris caught him with one hand and held onto him. He looked up at her and saw that she was looking across the courtyard. Ed connected his neural link to Iris's implants so he could see what she saw.

A Boxan stood in full power armor in the middle of the courtyard. He was so still that Ed would have missed him. The scan from Iris's implants had broken down the power armor into units.

"What do you suppose he's doing there?" Ed asked.

Iris frowned. "Ed, you need to go back to the car and get out of here," she said.

"What is it?"

The Boxan's identity appeared on his HUD. Eavoth, Strike Commander.

"That's the one who went with Kyle Mathews to investigate the Shroud monitoring devices," Ed said.

He'd made it a point to familiarize himself with all the joint Human-Boxan missions since they were still so infrequent. When that changed, there would be no way he'd be able to keep track of it all.

The Boxan Strike Commander noticed them and charged.

The breath caught in Ed's throat and Iris shoved him back. Then she ran towards the charging Boxan, pulled out her stun baton, and leaped to the side, jamming the baton into the Boxan's side. The maximum amount of voltage released through the baton, but the Boxan didn't slow down.

Iris ran in front of the Boxan. He tried to grab her, but she scrambled out of the way. She grabbed his hand and tried to use the Boxan's momentum, but he pulled her into the air.

Iris held on and glanced over at Ed. "Detonator," she said through gritted teeth.

Ed backed away several steps and froze for a second, not knowing what to do. The Boxan seemed focused on him despite Iris's attempts to fight him off. Ed sent a coded message to the UN Security force and alarms started going off. Automated bomb detection units would be dispatched, but Ed wasn't sure if they could detect whatever the Boxan had done.

The Boxan threw Iris off of him as if swatting a fly and focused his flaxen-eyed gaze on Ed. Ed glanced over at Iris's crumpled form on the ground. The Boxan took a few steps toward him and Ed started running, hearing the heavy footsteps of the Boxan chasing him. He veered off toward the streets and heard people screaming. Why was the Boxan suddenly trying to kill him? It didn't make any sense.

There was a loud pop, followed by a bright flash, and Ed was pushed to the side. He tumbled to the ground, people still running and screaming around him. There was smoke rising from the UN and a large chunk of the building was gone.

The UN Security forces arrived, firing their weapons at the Boxan while Ed scrambled back, his eyes wide. Their weapons had hardly any effect on the Boxan, and the ten-foot-tall alien closed in on him.

Seemingly out of nowhere, a plasma bolt slammed into the Boxan's chest, followed by another that ripped through the armor, and the Boxan collapsed to the ground. Ed gasped as the security force turned and pointed their weapons toward him. Glancing behind, he saw Scraanyx, but the Boxan glanced at the security force and held up his weapon, slowly placing it on the ground in front of him.

The UN security force shouted for Scraanyx to get on his knees and Ed watched as the Boxan complied with the security force's commands amid the sounds of other law enforcement agencies arriving.

Ed got to his feet and found the UN security force captain. "He just saved our lives," he said.

The captain spared him a look. "My orders come from the top. All Boxans are to be detained. This is one of three UN headquarters that were attacked today."

Ed glanced at the Boxan. Scraanyx looked as if he wanted to fight, but the enemy he was looking for wasn't there. He looked over at Ed. "Xiiginns," he said.

Ed's stomach clenched and his mind became a jumble of questions. "We'll get this sorted out," he promised.

Scraanyx regarded him for a moment. "None of us are safe. You must prepare yourself."

Sirens blared from the arriving fire trucks. Ed glanced around at the chaos before him. People were hurt and smoke billowed up to the New York City skyline. Ed couldn't help but think that this was only the beginning. Somehow the Xiiginns had made it to Earth.

He turned back toward the UN building. Iris had been close to the building, but he wasn't sure if she'd been caught in the blast. His implants had recorded the entire event and he took it back to when the Boxan had charged him. The glint in his eyes told of a being that was ready to kill. Ed froze the image and looked for some sign of an internal struggle, some sign that the Boxan hadn't totally succumbed to the Xiiginn influence, but there was none. He glanced around, hearing all the sounds of the city, and felt utterly exposed. This was only the beginning.

CHAPTER 34

Kaylan's mouth was dry and she tried to swallow.

"Here, drink some water," Zack said and held a straw to her mouth.

She sucked in some water and drank it down.

"Brenda, she's awake," Zack said.

Kaylan opened her eyes to see Zack and Brenda looking down at her. She tried to sit up but Brenda held her down.

"Take it easy. It's only been a few hours and you've broken a couple of ribs. Need to give the nanobots time to speed up the healing," Brenda said.

Zack used the bed controls to raise her up. Her ribs ached but nothing like what she'd felt in the strike-fighter. He placed his hand gently on her shoulder. Kaylan's whole body ached.

Brenda told her to look at the light as she tested Kaylan's responses. "You're going to be fine. I'll give you something for the pain, but you just need to rest for a bit."

"Where are we?" Kaylan asked.

"We're in the med bay on the cruiser," Zack said.

"Have we left Sethion's star system?"

Zack shook his head. "No, there's been some debate about where the refugees are going."

Zack told her that they were still bringing up the star carrier's systems and an engineering team was checking over the critical systems before they opened a wormhole.

Kaylan swung her feet to the side of the bed.

"What do you think you're doing?" Zack asked.

Kaylan winced. "The Boxans could give a rock lessons in stubbornness. We can't stay here any longer than necessary."

Brenda came over from across the room. "Can't you sit still for five minutes?"

"There's too much to be done. Can you give me something to help get me going?" Kaylan said.

Brenda glanced at Zack imploringly.

"Just for a few hours and then I'll rest. I promise," Kaylan said.

"A few hours," Brenda said sternly and then looked at Zack. "You'll see that it's only a little while."

Zack nodded. "I'll have the Athena lock her out of the systems temporarily."

Kaylan scowled at him, but it lacked any real vehemence. Brenda returned with a cigar-shaped device and pressed one end to the skin of her neck. There was a snap-hiss as the stimulants entered her system. The skin on her neck burned and Kaylan winced, but the bone weariness abated and the pain in her ribs faded to a dull ache.

Kaylan got to her feet, expecting to be a bit wobbly, but she was fine. She glanced at Brenda. "Thank you. I promise, just a few hours."

Zack mumbled something about keeping an eye on her as they left the med bay. Boxan soldiers were walking past them and Kaylan suddenly stopped. She turned to Zack, the breath catching in her throat. They'd almost lost each other, and the two of them gazed into each other's eyes. Zack's were red-rimmed with worry, but his gaze softened when he looked at her.

"Kaylan . . ." he said.

She grabbed him by his shirt and kissed the hell out of him as they stood in the corridor, then pulled him into a hard embrace and pushed herself away. "I needed to do that."

"You can do that whenever you want for as long as you need," Zack said.

Kaylan lips curved. "Let's go to bridge and see what the holdup is."

They headed for the bridge and Kaylan felt better than she had in a long time. It could have been the drugs Brenda had given her, but she also thought it was the fact that they were still alive. They'd done what the Boxan High Council had been reluctant to do.

They reached the bridge and the doors opened. Zack gestured for her to go first and she led the way in. Kladomaor was seated on the command couch with Ma'jasalax at his side. Etanu and Ezerah stood off to the side, listening to High Councilor Awan speak. Councilor Essaforn and Valkra were there, along with a wizened old Boxan Kaylan had never seen before. The old Boxan glanced over at them and there was a flash of recognition when he looked at Zack.

"As I've told you, if you bring the star carrier to Olloron, you won't be allowed to land or even enter the system," High Councilor Awan said.

Councilor Essaforn fixed her gaze on him. "We're Boxans. We deserve a place at the colony."

They stopped speaking when they noticed Kaylan and Zack standing there.

Councilor Essaforn's hard gaze softened when she looked at Kaylan. "I'm so glad you're feeling better. Ma'jasalax has told me how you pleaded with the High Council on our behalf. High Councilor Awan is convinced their fleet will shoot our ship down should we try to enter Olloron's star system."

"He's not misleading you at all," Kaylan said.

"Then what is to become of us? We have wounded and very few resources of our own," Councilor Essaforn said.

"You should leverage the Boxans' only ally in this and then open communications with the colony. The Nershals' generous offer is the best you're going to get at the moment. They might not allow you to go to Nerva, but there's certainly room on Selebus moon to get settled and regroup," Zack said.

Councilor Essaforn glanced at Etanu and Ezerah. "I appreciate the sentiment, but as you've stated, you're not official emissaries for the Nershals. What if we were to go there, only to be turned away again?"

"Ezerah's family stands high in the Nershals' global congress. They won't turn you away," Kaylan said.

"You will not be turned away, I assure you," Ezerah said.

"There are three hundred thousand of us. Given the state of things, some might view this as an invasion force. But miscommunications aside, there are Boxans from the colony there and part of the fleet. You can see how our presence might be the catalyst for things to get out of control?" Councilor Essaforn said.

Kaylan cleared her throat. "I suggest you be open and honest about the situation. The Boxan fleet is there to support the Nershals' defense of the system against the Xiiginns. We can't stay here. The Boxans aren't the only ones monitoring the quarantine zone. You should go to Selebus and ask the Nershals to act as intermediaries between the Boxans that are of the colony and yourselves. I believe that if you do this, the colony will become open to you eventually, or at the very least they'll send aid."

Councilor Essaforn glanced at Kladomaor and Ma'jasalax.

"I agree with Kaylan," Ma'jasalax said.

"I do as well," High Councilor Awan said. "And I'll do everything in my power to see that your voices are heard," he said, looking at Kaylan. "You were right and we should have heeded your warning from the beginning. We should have returned to Sethion much sooner."

Kaylan regarded the high councilor for a moment. "And the colony? You know as well as I that it's not a viable place for you in the long term."

High Councilor Awan pressed his lips together and frowned. "Has anyone ever told you that you're relentless?"

"Welcome to dealing with Humans," Kladomaor said.

Kaylan smiled and heard Zack mumble something under his breath.

"One thing at a time. I understand your intentions are for the betterment of our species, but it will take time," High Councilor Awan said.

It was something, at least. Kaylan nodded.

Councilor Essaforn looked at Kladomaor. “Have you considered my offer?” she asked.

“Let’s get to Selebus and take care of everything there first. Then we’ll discuss your offer,” Kladomaor said.

Kaylan glanced at Zack and he shrugged. The meeting ended and preparations were being made for them to leave shortly.

Ma’jasalax made her way over to Kaylan and Valkra followed. “You’ve done enough for one day,” she said.

Kaylan frowned. “I'm feeling fine. I just needed to make sure things were in hand.”

Valkra bowed her head to Kaylan. “After you’re rested, I’d like to discuss the connection we shared through the Mardoxian chamber.”

“Of course,” Kaylan said.

Zack urged her to leave the bridge and get some rest, occasionally glancing worriedly over at Kladomaor. When they left the bridge she asked him what was bothering him.

“I, uh, threatened Kladomaor while we were on the shuttle,” Zack said.

Kaylan’s eyes widened.

“I apologized, but you know. Sometimes the heat of the moment gets the better of us,” Zack said.

Kaylan took his hand and let him guide her back to the med bay for some rest.

CHAPTER 35

Kyle glanced at the time. It had been six hours since he and the others had escaped from their holding cell. No alarm had been raised, which he knew couldn't last much longer.

"Another patrol is coming," Tom whispered.

Six hours wasn't enough time to determine whether these were routine patrols or if the Xiiginns had been alerted to their presence. They were due to meet Dawson and Pearson, and Kyle hoped they'd found a way for them to get off this ship.

Kyle tried to blend in with the dark corner behind a network of piping. At his feet, the unconscious Xiiginn they'd surprised earlier began to stir and the Xiiginn patrol was almost upon them. Tom glanced down at the Xiiginn and his eyes widened when he saw the alien's tail begin to twitch. Kyle raised a finger to his lips so Tom would keep quiet.

The Xiiginn soldiers' heavy footfalls tromped toward them and Kyle held his breath. At his feet, the Xiiginn's arm started to move. Kyle gritted his teeth and squatted over the Xiiginn, wrapping an arm around the alien's neck. The Xiiginn started to struggle and its tail flicked to the side so Kyle planted his foot on it. He'd learned the hard way how much trouble those things could be. The Xiiginn started making choking sounds and Kyle clamped his hand over the alien's mouth, hoping the noise would be drowned out by the steady hissing of the piping network. He squeezed as hard as he could. The Xiiginns were strong, even the lowly tech they'd found working in these tunnels. Kyle didn't think he could break the alien's neck, but he knew they breathed oxygen, and if he could cut off the supply long enough the Xiiginn would lose consciousness again.

They were off to the side in a maintenance alcove, utterly exposed should the soldiers bother to look. The choking sounds became louder as the soldiers were almost upon them so Kyle gritted his teeth and squeezed. The Xiiginn's struggles weakened and stopped altogether, but Kyle held on until the end. He couldn't risk him regaining consciousness again.

"They're gone," Tom said.

The young tech comms specialist looked down the dead Xiiginn as if he wasn't quite sure that he was seeing a dead body. Kyle pushed the body to the side.

"You killed him," Tom said.

"I couldn't risk him waking up," Kyle answered while searching the dead Xiiginn.

"I know they'd do worse to us if they caught us, but it's just so . . ."

"Real," Kyle said. "Stay focused. Were you able to access our shuttle's systems before it left?"

Tom tore his eyes away from the dead Xiiginn. "Yes, I was able to insert a message under the maintenance cycle, but I don't know when the cycle will be run. Even if they return to the ECF base, it still could be some time before the two computer systems run the routine, and then the person monitoring would have to notice the message."

"It's the best we can do right now. I didn't plan on Eavoth and the others leaving so soon. Also, I don't think they're returning to the ECF base," Kyle said.

Tom frowned. "Why not?"

"We won't be on the shuttle, so if they returned to base without us, they'd need to explain our absence," Kyle said.

He scampered to the edge of the alcove and peered around the corner, finding the way empty. He gestured for Tom to follow and they headed to where they were due to meet the others. Since the Boxans had left them, Kyle assumed they were getting close to Earth. Unfortunately, once the shuttle was gone they couldn't communicate with each other using their implants and their PDAs had been taken from them. They returned to the tunnels beneath the hangar area and waited for the others. Tom kept shifting position and fidgeting in place.

"We're going to be fine," Kyle said.

He wasn't sure if he believed it himself but knew that a little bit of hope could get the people under one's command to focus. It just might be enough to do what they needed.

"What if the Xiiginns caught the others?"

"They didn't."

"How do you know?"

"Because these tunnels would be crawling with Xiiginns if they had," Kyle said.

Tom frowned and then sighed. "I didn't think it would be like this . . . coming out here."

"You and me both. I never imagined that any Xiiginns made it through the barrier. Now it seems really foolish for us and everyone else to have believed it," Kyle said.

Tom glanced at him, his eyes wide.

Kyle looked away, keeping an eye out for the others. Within a few minutes, Lieutenant Dawson and Corporal Pearson came around the corner. They each were armed with the same rifles the Xiiginn soldiers used. A cold icy pit settled into his stomach. Could they be under the Xiiginn influence?

"Colonel," Dawson said, "we ambushed a patrol and took their weapons. They're strong, but take them by surprise and they're just as vulnerable as anyone else."

Kyle nodded. "Good work. Did you find a way to get out of here?"

He glanced at Pearson, who was keeping an eye on the tunnels.

"Yeah, but not here. This hangar is much too secure. We've found a smaller hangar where they're adapting escape pods," Dawson said.

"Adapting them for what?" Kyle asked.

Dawson frowned. "We don't have much time. We should head over there. We observed a shift change and heard the Xiiginns talking about how hard they're being worked. They're following a rigid schedule, but there are a few minutes when we can get inside and take one of the pods. Did you guys have any luck contacting Earth?"

"Tom was able to embed a message in the shuttle's maintenance systems before it left, but by the time the ECF finds the shuttle it might already be too late," Kyle said.

"Then it's up to us," Dawson said and glanced over at Pearson, who was still keeping watch.

Kyle looked at Tom and gave a slight shake of his head. He'd have to trust that Dawson and Pearson weren't under the Xiiginn influence.

"Alright, lead the way," Kyle said.

Pearson brought up the rear while Lieutenant Dawson led them through the tunnels. Kyle supposed he could have asked for one their weapons. As a superior officer, he'd be within his rights to do so without question, but if one or both of them were under the Xiiginn influence, his order for them to surrender one of their weapons could lead to a confrontation. He thought about warning Tom but ruled it out. The young tech comms specialist was barely keeping it together as it was.

Dawson led them through a series of adjoining, low-ceiling tunnels and they spent much of the time crawling on their hands and knees. Eventually they came to a maintenance hatch and Dawson motioned for them to stop. The lieutenant cocked his ear toward the hatch, listening for a moment, and then opened it. He stepped out and the rest of them followed. Pearson closed the hatch. Dawson led them down a dimly lit corridor and into a dark room. It seemed that the Xiiginns were conserving power.

Dawson led them over to the far side of the room and, looking through a window, they saw a group of Xiiginns working on circular pods. They quickly squatted back down below the window to avoid being seen.

"See, it's a small hangar and they put the finished pods close to the exit," Dawson said.

Kyle took another look to get a better feel for the layout and then came back down. "I count at least seven Xiiginns in there."

"Why would they be modifying escape pods?" Tom asked.

Kyle pressed his lips together for a moment in thought. "The only thing I can think of is drop ships."

Tom frowned. "By drop ships, you mean to get their troops to the surface of Earth?"

Kyle nodded. "We've got to be close to Earth. We know from the Boxans that the escape pods they use have homing beacons on them. They're likely disabling the beacons."

"If there's a beacon on it, I can use it to send a signal to ECF command," Tom said.

"What we don't know is how much flying we're able to do in one of those things," Dawson said.

"It's about time we find out. Good work you two. This is our best chance of getting out of here," Kyle said.

An audible tone sounded above, silencing them all at once. Thinking the Xiiginns had finally discovered their escape, Kyle glanced back into the hangar to see the Xiiginns leaving their posts. He ducked back down, noting that several were heading towards the room they were in and there was nowhere for them to hide. Kyle held up three fingers for Dawson and then gestured at the door nearest them. Dawson nodded and then motioned for Pearson to get ready.

The door opened and the Xiiginns came inside. Dawson fired his weapon and bright flashes from the green bolts dropped two Xiiginns, but the last one screamed before Pearson shot him.

"Go," Kyle said.

Dawson went through the door first and they filed to the side, taking cover behind one of the round escape pods. Kyle heard more Xiiginns running over to investigate the noise and more shouts soon followed. They ran toward the hangar exit and green bolts zipped past them, narrowly missing. Pearson turned around and fired a few shots back, giving them some time to reach the pods. They came to the hangar exit, and in the distance, beyond the atmospheric containment shield, was a bright blue ball. Dawson took position behind them and they traded fire with the Xiiginns in the hangar. They were out of time. Kyle knew more soldiers were coming and it was only a matter of time before they'd be overwhelmed.

He and Tom circled around the escape pod, found the entrance, and went inside. There were seats around the edge with a control panel in the center. Tom went to work bringing up the interface and Kyle shouted for the others to get inside. Pearson came in first and Dawson took up position inside the doorway.

"Now would be a good time to get us out of here," Kyle said.

Tom was waving his hands, navigating through the controls, his face twisted into a frown. "I've got it. Doors closing," he said.

The escape pod doors began to shut and Dawson took a seat. The Xiiginns continued to fire from outside the pod.

Kyle glanced at Tom. "What are you waiting for?"

"Colonel, the navigation system already has preprogrammed coordinates—"

Tom was cut off by a loud blast from outside the pod.

"If it takes us to Earth, then I don't care. Get us out of here," Kyle said.

Tom hit the button and the escape pod's engines ignited. The burst pushed them back in their seats and Kyle held on. It felt like the pod was spinning out of control. Secondary engines fired and the escape pod leveled off. They couldn't see anything, and Kyle heard Dawson muttering a prayer.

CHAPTER 36

Mar Arden stood on the bridge of what remained of the warship. Hoan Berend sat on the command couch and was busy going through the reports on his console. Once he finished, he came over to Mar Arden.

"They've escaped," Hoan Berend said.

Mar Arden glanced at the commander. "You think letting them go is a mistake?"

"I've learned to trust in your plans," Hoan Berend replied.

Mar Arden glanced at the main holoscreen that showed the planet Earth, home to the Humans. "There's a planet full of Humans down there for us to exploit. I'm not concerned about losing four of them."

The door to the bridge opened and Kandra Rene walked in, striding purposefully to Mar Arden's side. "The Humans killed a few of our crew while escaping and we found some dead in the engineering tunnels," Kandra Rene said.

Mar Arden nodded. "If they were better soldiers, they'd still be alive. The methods the Humans used to escape reveals much about their species, however."

"The tunnels are a weakness, but the fact that the Humans managed to arm themselves is another matter," Hoan Berend said.

"Don't waste your time trying to secure this place any more than you already have. We won't be here that long. Our destination is out there," Mar Arden said and gestured toward the distant blue orb.

Hoan Berend looked at Kandra Rene. "You're positive that compulsion has worked on at least one of them."

Kandra Rene's gaze narrowed menacingly. "They're under my power and will initiate contact at the appointed time."

Hoan Berend nodded and looked at Mar Arden. "What's our next move?"

Mar Arden switched the view on the main holoscreen, which now showed multiple communication signals. They hadn't needed to initiate any scans to detect these signals. Their proximity to the planet was enough to start receiving them.

"The attack was a success. The Human and Boxan alliance is still tenuous, and with recent events, those relations will be further strained. The Humans will learn that they can't rely on the Boxans, and while they're scrambling around trying to figure out who to trust, we'll move into position," Mar Arden said.

"You still believe the reason the Boxans are here is because the Mardoxian potential is in Humans?" Hoan Berend said.

"I'm certain of it," Mar Arden said and brought up one of the recorded video streams.

An aged Human male came on screen and began to speak. "The Earth Coalition Force is humanity's answer to the alien threat. Would you like to work in space and fly on one the ships we're building for the first Human fleet? Perhaps the challenge in researching the latest in advanced technology calls to you. To realize your true potential, report to your local testing center and participate in the ECF's prescreening initiatives to help find where you'd best serve to protect our home."

The recorded video ended and Mar Arden looked at them.

"You see, they've already initiated a screening process, essentially doing our job for us. Now we'll know who to target once we get down there. So, you see, I'm not overly concerned with four prisoners escaping. The attacks already announced our presence, and before long, Humanity will learn to fear the Xiiginns even more than they already do," Mar Arden said.

He crossed his arms in front of him and the main holoscreen changed back to a view of Earth. Humans and Boxans were working to protect themselves, but it wouldn't be enough. He was just getting started and now he had a whole planet to use. Early in the Confederation's history their allies had believed the Boxans could never be beaten; their hold on the Confederation was too strong. But those who had doubted the Xiiginns were wrong. The Boxans were a shadow of their former selves, and with another species that had the Mardoxian potential, the Xiiginns would be the most unstoppable force the galaxy had ever witnessed. The Boxans revered the Drar, but even their vast empire was gone. The time for the Xiiginns was here, and Mar Arden would see that the entirety of the great expanse would be brought under their dominion.

CHAPTER 37

A few days had passed since the Boxan refugees from Sethion had landed on Selebus moon with the blessing of Nerva's global congress. It had been quite a shock when the star carrier had shown up in their star system, but after some quick communication from Kladomaor and High Councilor Awan, the Boxan fleet had been allowed to pass. Kaylan was pleased that the high councilor had kept his word.

Temporary shelters were being built and the resiliency of the Boxan refugees was something to be witnessed as they set to work. Most of them stepped off the transport carriers onto the forest moon and simply looked up at the sky in awe. They were initially afraid to remove their helmets despite knowing that the atmosphere was perfectly safe. Some were fearful of the forest, as if they expected the Protectors to attack at any moment.

Kaylan couldn't imagine living for so long with the harsh realities that the Boxans who'd been left on Sethion had been forced to endure. They were quite different than the other Boxans she'd met, and she wondered if the two factions would be better off going their separate ways. She didn't like those thoughts, but she had to consider them because it was a real possibility. She'd much rather see the two Boxan factions working together and uniting, which would put them both on a path to filling the large gaps between them now. The refugees would be redeemed for the trials they'd endured on Sethion and the colonists could exist without the haunting guilt that they'd left free Boxans behind. Neither could heal without the other, and in the end, they needed each other now more than ever before.

They'd buried Vitomir on Selebus. The cosmonaut had sacrificed himself to help the others restore the star carrier's systems. Vitomir was honored among the Boxan refugees for his sacrifice, but for the crew of the Athena, it was more complicated. The former Titus Station commander had sabotaged the space station, killing four people to join the Athena's mission. Kaylan had loathed the cosmonaut for what he'd done, which was nothing to how Vitomir viewed himself. His actions had led to the death of his own wife. After the Athena had been stranded in the Nershal star system, he'd worked to help them survive. She'd have let him rot in his quarters if it hadn't been for Hicks and the AI pointing out to her that they needed to use all available resources if they were to survive. So she'd made Hicks responsible for Vitomir, and throughout everything they'd been through, Vitomir had helped them. The cosmonaut knew how the rest of the crew felt about him, but in the end all they had was each other. She listened to Efren has he recounted the details of what had occurred on the star carrier—how they were pinned down and Vitomir had lured the combat mechs away so Efren could turn the power back on. She heard the same conflicted feelings in Efren's voice that she felt. In the end, she acknowledged that Vitomir had become part of the Athena's crew despite how they'd all felt about him. They all would have to make their peace with it because Vitomir was no longer with them.

Kaylan glanced at the tall trees and listened to the sounds of the forest. The day was drawing to an end and work would begin anew in the morning. Kladomaor spotted her and walked over.

"Adjusting to your new position?" Kaylan asked.

"I've been a Battle Commander for a long time," Kladomaor said.

"Essaforn and the others trust you," Kaylan said.

"Prax'pedax was the Battle Leader. I guess in Earth terms he'd be a General, except the refugees don't have a fleet to command," Kladomaor said.

"There's more to being a Battle Leader than commanding fleets. They've made you their advocate and have placed you in the most trustworthy position," Kaylan said.

"Their honor is misplaced. We wouldn't be here if it weren't for you. I'll see to it that no Boxan forgets, and when it's time to return to Earth, we'll be with you," Kladomaor said.

Kaylan felt her cheeks start to redden in embarrassment. "It's not just for Earth. We've seen what the Xiiginns are capable of, but Sethion was monstrous. If we don't stop them, countless other species will suffer the same fate."

Kladomaor regarded her for a moment. "I once thought of your species as primitive and brash. Weak. But I was wrong.

Those characteristics do exist in Humans, just as they do in Boxans, but you've become a force to be reckoned with. Ma'jasalax has said that the Mardoxian potential in you is equal to the most gifted priests in the history of the sect. Whether you meant to or not, your actions have put us all on a path that I believe will lead to the defeat of the Xiiginns."

Kaylan's mouth hung open and she was rescued from a response by Zack calling out to her. He came over, leading the old Boxan refugee she'd seen on the cruiser's bridge.

"This is Cardaleer. He's something of a scientist," Zack said.

Cardaleer bowed his head. "Mardoxian blessed," he said.

Kaylan bowed her head back to him.

"What's Mardoxian blessed?" Zack said.

"It's an honored title given to only the most gifted of the Mardoxian Sect," Kladomaor said.

Zack glanced at Kaylan, but she could tell he was much too excited about something to pay any mind to the title Cardaleer had used to address her.

"Before the Chaos Wars, Cardaleer studied Drar technology and was the foremost expert. He's agreed to help us with the Athena," Zack said.

"I'm afraid the Human is much too excited by what I said," Cardaleer said. "I merely stated that before the wars I worked with what Drar technology had been discovered. I was part of the teams that reverse-engineered its uses. Zack told me about the Shroud barrier."

"Do you think you can help?" Kaylan asked. The thought of returning to Earth sent waves of excitement through her.

"I will do everything I possibly can," Cardaleer said.

"And Etanu is getting us the materials we need to build a Star

Shroud model so we can learn more about the barrier," Zack said.

Kaylan smiled. For the first time since the barrier had gone online, protecting Earth from the Xiiginn fleet, she felt they were much closer to getting home than they'd ever been before.

CHAPTER 38

The days that followed the UN attacks strained Human and Boxan relations. Given the ineffectiveness of security forces to subdue Boxans in full power armor, there were motions to increase the production of more powerful weapons for law enforcement agencies across the globe. Ed Johnson knew that handing out more powerful weapons wasn't the answer. They needed specialized teams to be available to investigate alien threats on Earth, and this wasn't something the Earth Coalition Force had the authority to do. Ed thought back to the attack and remembered how Iris's weapons had failed to slow down Strike Leader Eavoth, and Scraanyx had explained that Eavoth's power armor had been modified to handle the stunners used by UN security forces.

Ed was in a conference room with General Sheridan and Scraanyx.

"So, nothing short of a hand cannon capable of shooting

plasma bolts can stop them? This isn't going to work. We need a better way to neutralize the threat," Ed said.

They had just gotten Scraanyx released.

"Death is the only release for any Boxan under the Xiiginn influence," Scraanyx said.

"Yeah, but we can't start handing out hand cannons with the advice to shoot any Boxan anyone thinks is acting suspiciously," Ed said.

"We'll need to do a better job of keeping track of Boxan activities, but there are more far-reaching repercussions to this," General Sheridan said.

Ed nodded and didn't like it one bit.

"Our protocols have been allowed to lapse. Cooperative mission protocols will need to be updated so a simple lie can't get anyone past security," General Sheridan said.

"That will help, but we still don't know if the Humans on those missions will be affected by the Xiiginns as well," Ed said.

"We're not going to figure everything out in this room. We'll get the right people working on it, but the threat level has just gone up. We thought the Xiiginns couldn't get through the barrier, so if that's the case, how'd they get here?" General Sheridan asked.

"They would have had a chance to slip through as the barrier was being formed," Scraanyx said.

"Which means they've been loitering out there somewhere for almost a year," Ed said.

"We need to find their ship and we'll need strike-fighter patrols to protect all the construction on the new moon," General Sheridan said.

Iris Barrett waved to him and Ed motioned for her to come

over. Her injuries hadn't been extensive and she'd gotten back on her feet shortly after the attack.

"There's an incoming call from General Heng Shang," Iris said.

Ed glanced at Sheridan and the ECF general's face hardened.

"Put it through," the general said.

The nearby wallscreen flicked on, showing the aged face of General Heng Shang.

"Thank you for taking my call," General Heng Shang said.

Ed knew Sheridan was still seething about the Chinese general's appointment to the ECF.

"What can I do for you?" General Sheridan said.

Shang nodded. "We've found something that will help shed some light on the Xiiginns."

The video cam shifted away from Shang to four people standing on his right. Ed's eyes widened when he recognized Colonel Mathews.

The camera shifted back to Shang. "They crash-landed in a small pod in the Kunlun Shan mountain region."

Sheridan came to his feet and walked toward the wallscreen, and Ed joined him.

"Are they alright?" Ed asked.

"We're looking after them," Shang said.

"What do you want?" General Sheridan asked.

The barest hints of a smile showed on Shang's face. "For you to acknowledge me and my own staff as part of the Earth Coalition Force as agreed by the UN Security Council."

General Sheridan's nostrils flared and then he nodded. "Understood. If you want to help the ECF, you can bring Colonel Mathews, Lieutenant Dawson, Corporal Pearson, and

Tech Comms Specialist Blake with you when you report for duty."

Any satisfaction General Shang had felt disappeared.

"A shuttle will be dispatched to you and we'll see you in a few hours' time," General Sheridan said and ended the call.

He glanced over at Ed. "You said I needed to work with him. This is me working with him."

Ed nodded and was silent for a few moments. He noticed Scraanyx frowning. "What is it?" he asked.

The Boxan regarded them for a moment. "Did they escape, or were they set free?"

Ed drew in a deep breath and looked at Sheridan. They'd thought that if they could build their fleet and race to upgrade their technology, they could keep the Xiiginns from reaching Earth. They'd failed, and now at least some of the Xiiginns were here. He didn't know how they were supposed to keep things running and stop the Xiiginn compulsion from infiltrating their ranks at the same time. Dark times were coming, and they needed to stick together now more than ever if the people of Earth hoped to survive.

Thank you for reading Rising Force.

If you loved this book, please consider leaving a **review.** Comments and reviews allow readers to discover authors, so if you want others to enjoy *Rising Force* as you have, please leave a short note.

ABOUT THE AUTHOR

Ken Lozito is the author of multiple science fiction and fantasy series. I've been reading both science fiction and fantasy for a long time. Books were and are my way to escape everyday life. What started out as a love of stories has turned into a full-blown passion for writing them. My ultimate intent for writing stories is to provide fun escapism for readers. I write stories that I would like to read and I hope you enjoy them as well.

If you would like to get an email when I release a book please visit my website at **KenLozito.com**

One Last Thing.

Word-of-mouth is crucial for any author to succeed. If you enjoyed the book, please consider leaving a review at Amazon, even if it's only a line or two; it would make all the difference and would be greatly appreciated.

ALSO BY KEN LOZITO

Ascension

Star Shroud

Star Divide

Star Alliance

Infinity's Edge

Rising Force

First Colony

Genesis

Nemesis

Legacy

Sanctuary

Safanarion Order

Road to Shandara

Echoes of a Gloried Past

Amidst the Rising Shadows

Heir of Shandara

89134147R00202

Made in the USA
Columbia, SC
09 February 2018